BECOMING MORE

JENNIFER L. MOORE

Print Edition ISBN: 978-1-952640-02-5

Ebook Edition ISBN: 978-1952640-03-2

❁ Created with Vellum

For my Family

*L*yn stood at the fifty yard line of the practice field, her brown curls tickled her face in the cool breeze. Stood was a generous word at 5:30 on a Monday morning. She wavered on the edge of the field. Without coffee pumping through her veins, she had to fight for awareness of her surroundings. The scent of the fresh cut grass and the sound of jocks on the scrimmage line did little to convince her she was awake.

"Lyn?"

Lyn turned toward the voice and blinked until the figure came into focus.

Scout stood a good distance down the side of the field. "You can hear me?"

"I'd hear you better with coffee." Lyn focused on him and let the scrimmage become background noise.

"Coffee after. Sound first. You can hear me whisper from fifteen yards, your best so far is twenty-five. Let's see how far we can extend it this morning." Scout walked backward to the next painted line on the edge of the field.

"Can you hear me now?"

Lyn smiled. She felt like she was in a cell phone

commercial instead of at shifter training. "Why are we even here? It's the last week of school, surely even the football team gets a summer break."

Scout smiled back and stepped farther away again. "Would you rather be cleaning out boxes from your garage?"

Lyn grimaced at the reminder of Jonathan's boxes. When he'd died, her friends helped pack up his apartment, but Lyn didn't want to deal with them and they were relegated to stacks in her garage. She still didn't want to deal with them. If she dealt with them, she'd have to think about her failure. She'd told him she would find his real daughter, maybe not in those exact words, and maybe it wasn't even a promise, but she hadn't done it, hadn't even known where to start. "I should just set the boxes out for bulk trash pick-up."

"You have all summer to deal with them and I'll help." Scout stepped back again.

She'd been training with the team since November. Once in the morning, three hours before she'd usually be awake, and while she skipped the boys after school practice, she was required to meet at the skate park on the edge of what passed for a forest in Cedar Oaks.

Greg had convinced, no, coerced her into shifter training with Killian and his crew. She'd attempted to get out of it several times, but each time her alarm went off in the morning and she rolled over after hitting snooze, she had a sudden urge to throw up, forcing her out of bed and across the hall to the bathroom.

Once she was out of bed she couldn't go back, not with what awaited her in her dreams, and although she wouldn't admit it, she enjoyed the sprints and the other physical parts of the morning workout. Scout even squeezed in some additional training, like today's hearing session. It wasn't all bad, it was just early.

Lyn conceded that Greg had a point about needing to know how to control the things she was capable of, but she didn't want to let it change her, make her more like Killian. A bully. A predator. She needed to learn to control her shifter side so that she could tame it, but Killian was a jerk and just being in the same space as him made her hackles rise. She felt the hair on her arms stand even now, focused on Scout.

"Don't think about him." Scout whispered from halfway to the end of the field.

Scout knew how she felt about Killian and how much she hated this arrangement. He made it more tolerable, but only just. If she could train one on one with Scout, she'd be fine, but Greg's arrangement involved Killian, her least favorite person in Cedar Oaks.

"Can you still hear me?"

Lyn took a breath in through her nose and blew out through her mouth. She raised her arms and placed her thumb and forefinger an inch apart.

Scout nodded and stepped to the next line.

"This...thirty-five..."

Lyn squinted her eyes like that would help his voice come into focus. She shook her head. "You're breaking up now," she said at a normal volume.

"Thirty yards is good, especially since you haven't had coffee and you look like you'd fall asleep standing up if you could." She could hear him better now that he stopped whispering.

"Can I?"

"No." Scout laughed and picked up the stopwatch hanging around his neck. He stepped back to the end zone and lifted his free hand. "But I have coffee if you can get here faster than last time." Scout's hand fell to his side.

Lyn snarled and ran. She really wanted that coffee.

~

*L*yn sat alone at the bottom of the bleachers with her coffee in her hands and her eyes closed. The scent of roasted beans, caramel, and steamed milk made her smile. Scout knew how to motivate her.

"Good morning."

Lyn didn't need to open her eyes. The voice, mixed with the scent of fresh cut grass and open spaces, along with his deodorant and aftershave was distinctly Greg. She took another sip of her still hot coffee and ignored him.

She and Greg had been a perfect couple for three months. She wasn't sure what they were now besides complicated and she had been too tired for too long to figure it out.

No matter what their relationship status was, she wasn't ready to let Greg off the hook for his part in her early morning torture sessions. The ones that apparently weren't going to stop even though it was summer break. She tamped down a growl while picking out a familiar form from the huddle in the middle of the field.

Killian turned his eyes to meet her glare and his lips curled up into a smirk.

"I brought coffee, but it looks like you already have some." Greg's voice broke her stare with Killian, but she kept her eyes glued to the mass of sweaty bodies as they fought over the ball.

"Too early?" Greg sat down beside her, not quite touching, and looked at his feet. He set the carry tray of coffee between them and took out one of the cups.

She grunted and took another sip of her coffee to keep her snarky comment to herself.

She could have stopped coming out to practice with the team. At least that's what she told herself, but Scout wasn't the only team member that was nice to her, most of them were, actually. They made her feel like one of them. Well, everyone except Killian, who went from hot to cold so fast she got whiplash. Sometimes she thought he might actually enjoy her company, and others she was sure he hated this arrangement as much as she did. It made her wonder why he kept trying to train her.

Killian and Greg didn't get along and that was putting it nicely. Killian didn't accept her training as a favor to Greg. No, more likely it was to control her, just another hold over from his bullying behavior. Thankfully, that had let up, mostly. The team accepted her, and Killian didn't need to keep on her at school, since he had her cornered every morning and night while he and his pack taught her to be a good little shifter wolf.

Lyn felt a growl in the pit of her stomach and she stifled a smile when Greg squirmed and put more space between them. Then she bit her lips to stop both. That was not the type of person she wanted to be. She refused to turn into a predator just because her biology told her she was one. She swallowed the last of the caramel goodness from her cup and eyed the fresh one that Greg had brought.

"Only two days left of school." Greg straightened his posture. "Do you have plans for summer?"

"You'll have to ask Killian."

Greg flinched at her tone. "I still think this is for the best. I don't like him either, but..."

"It's not working." Lyn interrupted.

Greg made a sound that Lyn couldn't interpret and hung his head. "Are you able to sleep at all?" He looked at her.

Lyn looked at the cardboard coffee tray between them and shook her head.

That wasn't quite true, but it might as well be the case. It's not like she didn't try, but any amount of sleep she did get was tainted by nightmares.

The memory of which made her tense. Tightness closed around her. Her pulse increased and her breathing became erratic. She tossed her empty cup into the trash can at the bottom of the bleachers.

Earlier this year, she would've missed, and the cup would have bounced off the fence, or fallen shy of the can, but even though she was tired, shifter training had improved her hand-eye coordination.

"We should tell someone." Greg held out the new cup of coffee.

Lyn bristled. "No," she said, unable to suppress a snarl. "I'm holding up my end of our bargain. You'd better hold yours." She reached for the coffee and her fingers brushed his.

"But if it's getting worse…"

Lyn snapped her head around and stared down at Greg. She didn't remember standing. "No." The word dripped venom.

"You guys okay?" Scout's voice asked over the buzz of tension in her ear.

A quick check with her wolf's senses told her that Killian and Scout stood close enough behind her to restrain her, while the rest of the team were within sprinting distance. They could be on top of her in moments if her temper got the best of her. She knew, because it had happened before.

She kept her eyes glued to Greg's and watched as he considered breaking his silence, but after a moment he shook his head.

"Lyn, where's your phone?" Scout's voice was calm and quiet as he stepped up onto the bleachers to stand beside her. He held out his hand.

She lifted the device and looked down. Her hand was shaking and her claws were extended.

"Do you need help?" Scout whispered.

"No," she snapped. Her fingers curled around her phone. She thought she might crack it this time.

Scout's hand remained open, palm up, and she placed her phone in his hand. "Earbuds?"

Lyn closed her eyes and shook her head. She tried to use the breathing exercises he had taught her to control her temper. She knew her wolf was a hair's breadth away from the surface. Close enough that she could tap into that heightened awareness to sense the team behind her, closer now.

She knew that August was biting a single fingernail, and she wanted to punch him for it. Steve and Archie moved to flank their Alpha. Killian stood tense. Lyn knew he was staring at the back of her head. He was probably smirking. That stupid upturned corner of his lip that made Lyn want to punch him in the face.

Scout pressed play and the sad sounds of stringed instruments lifted up from the speaker.

She took her phone back and closed her eyes until she felt her claws retract. "I should shower before class," she said after a few moments and stepped off the bleacher and toward the locker room, leaving the boys staring after her.

CHAPTER TWO

*G*reg watched Lyn walk away. The tension clear in her posture.

"You are supposed to be helping her control it." Greg stood and looked down from the bleachers at Killian.

Killian crossed his arms and smirked. "We are. Last month she would have shifted more than just her nails and eyes if she'd gotten that angry. Maybe you should check yourself. She only gets that mad around you."

"That's not true," Scout said without taking his eyes off of Lyn's retreating figure.

Greg turned to him. "What part?"

Killian glared at Scout.

Scout looked at Greg. "She's getting better at her control. But you aren't the only reason she's angry. It's like... she's haunted or something."

Greg watched Scout shake his head and had the urge to break his deal with Lyn. Scout might be able to help her, where he and Killian had failed. He turned toward the building and watched as Lyn stepped inside. He turned back to Killian. "Just do what she asked you to do." Greg stepped off the bleachers and walked away from the Killian and his crew.

"I will, but you need to back off, Gregar. You're making it worse."

"Shut up, Killian!" Greg didn't turn around. He didn't want to see the smirk on Killian's face. The urge to punch him would be too great, and he was better than that. He knew his problems wouldn't be solved by hitting them and he couldn't lay all of them at the shifter's feet either. His problems began before he enlisted Killian's help training Lyn.

The first week after Lyn found out she was part shifter was fine. He thought they were at least. They had spent a lot of time together getting to know each other. He thought their relationship was going well.

He knew Lyn wasn't happy about being a predator, far from it, and she was adamant about learning to control it. But Killian and his team had backed off from their bully tactics and she smiled more at school.

He wasn't sure when it had changed from a genuine smile to a fake one, but by Halloween there was no mistaking the depression she had slipped in.

Even before, when Killian had been more bully than not, Lyn had always seemed light. Now, it was as if she carried darkness with her wherever she went.

Greg had not seen her carefree in months. She didn't dance. She backed out of plans. She went from home to school and back again. Umiko told him that it was almost as bad as the weeks after her mom died.

One day he walked Lyn home after school and confronted her. He started off asking, but didn't get anywhere being gentle. Just 'it's nothing' and 'I'm fine.' Greg knew she was lying.

He forced her to talk until she finally came clean about the nightmares. She wouldn't tell him what they were about, but she admitted that she wasn't able to sleep because of them.

He made a deal with her, thinking that her wolf was the problem. Killian would train her and he wouldn't tell anyone about her nightmares. He thought it would help her in the long run.

Greg rubbed his hand through his hair and it stood up. That agreement had been a stupid idea, but now he was stuck with the consequences. She would hate him if he told any one. He would lose her trust and that was just about the only thing he had since their relationship had imploded. He was grateful they had managed to remain friends, albeit icy ones, but if he lost her trust, there would be no coming back from it.

He sighed as he stepped through the cafeteria door to wait for the bell to ring. Lyn's spark was gone and he didn't know if he could help her.

CHAPTER THREE

The motion lights on Lyn's driveway flickered to life as Jake's truck pulled in to drop her off. It was full dark outside and they were just getting back after a run and a successful hunt.

"You did great tonight," Jake said as he put the truck in park.

Lyn opened the passenger door and stepped out. "Thanks." She walked toward her front door without looking back, her head low on her shoulders.

Scout stepped out of the back passenger door and closed it. "Lyn?"

She stopped walking and turned back to him. "It's late and I'm tired," She glanced at Jake behind the wheel. "Thank you for the ride home."

"Anytime," Jake said and flashed her a smile.

Lyn didn't return the gesture, instead she turned and walked up her sidewalk.

"Get some rest. I'll see you tomorrow." Scout moved to get into the front seat. He turned back again as Lyn stepped onto her front porch. "I'm… we're… If you need to talk, just call. Okay?"

Lyn nodded, stepped into the dark house and reached back to lock the door. She leaned against it and slid down to the floor. She watched the spray of Jake's headlights illuminate the room as he pulled out of her driveway. When the light was gone, exhaustion overcame her and tears flooded her eyes. She wanted to go upstairs for a shower then snuggle under her blankets and sleep for three or four weeks, but she knew what would happen.

She'd toss and turn for an hour, finally get comfortable and drift off to sleep only to wake up covered in sweat and struggling to keep her wolf under control.

She was getting better at the last part. She hadn't shredded her blanket in a few days, though she was still finding stuffing stuck here and there from the last time.

Lyn picked herself off the ground and walked to the couch. She turned on the T.V. and flipped through the movie choices. She'd tried romances, comedies, cartoons even. Nothing kept the nightmares away.

She briefly considered a horror movie. Maybe a really scary one would give her nightmares something else to focus on. Something unreal and therefore less threatening than her current reoccurring themes.

She continued flipping past mediocre choices and took a deep breath to calm herself. "Eww. Gross." She wrinkled her nose at the scent that accosted her.

She smelled of dirt and sweat mixed with blood and death. She needed to shower and brush her teeth to remove the taste of coyote. After that, she'd pick a movie or watch stupid cat videos from the internet while she tried to get some rest.

CHAPTER FOUR

"Just give up. It's not going to work," Lyn said to Umiko's reflection in the bathroom mirror.

"How did your mom deal with the frizz?"

Lyn yawned. She made it through her last day of school and only nodded off twice. Once in Algebra while Umiko played with her hair and again in Chemistry after she finished her test early, which might or might not be indicative of understanding the material. Lyn tried to keep her grades up the last few months, but with the exhaustion, they were what they were.

When the last bell of the year rang, everyone still trapped in the walls of Cedar Oaks High bolted out the doors and off to whatever celebratory plans they had made. Lyn had no idea what her summer would look like other than shifter training and not sleeping, but she didn't have time to dwell because Umiko had roped her into afternoon plans with Greg and Clark today, and if Lyn knew her friend at all, she had plans for the entire break too.

"Are you still not sleeping?" Umiko asked Lyn's reflection in the mirror.

The bathroom counter was littered with various bottles,

tubes, and brushes, most of them Umiko's and not at all suitable for Lyn's skin tone.

Umiko held a curling iron with white hair wrapped around the shaft against Lyn's head. She loosened and pulled it gently through as white curls fell beside Lyn's face for a moment before they fell out.

Her hair was strange to say the least. Today, she had a mix of brown, red, and white. The brown parts were curly but frizzy, as usual. The red streaks formed soft curls that interspersed the rest, while the stubborn white hung straight down her back no matter what they tried.

"I'd sleep for the rest of the week, if I could." Lyn picked up a tube of bright pink lip gloss and brushed it across her lips. After pressing her lips together, she wiped it off again. The color made her look even more washed out. She searched among the bottles for a paler shade.

"Do you want to talk about it?"

Lyn shook her head.

Umiko already knew about the nightmares. Lyn had told her everything when Umiko had helped her clean up after the first destroyed blanket.

"This just isn't working." Umiko put down the curling iron and looked at Lyn in the mirror. "I curl it, but it just falls back out." She pouted at Lyn's hair as she held it in her hands. The white ends fell below the brown and red curls.

Lyn held in an 'I told you so' and looked at her hair in the mirror. She was perfectly fine with its straightness. It was Umiko who was determined to make it more than it wanted to be.

"Maybe we can trim the white to be the same length, at least then it wouldn't look so weird."

"Don't worry about it." Lyn wouldn't. She'd grown used to the rebellious locks. At least she could brush it now, without creating what looked like a lion's mane around her face.

Her old curly, brown hair never enjoyed being brushed. It was more carnivorous plant than cooperating hair. It had broken more than one brush and a larger number of combs over the years. Only her mother could get it to behave, and she wasn't around to help anymore. Luckily, Lyn only had to deal with the monster curls occasionally now.

For months, Lyn had been trying to figure out her hair. Sometimes she would wake up and it would be brown and curly, others times it would be white as bone. It seemed to have three styles. Old Lyn brown, Umiko red, and new Lyn white. Four if you counted the mix she was sporting now. Lyn never knew which one it would choose to be for the day. She didn't seem to have any say in the matter. Just like a lot of things in her life.

Umiko ran her fingers through the red curls and loosened them to gain length.

"Just leave it."

"Are the nightmare's getting worse?" Umiko asked after checking her reflection in the mirror.

Lyn shrugged. "They are all a variation on the same theme. I'm either being trapped or hunted." Lyn shivered at the thought. "Can we not talk about it right now? The boys will be here soon," she paused to consider her reflection, "and I still have to meet the team at dusk." Lyn stood up and walked to her closet. She pulled out a black and white thigh length dress and held it close to her chest for Umiko's opinion.

"Even tonight?"

"Every morning, every night." Lyn spoke into the closet.

Umiko changed the subject. "You're wearing a lot more dresses lately. I like your new style."

Lyn looked longingly at her discarded jeans on the back of her desk chair. Lyn wore more dresses, but not because her style had changed. She still preferred T-shirts and jeans. At least she did until the night she shifted fully clothed because

Killian wanted to prove a point. That outfit had not survived. Scout had to cut Lyn out of her mother's most worn pair of jeans and an altered T-shirt. Lyn still had the T-shirt, but the jeans weren't going to live again.

If she could just get her temper under control and get through the fear, she might be able to go back to her trusty denim. But not sleeping combined with recurring nightmares scarier than horror flicks weren't making that easy.

Lyn unzipped the dress and slid it off the hanger.

"Wait, before you change, I brought some things too." Umiko stepped over to Lyn's bed and unzipped her bag.

Lyn sighed. Whatever Umiko brought, it was not Lyn's favorite pair of broken in jeans and well worn T-shirt, but she joined her best friend beside the bed and laid the black dress on the wrinkled comforter. She moved her phone out of the way so it wouldn't get lost in layers of clothing.

Umiko handed Lyn a pale green dress with three-quarter sleeves and laid out a bright royal blue short sleeved dress on her side of the bedspread. "Do you want to choose first?" she asked.

Umiko's smile was so wide that Lyn didn't tell her that she had no opinions good or bad about the three choices laid out for her. "Why don't we just try them all on?" Lyn handed Umiko the black dress and Lyn picked the royal blue for herself.

"Great idea!" Umiko took the proffered dress and ran into the bathroom to the other mirror.

Lyn held the bright fabric up to herself and looked at the full length mirror in her bedroom corner. Her face contorted as she yawned though a grimace. Bright colors were intense next to her pale skin. They either looked great or awful, with no in-betweens.

"Ew! Not that one,"Umiko said coming out of the bathroom a few moments later wearing Lyn's black and white dress. "But this looks great, right?"

The girls spent the next ten minutes trying on and critiquing the dress choices. Umiko decided to wear the black and white dress from Lyn's closet and Lyn borrowed Umiko's pale green one.

Lyn's complexion tolerated pastels much better than intense colors. Unless it was red or black. Lyn could pull off red and black, they just made her look more otherworldly.

"I am so glad we are the same size," Umiko said and twirled once. She watched the dress flare out in the mirror. "Now all we need are shoes," she looked at her bare feet and wiggled her toes.

"I'm sticking with sneakers, but I have a white pair." Lyn held up a pair of dingy white tie shoes, not quite athletic quality.

Umiko frowned. "At least clean them up a little first," Umiko said with her hand on her hip. "What about me? I brought white sandals, but I think black would look better."

"I think the white sandals would go well, but I have some black wedges, if you want to borrow those." Lyn rummaged around in her closet and handed Umiko a single shoe.

Umiko slipped the wedge on her foot and buckled a white sandal on the other. She turned her ankles and admired the effect in the mirror. "I'm going to stick with sandals." Umiko leaned down to pick something small and white off the ground. "I thought we picked up all the stuffing from the ruined comforter?" Umiko looked around the room.

"I guess we missed some."

Umiko stepped over to the trash can beside Lyn's desk and dropped in the white fluff. "Is this another letter from that boarding school?" Umiko lifted an envelope from beside Lyn's trash can.

"It's just junk mail. I think Ms. Sanchez put my name on a mailing list. Just toss it in the trash." Lyn shrugged at the envelope in Umiko's hand.

"Have you opened any of them? What do they say?"

Umiko slipped her finger under the red wax seal. "It's fancy." Umiko smiled. "Ouch." Her smile flipped. "It bit me."

"Why did you even try to open it?"

"Because you didn't."

"I opened the first one. Since I'm not going, I didn't figure it was important. Maybe they'll give up." Lyn looked away from her best friend's curiosity.

Lyn wasn't going to move anywhere. This is the house she shared with her mom. All her mom's things were still here and Lyn was not going to part with them to move halfway across the country to a boarding school.

She uncovered her mother's black hooded sweatshirt half buried underneath her pillow. She brought it to her nose. The fabric still smelled like love and safety, her mom's scent, even after a trip through the washing machine. Smelling it made her miss her mom and a tear threatened to fall. Her mom could have helped her with her nightmares. Maybe if her mom were here she wouldn't be having them in the first place.

Umiko laid the envelope on Lyn's desk before turning around. "Lyn?" Umiko's voice was strained.

"Yeah?" Lyn pulled the hoodie away from her nose and looked at her friend all dressed up.

"Are you thinking about your mom?" Umiko asked.

Lyn nodded and laid back on the bed. She drew her legs up and curled around the ball she had made with the sweatshirt. She wanted to wear it over the dress, but she knew Umiko would just make her take it off again. Lyn closed her eyes, but the idea of sleeping and the memories of her nightmares made her open them again.

"Do you want to talk about her?" Umiko retreated to the bathroom sink, but left the door open.

Lyn heard her friend rummage in her make-up case, amazed that there was still anything in it that wasn't already spread out on her counter. She pulled a pillow under her head and sighed.

"She could have gotten this hair to curl. She could always get it to do what she wanted," Lyn said. "My hair listened to her better than anyone." Lyn lifted a hand to her hair and brushed it with her fingers. "I used to fall asleep when she brushed it." Lyn wrapped and unwrapped a few strands around her fingers.

"It was probably because she was used to dealing with her own. I swear you two had matching hair," Umiko said stepping to the door. "Except for the frizz, of course."

Lyn saw Umiko's eyes widen. "What?" Lyn brought her fingers away from her hair.

"What were you doing just now?" Umiko asked from the bathroom doorway. A smile slowly spread across her face.

"Remembering my mom?" Lyn looked at her friend sideways. "You asked…"

"No, what *exactly* were you doing." Umiko took a step closer to the bed.

"Just remembering the way my mom would touch my hair." Lyn's hand went back to the top of her head and brushed down her strands. The hair curled around her fingers.

"Look in the mirror," Umiko pointed to the full length mirror in the corner of the room.

Lyn's pulse started to speed up as she stared at her friend. "Why? What happened now?" Lyn stayed where she was, torn between wanting to know what was new and wanting Umiko to just tell her instead of doing some stupid slow reveal thing. Lyn didn't like surprises, they usually complicated things. Lyn was sure this was going to be just another complication.

"Come on, just do it." Umiko reached out with both hands and pulled her friend to standing. She half led, half pushed Lyn to the mirror.

Lyn closed her eyes and let Umiko lead her. When they stopped moving, she slowly opened one eye and prepared herself for a shock. It was one, but one she was more used to than she thought.

Brown curly hair framed the face in the mirror. The white and red had vanished completely and the frizz was tamed.

"Did you know you could control it? I thought you said it was random. Why didn't you tell me?" Umiko asked with a pout.

"I can't control it. At least, I don't think I can." Lyn tried to find a pattern. "It's always white after I get home from training at night and mostly normal again after I shower. But I wake up with some mix between the three every morning."

Umiko straightened her lips. "Okay, do the hand thing, but this time think of my hair."

"What hand thing?"

"The thing you did to change your hair." Umiko mimed Lyn's hands on her hair. "Just try it. But think of my hair instead of your mom's." Umiko put her hand on Lyn's back and waited.

The expression on Umiko's face was familiar. It was the look that meant she was not going to let this go. It was the same look a street peddler gave his trained monkey when he wanted it to perform for a crowd of passersby.

Lyn lifted both hands to the top of her head and closed her eyes. She ran her hand over the tight brown curls while imagining Umiko's hair on her own head. She opened her eyes.

She turned her head left and right. The brown from a few moments ago was gone and there was no white. Umiko's red color fell from Lyn's scalp to just below her shoulder blades. A perfect mimic of Umiko's.

"That is amazing," Umiko cooed and performed an excited little hop in the borrowed wedges. She completed the maneuver with clapped hands, as if her inner child had just been offered a candy store shopping spree. "Try Clark's," Umiko pleaded. Her hands clasped in front of her chin and a smile spread across her round face.

Lyn stared at her reflection. She squinted and un-squinted her eyes as she moved close and farther away from the mirror. She let out the breath she had inadvertently held. She met Umiko's gaze in the mirror, they beamed back at her with child-like excitement. Exactly what Lyn was missing. Instead, Lyn felt anxiety and a growing need to flee.

"Come on, just try." Umiko nodded at her.

Lyn picked out a few strands and pinched the top of the shaft with her fingers. She pulled the strands of straight red through her fingers and thought about Clark's shorter jet black hair. When her fingers moved along the strands, white was left behind, like her fingers had erased the color. Beneath the pinch in her fingers the hair was still Umiko's shade of red.

"Did you even try?" Umiko asked as she stood behind Lyn with her hands on her hips.

"I did." Lyn looked at Umiko through the mirror.

"Are you sure?" Umiko softened.

"Yes," Lyn said and walked away from the mirror and back to bed. She sat down and shifted her weight when she felt the hard press of her phone at her hip.

"Then that's a limitation." Umiko turned to her friend and smiled. She stepped back into the bathroom and rummaged in her make-up bag for a skinny bottle. She untwisted the lid and pulled out the mascara wand. "Now, we just need to know what the limitation means. I wonder what is different about Clark's hair that makes it not work."

"This doesn't freak you out?" Lyn laid back on her bed and cast her eyes toward the ceiling. She watched the fan spin and let her eyes drift closed as she counted her breaths.

"Of course not." Umiko scoffed.

Lyn rolled over to face her friend.

"I can change my legs into flippers." Umiko glanced down to Lyn's legs.

Lyn could just about see the lightbulb brighten over her friend's head as an idea took root.

"Oh, no." Lyn shot up to sitting. She shook her head. Umiko's ideas had a way of getting bigger than Lyn wanted. Way bigger. Defeat the evil witch type of big.

Last time, her idea had ended with Lyn finding out that her parents were not her parents and that a witch had killed the only mom she had ever known. Lyn didn't want to know where this mission might lead. What was worse than a witch? With Lyn's luck, that would be where this would end up.

"It'd be cool though, right?" Umiko asked, a huge grin across her face. "You've got to try it!"

The doorbell rang.

Lyn jumped up from the bed. "Thank God," Lyn said to herself and walked through the bedroom door, leaving Umiko's plan for another day. One when she'd be prepared with an excuse to combat Umiko's persistence.

Maybe she could say she wanted to finally go through the boxes from Jonathan's apartment. She could play the grief stricken daughter card, though Umiko would see through that. Lyn hadn't known Jonathan much at all and his recent death to cancer didn't trigger much in the way of sadness, just obligation, with a heaping dose of failure.

Lyn knew Umiko was getting an itch to figure out the rest of Lyn's creature heritage and she'd need an excuse with more truth to it than clearing out boxes if she was going to be able to put Umiko off the idea. She would need either a really good excuse or a distraction.

Her current distraction rang again.

CHAPTER FIVE

*L*yn opened the front door without asking who it was first. Now that she didn't have to worry about the neighborhood witch being on the other side, she had been doing that more.

Of course, sometimes it was Killian coming to get her for training when she'd overslept. She wasn't sure that was much better, but at least he wasn't actively trying to hurt the people she cared about or steal Lyn's power for his own ends.

This afternoon, Greg stood on the porch dressed in a well-fitting pair of jeans and a plain black T-shirt. He handed Lyn a small white clover blossom as he stepped into the house. "It's all they had at the sidewalk sale." He smiled and kissed her on the cheek.

"How thoughtful," Lyn responded and put the bloom behind her ear. She could put her animosity toward Greg away in order to distract Umiko.

"You are rocking the red today," Greg lifted his finger to point at something on her head, "The white bit is... Does it only go half way?"

Lyn's hand flew to the section of hair that had erased itself. She moved to the hallway mirror and concentrated on fixing it. Red, red, red, she thought, but nothing changed. Her reflection taunted her with her face covered by Umiko's hair, except for that one pinch of white at her temple.

"I like it." Clark said from around a glass vase with a large arrangement of flowers. She couldn't name them all, but she noted carnations in a variety of colors. "It's interesting."

"Umiko," Lyn called up the stairs. "Clark is here, with flowers."

"Down in a sec." Umiko's voice carried back down. "I'm on the phone."

"Sorry, Clark. Umiko is too busy with her social calendar to meet you at the door. Even if you are carrying an expensive flower arrangement." She stepped back to let Clark enter.

"No worries. Besides, they cost me as much as that flower in your hair." Clark winked.

"Wow. That must be some sidewalk sale," Lyn teased. The exchange helped loosen the tension in her shoulders.

"We'll go with that. It sounds much better than dead people flowers." Clark walked to the living room.

Greg gathered a pile of junk mail into a neat stack and moved the remote for Clark.

"Ah, they're from the nursing home." Lyn said. "Did you get to see your dad?" She closed the door.

"No." Clark placed the vase on the table and took a step back. "Mrs. Sheila had a lot of loved ones around when she died. This side and the next. She didn't need a ferryman to help her find her way."

Lyn didn't know how he handled being perpetually disappointed in not getting to see a father he knew existed. Lyn knew nothing about her biological parents, besides that her sperm donor was a shifter and her egg donor let a crazy woman baby switch Lyn. At least, she thought that was the order of things. She'd been a bit out of her mind when the witch was ranting and Umiko was better at embellishing stories than delivering facts.

"Okay. I'm done," Umiko said from the top of the stairs. "Are those for me? Who died?"

"Sheila. She was 97," Clark smiled as Umiko walked down the stairs in the black and white dress that perfectly coordinated with his black jeans and T-shirt.

"Aw. I liked talking to her." Umiko pouted as she stepped from the last stair and looked at the colorful arrangement of carnations.

"She told me to give these to you." Clark swept his hand toward the flowers.

"She is such a sweetheart," Umiko said. "I mean 'was.'" Umiko walked over to smell the flowers and take Clark's hand. "There's been a development," Umiko almost sang to the room.

Here we go. Lyn thought as she stepped away from the foyer.

Greg took a seat on the end of the couch nearest the door.

Just as Lyn was about to sit in the arm chair on his side, there was another knock. She returned to the door and opened it, wondering if maybe she had a package arriving that she had forgotten about.

"Killian?" Lyn's eyes went wide as she took in the tall muscular alpha standing on her porch. "What are you doing here?" Lyn crossed her arms over her chest but didn't move to let him in.

"Umiko called me," Killian stepped into the house without waiting to be invited. He didn't bother to avoid bumping into her.

"What?" Lyn turned to look at her friend.

"That was fast. Come in, I was just getting started." Umiko waved Killian in. "Hey, Scout." Umiko joined Clark on the couch.

"Hi, Umiko."

Lyn turned to her second uninvited guest. Only, she supposed they had both been invited, just not by her. She looked to the left of the door to see her house numbers on the door frame. *It certainly looks like mine.*

"What are you doing?" Scout asked.

"Just checking to see if this is my house."

Scout's brow wrinkled.

"I didn't know Umiko had invited more people."

"I hope you don't mind."

"It's Umiko's war council, how can I possibly mind?" Lyn sighed and stepped back to let him in. It wasn't the rhetorical question he took it for.

"War council?" Scout asked, confusion knit on his brow. He stepped inside but stayed near the door with Lyn.

"Never mind," Lyn said under her breath and turned to her friend. "Umiko, will anyone else be joining us?" Lyn's determination to have a good afternoon suddenly left and her exhaustion returned.

"I don't think so. Did you call anyone?"

Lyn closed the door a little harder than she intended. She took a deep breath before she turned to the now larger party.

Scout put his hand on the small of her back and looked at her. "Are you okay?" he whispered.

"I'm starting to feel like I need a run. A really long one where I'm too tired to come back." She lowered her eyes to the floor. "Or a Rip Van Winkle length nap."

"We could bail," Scout whispered, removing his hand from her back.

Lyn looked up into his brown eyes to see if he meant it.

His eyebrows lifted.

Could she? Lyn looked around at everyone gathered in her living room like they lived here. Umiko and Clark on the far end of the couch, Greg on the other. Could she just leave them here and run off with Scout? She found herself tempted by the offer. She glanced from Scout to the front door.

"You might be wondering why I called you all here," Umiko said with a giggle.

The door shrank. Her opportunity to escape going with it.

The walls began to close in and dread clung to Lyn's chest like a capuchin monkey. She knew things were about to get out of her control and she hoped she could keep her wolf contained.

Maybe she could go into the garage and a pile of dead man's boxes would fall on her and break a bone or put her in the hospital or something else more palatable than whatever Umiko had planned.

CHAPTER SIX

"What's the big drama, Umiko? Did she shift in front of you?" Killian plopped down in the arm chair across the room from Lyn.

Lyn's head jerked from Umiko's face to Killian's. That was not what she expected this war council meeting to be about.

"What? No." Umiko shook her head. "Why would you think that?"

"On the phone, you said she changed." Killian sat back in the chair and put his shoes on the coffee table. "Was it teeth or claws or both? I doubt she went full wolf." He crossed his arms over his chest.

Lyn wanted to scream at him to get his feet off the table, at all of them to stop talking about her like she wasn't there. Instead, she folded her hands into fists beside her and fought to keep her claws contained. If she let her anger out, she would be playing into his hand. She pushed the fury down and bottled it for later.

"I didn't mean change like that."

Lyn caught the sour look that crossed Umiko's face. She'd seen that disgust before, in her nightmares.

Killian stared at Lyn, who was still standing by the door. "She's supposed to."

"I haven't found a good time." Lyn crossed her arms over her chest and glared back at the alpha.

"Now's good. They're all here." Killian sat up in his chair, planted his feet on the floor and challenged her. His shoulders tensed as he made eye contact.

Lyn stared back. This was not shifter training, and this was not his territory. It was her house and she wasn't about to let him start making the rules in her home. Umiko apparently had that function covered. She glared at him. "It's not happening."

"Scout sent me the playlist." Killian slid his phone out of his pocket and waved it with his wrist. The smile on his face and the tone of his voice made him look like a child with a new toy, but Lyn heard the threat underneath.

Scout looked at Lyn and mouthed the words, "I'm sorry." He knew Killian well enough to hear the threat too.

"I knew you wouldn't be able to do it on your own," Killian said. "You're too worried about what they think." Killian growled like it was the stupidest reason in the world.

"Back off, Jacobs." Greg shifted forward from his seat on the couch beside Umiko.

The pair faced off over the corner of the massive flower arrangement.

"Well, aren't these nice flowers? Who brought them?" Scout asked, but his ploy to change topics was lost.

"You back off, Gregar. You wanted me to train her. She needs to shift in front of her friends, and her friends need to see it." Killian said friends like the word tasted bad in his mouth. "Otherwise, if it ever comes down to life or death, she will get stuck in her head caring about your reactions and someone will get hurt."

Scout lifted the glass vase from the coffee table and

relocated the flower arrangement to the kitchen, giving weight to Lyn's expectation that this was going to get messy.

Lyn suppressed a growl. "Quit being dramatic."

Scout returned to the side of her chair and leaned his weight on the arm rest.

"Quit being so embarrassed by what we are," Killian countered, "and don't say you're not one of us."

Lyn met his eyes and a contest of wills ensued. Both sat up straighter in their chairs and squared off across the low coffee table.

"Well," Umiko tried to regain control, "this is my meeting, Killian. You can call your own later. Have any of you fine men noticed Lyn's hair?"

Lyn sighed and leaned back. She closed her eyes and forgot about Killian. This was more of what she imagined would happen as soon as Umiko got her lightbulb moment upstairs. Any moment now, Umiko would want to start an expedition to figure out the rest of Lyn's heritage.

Scout was the only one who raised his hand, the other three guys in the room took a moment to look at her.

Lyn rubbed her forehead and tried to forget that everyone was staring at her hair. Her freakish, did what it wanted and made a scene, hair.

"It's red, who cares?" Killian said.

"Right? It's no big deal. Everyone out." Lyn didn't expect it to work, but she tried.

"She did that herself," Umiko answered.

Clark leaned forward on the couch and stared at Lyn's hair. "I'm assuming you mean without a bottle of hair dye and a straightening iron."

"I do," Umiko said, her lips curled up in excitement. "No tools or products of any kind. Not even a hair brush."

"How did you do it?" Greg's eyes were glued to Lyn's hair. He wasn't so much looking at her as through her, or around her, almost as if he wasn't even seeing her, sitting there, melting under the gaze of everyone in the room.

"Magic." Lyn filled the word with all the sarcasm she could muster and looked away. She let her eyes drift to the flowers in the kitchen.

"She can show you," Umiko said and clapped her hands.

Lyn sighed. She knew Umiko wasn't going to let it go without a show. Lyn hated the idea of performing, of being the center of attention in a freak show stage act. How could she get them to just leave?

She looked around the room at all the expectant faces. They were watching her hair as if it might change at any moment.

She closed her eyes with a huff and lifted her hands to her forehead. She imagined the brown curly locks of her mom's hair, the kind Lyn had until the binding started to fade. She ran her hand up and over her scalp and down her hair until the ends fell through her fingers.

"See. It's definitely a creature trait, right?" Umiko beamed.

"That's your mom's style," Clark said. "I remember from the hospital."

"It is. She can do mine and her mom's, but she can't do Clark's," Umiko said. "I tested that already. So, there are limitations, but I don't know why, yet."

"That's why we're here?" Scout asked. "Because she has cool hair?" He moved his arm to rest on the top of the chair, over Lyn's head.

"Now that you've all seen my party trick, you can leave." To Lyn it was just hair, but to Umiko it was a puzzle to solve and Lyn did not want to be solved.

No one moved.

Lyn sank back into her chair and tried to fade away. She should have just run off when Scout offered. She was invisible, her presence didn't matter for the discussion currently going on around her. Her objections held no weight.

She noticed Scout shift on the edge of her chair, but she didn't know if it was discomfort or interest that made him move. She didn't look to find out, she wanted to think she had one person on her side.

"It's a glamor," Greg said.

"Like fairies?" Clark asked, "or vampires?"

"Oh. My. God. I am not a vampire!" Lyn shouted and grabbed the arm rests. Her claws digging into the upholstery.

No one cared.

Scout put a hand on her shoulder.

One person cared.

Lyn forced her nails to retract.

"The fae can change their appearance, or at least make you think that you see something different than what's actually there." Greg looked at Clark.

"You think I'm part fairy?" Lyn began to hear her pulse drum in her ear. She raised a hand to rub her jaw line and the space just in front of her ear.

"No," Greg said. "I'm sure you're fae. I just don't know what kind."

Lyn stared at him like he had three heads. "Excuse me? Why didn't you tell me? How are you so sure?"

"How do you know?" Umiko asked before Lyn had finished her own questions.

"She can't break promises," Greg said, ignoring Lyn's accusal. "When you make a deal with a fairy, neither party can break it without repercussions." He scooted forward to the edge of the couch. His knees bumped Lyn's.

"I can break promises. I promise not to stick out my tongue." Lyn stuck out her tongue. "See. A broken promise." She leaned back and crossed her arms over her chest.

Greg held out his hand for Lyn to take.

She eyed him suspiciously, but she took it. She wasn't sure why. She was angry and tired and she knew she wasn't thinking straight.

"Promise not to hit me," he said.

"Why would I hit you?" Lyn asked, but she already felt the urge to do just that. She narrowed her eyes. "Never mind, don't answer that." There were only two people in the room that Lyn didn't feel like wrapping her hands around their throats. One of them was sitting quietly beside her best friend, whom she did want to strangle. But not for a moment did she think Clark would choose Lyn's side over Umiko's.

Lyn took a deep breath and tried to lower her heart rate. If she didn't, she would call her wolf without meaning to and give Killian what he wanted. That was not going to happen, if she could help it.

"Just promise," Greg squeezed her hand.

Scout shifted on the arm of the chair again.

"Fine." Lyn sighed and rolled her eyes.

"Say it."

"I promise not to hit you." Lyn rolled her eyes.

Greg let his hand drop. "There are other signs, too. Like her connection with music. The way it manipulates her." Greg turned to face Killian. "Do what you came here to do," he said.

"What the hell?" Lyn said. She shot forward in her chair and knocked Scout from his precarious perch.

A pleased look spread across Killian's face as he looked at Lyn across the table. He pushed a button on his phone.

Lyn recognized the music. It was the same loud, discordant sound that the pack had used to cause her first shift. She covered her ears with her hands and turned toward Greg. "What are you doing?"

"Proving a point," Greg said with confidence.

"By force?" Lyn removed a hand from her ear and curled her fingers into a fist. She threw her arm in an arc toward Greg's face.

Greg didn't flinch.

Lyn's fist stopped less than an inch from his cheek. She growled at the impotent connection as her stomach lurched.

"You made a deal." Greg looked into her eyes and cocked his head. His brow wrinkled. "I thought your eyes were green?"

"Not in her wolf form," Killian's smile grew. He was enjoying her discomfort.

A familiar rumble started in her belly as the anger she had for Killian built. Lyn tried to block the music from syncing with her pulse. She covered her ears in a futile gesture and shook her head as if she could dislodge the sound taking root.

"Killian, maybe this isn't the best time," Scout said.

Lyn felt the touch of his hand on her shoulder even through the waves of pain trying to pull her under and release her wolf. She would have pulled away from his touch, but she was fighting on a different front at the moment.

Killian turned up the volume and leaned forward in his own seat. "If you fight it, it will be worse."

"But you've been teaching me to fight it!" Lyn yelled at him. Her emotions already getting the better of her.

"So I have," Killian smirked. "What are you going to do about it?"

Lyn funneled all her frustration at not being able to punch Greg into a new target. She stood up and leaped at Killian with her hands raised to wrap around his throat, but the shudder of her shift threw her off balance. She slammed her hands into the coffee table.

Lyn started to scream as the pain swept through her, but she managed to turn it into a growl. The shift in determination dulled the pins and needles of her changing form. Instead of trying to shut it off, she rode the wave of sound and the tempo of her pulse, there was no other way, not with the beat of the music pounding in her veins.

"You're going to ruin that dress if you don't get your head in the game," Killian taunted her.

Lyn looked at the five faces in her living room. She shook her head and fought back against the pull of her wolf as a scream tore from her throat.

Not everyone in this room had seen her naked, not yet, and she was going to keep it that way. She clamped her mouth shut and ground her teeth together. She tried to remember the songs from the other playlist. The one Scout had used to pull her back to herself the first time. She hummed a few bars of Rachmaninoff.

Pain shot through her legs and she lost the tune. She cursed under her breath and almost fell to her knees.

"Umiko," Scout's voice cut through Lyn's fear, "pass me the blanket."

"Scout?" Lyn said through her teeth.

"It's gone too far," he said. "You can't put her back in. She wants to be free."

Scout held the blanket between Lyn and the eyes scattered around the room as her knees buckled and she channeled the intense pain into a growl.

"It's going to be okay," Scout whispered.

She looked into his eyes and saw her pain reflected there.

The snap of bone echoed through her ears. She slipped off her underwear as she went down to the ground on four legs. She ripped the dress over her head as her body bucked one last time and was still.

Lyn's wolf panted as if she had run the length of the forest, but she didn't collapse. She stood weak on four legs and gathered her anger around her like armor.

Scout let the blanket fall. Almost as if he were a magician and she was his magic trick, only Lyn knew Scout didn't feel that way. Killian probably, but not Scout.

Lyn's wolf looked around the room with her amber and silver eyes and took in her companions.

Clark looked impressed and Umiko rubbed her knees

with a grimace. Killian was locked in a staring match with Greg.

Lyn's wolf snarled. Her head moved from Greg to Killian and back. Her jaws snapped. She wasn't sure which one was the biggest threat at the moment.

Umiko flinched and pulled her legs up onto the couch.

Lyn laughed on the inside at Umiko's misconception that making herself a smaller target could protect her from Lyn's wolf's jaws. She, who plucked rabbits from their burrows in the dead of night.

Clark pulled Umiko closer and wrapped his arms around her.

Lyn's wolf breathed in the scent of their fear. She was the biggest predator in the room and she surveyed her prey.

Greg and Killian faced Lyn's wolf, defiance clear in the set of their shoulders. The girl, however, was cowering and her ineffectual protector unconcerned. The latter pair would be easy kills, the former a challenge but not deadly odds. Lyn's wolf could already taste the blood she would shed. She turned toward her first target.

Lyn struggled for control before her wolf made good on her desire, but she had so much anger and so little sleep that her wolf was stronger. Her wolf snarled at the biggest threat in the room besides herself.

Killian was brutal in training. He was harder on her than his teammates and she hated having to do what he told her. She growled and stepped closer to him, her teeth dripped with saliva. Her sharp claws clicked on the wood floors.

He just smiled, which pissed her off more, but Lyn wrestled control and turned her wolf away from him. This was her house and there would be no bloodshed. Turning brought her face to face with the next biggest threat.

Right now, Lyn was angriest at Greg. Not only had he been the one to insist that Killian train her, he had forced this shift on her without giving her a choice. Her wolf faced the new target and growled.

Greg watched her, eyes wide, tension in his shoulders. He would fight back, but she didn't care. She'd taken down coyotes. He would be just as easy.

Lyn used to think Greg was nothing like Killian. His hero complex was at odds with Killian's bullish attitude, but right now, they were the same. Greg forced her change exactly like Killian had done to her the first time. The day she found out she was part predator.

She exposed her teeth mid snarl and stepped toward Greg.

CHAPTER SEVEN

Greg tensed and met the wolf's eyes.

"Gregar, I don't know exactly what you are, but the best thing you can do for Lyn and to save your neck is to submit," Killian demanded. "I don't think even you can heal if she rips your throat out."

Greg glared at Killian but let his stance relax. He sat back on the couch. "I'm sorry." His mouth made the shape, but Lyn heard nothing but the awful beat from Killian's phone.

Lyn growled. She couldn't stop it. She didn't care if Greg was sorry. It was too late. Her wolf was in control.

"Lyn, heel," Killian barked at her.

Lyn turned away from Greg and focused on Killian, maybe today would be the day she could snap his neck. She had the upper hand. She was already in her wolf form. He would have to waste precious time to shift. She snarled and saliva dripped down her fangs.

"Don't get any ideas." Killian's growl rumbled in his throat.

"I told you this was a bad idea," Scout chided. "Her wolf is pissed. Lyn can't reign her in." He stood near the chair, his phone in hand as he pushed and swiped on his phone screen.

"Thanks for that insight," Killian grumbled without breaking eye contact with Lyn.

Lyn's dual colored eyes demanded his dark ones look away first. She growled and showed her sharp teeth as she stepped onto the table to get closer to Killian.

"What's going on?" Umiko asked from the slim safety her position between Greg and Clark offered her.

Lyn snarled, ignoring the rabbit in favor of the wolf.

"Lyn's wolf is challenging Killian," Scout said. He increased the volume on his phone to combat the songs coming from Killian's. "Killian, silence your phone." Scout looked at his alpha, but spoke to Umiko. "If he breaks contact first, she will never submit to his authority, and his position in our pack would be suspect. He could lose his alpha status."

"She's challenging him for alpha?" Clark asked. "Now?"

"Yes and no," Scout said. "Lyn doesn't want to be alpha. She knows she should break eye contact first, but she's stubborn. Her wolf is more so, and strong, and thinks she'd be a better alpha."

The loud beats from Killian's phone stopped when the song ended on its own.

"They've done this before and he's always won?" Clark asked.

"Not exactly," Scout said sheepishly. "I cheat." He shook his phone. "With permission, of course." The first song faded and 'The Sound of Silence' began to pour out.

The haunting sounds of Scout's playlist finally made it past the thundering of Lyn's wolf's pulse. She breathed deep, taking in the lingering scent of fear. Beyond it she smelled sunshine and salt. Lyn's wolf turned to Umiko and blinked. She turned to the smell of open spaces and growled when Greg looked at her. She took another breath and followed the scent. Age and rust belonged to Clark and mixed with Killian's wildfire and smoke. Another breath and she found the calming scent of cedar wood. She stepped down from the table and stood on guard near the only person in the room she trusted at that moment. Her wolf's control began to fade and Lyn was able to take over.

She stared at Killian until her knees shook and she was forced to the ground for a second time, a growl in her wolf's throat blossomed into a gasp of pain in her human one.

Scout tossed the blanket over Lyn's changing form as she shuddered.

"You're getting quicker," Scout said to Lyn when she looked up at him.

White hair framed her face. Her eyes were still her wolf's. One amber, one silver.

He turned to Umiko as Lyn picked up her discarded clothing. "The music really helps. I haven't managed to get it to work on any one else." He looked down and smiled at Lyn. "Just you."

"It might not work for anyone else." Greg interrupted their moment. "I'm pretty sure her affinity for music is part of her fairy genes."

Lyn put her dress on while keeping the blanket wrapped around her. When she was dressed, she stood, letting the blanket puddle to the floor by the coffee table, and walked to the door.

Scout watched her

Lyn's pulse still pounded in her head. Her anger was louder than his phone but she heard David Draiman's haunting voice and clung to it.

A thousand voices, maybe more.

"Everyone out!" she yelled and opened the door. She exhaled with a force reminiscent of a bull before it pawed the ground.

Scout moved toward the door to obey her demand.

"No," Umiko, Greg, and Killian said in unison behind him.

Scout stopped in his tracks.

People hearing without listening.

Lyn glared at Killian. She knew he wouldn't submit to her unless it was what he wanted and it wasn't, it couldn't be. She had been down that road many times over the last few months, in training and out of it. He could never submit to her and keep his status and she did not want to be alpha.

She turned to Greg. His eyes were apologetic, but firm. She sensed it was only surface deep, not an apology for what he had done, more of an apology about how she felt about what he had done. He wouldn't back down and neither would she. The last tendrils of trust were broken.

Lyn looked at her best friend.

Umiko looked back, challenging Lyn in her own small way. But that was Lyn's fault. Ever since they met, Lyn had let Umiko call the shots, and look what it brought her. Umiko was in the planning stages for her newest mission, she wouldn't give it up just because Lyn was feeling ganged up on. Umiko would press on, even if it was without Lyn.

Clark sat next to her, and while his voice didn't join in the chorus of defiance, he didn't look like he was going to leave either.

Lyn closed her eyes, defeated.

And whispered in the sound of silence.

Lyn turned to Scout. The only person in the room she didn't want to eviscerate. The only person in the room that had offered her an out. She wished she had taken it then, but she would take it now.

She took a deep breath, stepped through, and slammed the door behind her. The windows nearest the door vibrated in their panes. Lyn's entire body vibrated with rage, but at least her wolf was still.

CHAPTER EIGHT

*S*cout looked around the room at the stunned faces. Only one appeared unconcerned with Lyn's departure. The rest were gaping at the space Lyn left bending. *Good,* he thought. *You should be concerned. What the hell kind of friends are you people?*

Greg and Killian stood beside their seats. Killian with a smile on his face. He had won, after all. He had forced her to shift in front of her friends and Greg had asked him to. The hero had wordlessly accepted that Killian knew best and Killian would never let him live that down.

Greg was more subdued. He was trying to figure out what just happened, but Scout recognized the look Greg cast at the door. He expected her to walk back in. He was waiting for her to come to him. Scout shook his head. Greg didn't know her very well.

Umiko stared at the front door, her jaw hung open. She gathered herself and spoke. "I can't believe she did that. She just ran off." Umiko looked puzzled. "She's never done that before."

"Sure she has," Killian sat back down in his chair and put

his shoes on the table. "She's a master of running away when things get difficult."

"She's never done it to me." Umiko stood up and faced Killian. "You deserve it. You're a bully."

"Really? I wasn't the only one she told to get out, nor the only one that defied her." Killian smiled.

Shock registered on Umiko's face.

Clark put his hand on her arm and pulled her back down to the couch. He began rubbing circles on her back.

Scout couldn't fault Clark for taking his girlfriend's side, but he could fault Greg, for not.

"I'll go get her." Greg stepped around the coffee table.

"I'm coming too," Umiko said and pulled her arm from Clark's light grasp.

Killian laughed. "Lyn doesn't need you. She'll be fine. She just needs to run it off."

"Don't tell me what she needs." Greg bristled and faced Killian with his finger lifted in the alpha's direction. "You don't know her as well as I do."

"Don't I?" Killian said. "I've spent more time with her lately than you have." He stood and squared off with Greg.

Umiko looked between them and said something that Scout couldn't make out over their posturing.

"None of you know why she left just now, do you?" Scout shouted above the din of voices.

Every face in the room turned toward him.

"She was angry," Killian said. "She'll get over it." He met Scout's eyes before he sank back into the chair.

"I ambushed her," Greg turned his gaze to the floor but kept on his feet.

Only Umiko held her opinion in.

Scout recognized the strength it took for her to do that.

"Why do you think she left, Scout?" she asked after a breath.

Scout chuffed. Could they really not see it? How could

they not? They were suffocating her and not a single one of her friends noticed. "She left because you all think it's your right to control her." Scout looked at Killian. "I know you're alpha, but she hasn't accepted membership into your pack and she will never submit to you. You need to accept it."

He turned to Greg. "You think that just because you're a big, strong descendant of Amazonian parentage, you need to protect her. Trust me, she can handle herself if you let her."

Scout turned to Umiko. She looked at him with a tremble in her cheeks. He didn't want to add to her pain, but he also knew she needed to hear his words. "Umiko..." He softened.

"I do. I don't mean to, but I do."

Scout nodded. He hoped she understood well enough to change, for Lyn's sake.

"What are you proposing, Scout?" Clark asked, pulling Umiko back to sitting again.

"Lyn's whole world turned upside down last year. She found out that everything she thought she knew was suspect because of a witch's binding spell. She lost her family and her humanity in the span of, what a month? She's slowly coming to terms with being a shifter, which she obviously does not fully control, and now we throw possible fairy blood into the mix. That makes two predator parents. There is no way that sits well with her. She will need some time to let that sink in. You need to trust her or she might run off for good."

"How do you know these things and I don't?" Umiko's voice trembled.

Scout heard regret tinged with sadness.

Scout lowered his voice. "Because I listen to her." He walked toward the door and stooped down to pick up Lyn's running shoes. He took her purse from the hook by the door and put his hand on the handle.

"It helps that his mom is a psychologist," Killian crossed his arms. "I stand by his assessment. He's a damn good judge of people."

Scout rolled his eyes. Of course Killian would take credit. Scout hadn't expected anything different.

"You should all go home. Lock the house when you leave." Scout opened the door. "I'll make sure she's okay." He closed the door and left the rest of them sitting in Lyn's living room.

Scout took a breath and found Lyn's distinctive rainstorm and long run scent. He moved the same direction she had, down the sidewalk and right along the street, but he didn't need to catch up to her. He knew where she was headed.

CHAPTER NINE

Storm clouds were brewing by the time Scout caught up to Lyn. The grey sky tempered the heat and brightened the green of the trees.

She stood inside a copse of cedar trees along the bank of a slow moving creek. This was not the first time she had come here, nor the first time he had followed her. Her white hair stood out amongst the greens and browns of her surroundings. No matter what she looked like before she shifted, she always came out of it with white hair and skin a shade paler than normal.

Her dual colored eyes didn't normally linger long after she changed, reverting back to their usual green within moments, but today was different. Scout saw the trouble she was having taming her wolf reflected in the set of her shoulders. Her wolf was still close to the surface, but he wasn't worried about scaring her, she was already aware of his approach.

"Can I join you?" he asked, stepping into the small clearing.

The space between the cedars was littered with white topped mushrooms and smelled vaguely of ammonia.

Scout knew she had chosen this spot for exactly that reason. She had already surpassed Killian in her scent tracking ability and she knew Killian would never be able to find her here. The ammonia smell was enough to mask her scent from most animals, and Killian was not the best tracker in the pack, not even close.

He was also sure that she knew the intense smell would not hide her from him. He was the one teaching her to track by scent. It was he who had pitted her nose against Killian's. He who had brought her superiority to her attention.

But she wasn't trying to hide from him.

"Did you forget something?" Scout walked to the edge of the creek with her shoes behind his back.

They looked out over the water. The darkened skies hinted at rain, maybe more, but it would mean nothing until it fell. The weather seemed to be more fickle lately. Broadcasting one thing then failing to deliver.

Silence hung in the air as Scout listened to Lyn breathe and try to tame her anger.

She stood with her fists at her side and looked down at the mushrooms around her bare feet. "My phone."

"I brought your shoes and your purse." Scout held the items up as he mentioned them. "Is your phone in here?"

Lyn shook her head. "My phone is on my bed. I accidentally left it in my room when I was trying to get away from Umiko and her mission the first time. I didn't get a chance to go back upstairs after people arrived."

"I can go get it for you. If you'd like." He didn't want to leave her here alone, not after her friends had ganged up on her. "Or you can borrow mine. I made a new playlist. Do you want to hear it?"

Lyn bristled at his words.

Scout lowered his head. "I'm sorry about earlier. I should have tried harder to stop Killian and Greg." He stepped in front of her and tried to get her to look at him. "I'm sorry."

"Thank you." She didn't meet his eyes.

He wanted to reach out to her. Pull her into his chest and hold her. Help her calm her wolf and her anger with his strength.

He took a breath and calmed the urge. "The new playlist starts with some a cappella. Straight No Chaser and Citizen Queen. After that I think you'll pick up on the theme."

Lyn wiped her eyes with the back of her hand. "I don't know Citizen Queen."

"Then I'm excited to get to introduce you." Scout smiled. "They are an all girl a cappella group. He thumbed through the myriad of playlists on his phone and found the one he made especially for her with a little help from Veronica, his brother's girlfriend.

He now curated most of his lists with Lyn in mind. He enjoyed having music in common with her. A reason to put his hobby and his mixer to use beyond school dances and side projects he had yet to let anyone listen to. He looked forward to sharing with her more than anyone else. He knew she would share his excitement and point out his failures and he would love both.

His heart skipped a beat. Scout handed Lyn the device, trusting that Veronica knew what she was talking about when she said he needed to put himself out there. His heart pounded in his chest. This playlist was far from subtle.

"What did Greg and Killian mean about my eyes?" Lyn took his phone. She pushed play and lowered the volume to an under current.

Scout took a breath and answered her question. "Your wolf shows a trait called heterochromia. It presents in several ways, but yours is two completely different colored eyes. It's usually caused by trauma but there are some cases that are hereditary."

"But my eyes are green. They always have been."

"You've never looked at your wolf's reflection."

"Do you have a mirror?" Lyn asked.

"No, but there's a camera in your hand. That might do, and there's me."

Lyn turned to look at Scout.

Scout heard the song in the background as it blended with the sound of the water gently flowing behind them and the birds chirping overhead. When she looked into his eyes, he nearly lost his calm.

"What color are they now?"

"Green," he said. He didn't elaborate on the gentle cresting waves that he saw in her eyes, or the fact that they sparkled like emeralds in the right light.

"So, in order to see this heterochromia thing, I'd need to shift."

"Maybe." He shrugged. "When you shifted back today, your eyes stayed for a while. Your wolf's eyes stared everyone down." He smiled. He had enjoyed watching her display of dominance.

"I was angry. How could they have ganged up on me like that?"

"You were more pissed off than I have ever seen you." Scout chuckled. "You left them all speechless."

"I did?" Lyn's eyes settled on his lips.

"Not for long," he admitted, "but yeah. They couldn't believe you walked out." Scout paused. "I think you should do it more often."

Lyn smiled. "Thanks."

"Anytime," he said. "I actually left them all in your living room. Between Umiko and Greg, I figured someone would lock your house up, right? Was that okay? I can go back and do it myself."

"It's fine. Umiko will lock the front door, after everyone leaves, and go out the back."

"Okay." Scout looked at his phone in her hand. The lyrics were loud in his ears, matched only by the sound of his pulse racing. "Do you want me to tell you more about your eyes?"

"Yes, but I need to move." She turned up the volume and handed Scout his phone. "I still feel trapped." She turned away from him and walked to the middle of the copse.

He stood near the trunk of a tree to allow her space to move. She motioned to him to increase the volume. *No going back now.* He did as she asked and slid the phone into his back pocket, speaker pointed up.

"Your right eye," Scout closed his eyes and pictured hers, "is amber. Dark red near the pupil radiates out to a deep gold. Your left is an ethereal shade of purple. It's pale enough that most people might think it was silver, like ice."

"Why do you see purple?"

"I pay more attention than most." Scout loved her eyes, whether they were green or silver and amber. The intensity of her gaze looked like it took everything in. Like she was memorizing every crease, gradient, and subtle shift in shape or color. When that gaze was on him it was like she could see through him. Like she could read his every thought, like she might know what it was like to be him.

He let his mind wander back to the first time their eyes met. The school cafeteria. He was on his way to the gym the day Greg and Killian got into their first fight of the year. Her eyes were green that day. A shimmering green that reminded him of tall grass dancing in a breeze.

Scout opened his eyes a few moments later to see Lyn stretching her arms above her head. She flexed her feet to stand on her toes making her appear even taller than she was. Her feet started moving with the voices in his pocket, although she looked sluggish and unsteady on her feet.

He stayed quiet as Straight No Chaser's "I Won't Give Up" faded into Citizen Queen's "Slow Burn." He watched her face for understanding, but saw none.

"So, one gold and one silver," she said as her head

whipped around in a turn and her white hair streaked behind it. She nearly twisted up her legs mid turn, but she recovered before she tripped.

He heard her words, but he was lost in her dance. Even faltering, she commanded his full attention. But where was her grace? A question formed in his head, but didn't make it to his lips.

Lyn slowed at the end of "Slow Burn." Lyn put her fingers in her ears as the next song started.

Scout took it as a cue to lower the volume on his phone. Half disappointed and half relieved that she wouldn't hear the end of his love themed playlist.

He snapped a picture of Lyn with the sun streaming through the cedar trees behind her. It tinted her skin with a warm honey glow and set off her hair like a crown of gold, but her eyes shined even brighter.

She sat down in the middle of the trampled mushrooms. "I know that's an awful smell, like a freshly cleaned hospital room or a janitor's closet, but it's also kind of intoxicating."

"Ammonia. It's from the mushrooms. I definitely don't think they're the edible type." He winked and sat opposite her.

"Good thing I'm not hungry."

"You, not hungry? I'm sorry, but are you the same Lyn I know?"

She looked at him and smiled. "Thank you for following me. The music helped. I needed a reset."

Scout lifted his camera. He tapped the screen's picture of her face and set the focal point. "You're welcome." Scout zoomed in on the photo's capture of her eyes and handed it to Lyn. "Heterochromia."

She looked at the phone and moved it closer to her face. She zoomed in on one eye, then the other. "So, why are they this sometimes," she handed the phone to Scout, "but green most of the time?"

Scout shrugged his shoulders and looked at the warm amber and cool silver of her irises.

"They were always green before," Lyn said with a far away look, "the same green as my mom's."

Scout watched as Lyn's eye color slowly shifted back to a sea green. Next to her white hair, they gleamed with color.

"What color are mine?" he asked.

"Brown with a touch of grey near the pupils." She stared into them. "Like looking down into a volcano from really high." She smiled.

Scout tried not to blink as heat rose to his cheeks. He liked the way she described his eyes. "Can you imagine having the same?" Scout asked.

She sighed. "You think I can change them the way I can change my hair?"

Scout nodded. He didn't want to push too hard like Killian and Umiko had. "You don't have to." He didn't want to give her any excuse to run.

"No. It's okay." Lyn closed her eyes and placed her hands in front of them, her fingertips barely pressing on the rounded eye through the lid. After a moment, she pulled her hands away from her face and put them in her lap. She looked at Scout.

Scout shook his head and put a hand on top of hers. "It must not be that simple." He squeezed her hand in what he hoped was encouragement, only he couldn't bring himself to let go.

Lyn stared into his eyes and he tried hard not to be the one to break eye contact.

He watched as the green of her eyes began to darken and shift. He thumbed open his phone without looking. When her eyes stopped changing he lifted the camera and snapped a picture. "It's a little strange to be looking into my own eyes." He handed her the phone. "Without a mirror, I mean."

Lyn held the phone and switched between the photos. It

was her face, but with Scout's mountain colored eyes.

"But what did I do that was different?"

Scout shrugged and moved his hand away. "Do you want to talk it out?"

Lyn shook her head and handed him back his phone. She picked up a broken mushroom and tossed it away.

"How long are you going to make them sweat it out before you go back?" Scout changed the subject

Lyn smiled. "A week. Two tops."

Scout loved it when she did that. The smile, the deadpan humor, the way she twisted the corner of her mouth, all of it."In that case, may I take you somewhere?"

Lyn nodded.

Scout stood and walked to the edge of the clearing where he had left her shoes. "Shoes or no shoes?"

"Shoes." She took the offering and reached inside them for socks.

Scout thumbed a quick message to Killian. *Safe.* He stood up and extended a hand to Lyn after her shoes were tied. "Would you prefer pop, country, or a rock playlist for our run?"

When Lyn took his hand, his whole arm tingled.

"Why don't you surprise me?" She stood up and released his hand.

Scout thought about continuing the one she'd just started, but his nerves won out. Now wasn't a good time. Maybe there never would be one. He chose a fast paced playlist and slid his phone into this back pocket. He smiled at her and started to run.

"Where are we going?" Lyn asked as she met his pace.

"If I tell you, you'll run ahead," he teased.

"What? You don't want to be beat by a girl?" She sprinted a few yards ahead.

"I wouldn't mind being beat by you," he whispered and increased his speed.

CHAPTER TEN

Scout and Lyn ran side by side through parks and neighborhoods and along sidewalks bordering busy neighborhood roads until Scout slowed down in front of a big, black, iron gate.

"Why did you bring me here?" Lyn froze at the cemetery entrance.

"Today is the anniversary of my dad's death," Scout said standing next to her.

They looked at the open gate as a dark sedan slowly exited from the gravel road that led into the hallowed grounds.

"I stop by every year to make sure the plot is clean and cared for. It's silly. I know he's not there, but it makes me feel better." Scout turned to her.

Lyn saw the worry spread across his face.

"Are you okay? We don't have to stay. We can go somewhere else."

Guilt and sadness warred within her. She had only been here twice. Once for her mom and once for her mom's husband. If it hadn't been for Scout, she wouldn't be here now. She felt like a horrible daughter. She wiped a tear from her eye and sidestepped her issue by latching on to his. "I didn't know your dad was dead."

"We don't talk about it. Well, my mom, Jake, and I talk about him all the time, at home. But there's pack drama, so we try to step lightly. Well, some of us do." He crossed the gate's threshold.

"How are you related to Killian, again?" Lyn was stalling. She knew they shared a last name. She also knew they weren't brothers. She just wasn't sure if their link was maternal or paternal.

"Cousins on my dad's side. Oddly enough, born on the same day. I'm older by seventeen minutes." Scout turned to face her. "Wait, didn't Umiko say you couldn't step on holy ground. Vampire, right?" He took two big steps backward into the cemetery and she swung at him, crossing the threshold to reach.

He let her fist connect with his bicep. "I guess not." He winked.

Lyn found herself matching his easy attitude for a moment, before she remembered where she was. She took a deep breath and the smile faded. "My mom is here."

"Oh. I should have realized. I'm sorry." Scout looked at her like a deer in headlights. "Do you want to…"

She shook her head. She probably should stop by to visit, but, like Scout said, it was silly. Her mom, or the woman she thought of as her mother, wasn't actually here, and though Jonathan lay at her side, her relationship with him was more complicated.

"We can leave." Scout pulled up close to her.

She felt his arm press against hers, like he could and would sweep her up and carry her away.

"No. It's fine. It will be fine." Lyn bolstered herself. "Where is your dad's marker?"

"Far right corner. The Jacobs' family plot."

Lyn nodded and took a step in that direction.

The cemetery was large, with a gridded one lane gravel road criss crossing to divide the property into squares almost as large as city blocks. Scout took her to the far right edge of the property and walked her along a black metal fence separating the grave stones from an overgrown field.

Scout kept looking back at her like he was afraid she'd disappear or run. Lyn tried to focus on putting one foot in front of another and not stepping on the resting place of someone's dead relative, instead of where her mom and Jonathan were waiting for her.

"Let's just leave." Scout pulled up short. "I can come back later."

She glared at him.

"Fine," he said, "You win. Back corner. I'll race you." Scout started running.

Lyn took the bait and chased. They leap frogged a couple of times before reaching the spot Scout had indicated.

"Back corner. Three rows over, two down. But this whole section is 'Jacobs.'" Scout walked over his relatives to stand in front of his dad's headstone.

Lyn followed, walking along the edge of plots, or where she imagined the edges to be since the ground was uninterrupted grass with vertical stones scattered throughout.

Scout kneeled on the ground and pulled out a weed.

"Taylor S. Jacobs," Lyn read. 1974 - 2008. "Is the S for Scout?"

"No. Scott, but that is where Scout comes from." Scout reached for and pulled another weed out of the ground by the root. He pulled a third and a fourth. "My birth certificate says Scout. It's not a nickname."

Lyn stood quietly by while he worked.

It was peaceful here, set off from the main road. There were hardly any traffic noises and there were trees shadowing almost every headstone. She wanted to lay down and rest like the cemetery residents. Just for a few moments.

The tweeting of birds and the chitter of squirrels were as soothing as a lullaby and a butterfly caught her peripheral vision.

It flitted between grave stones toward the other side of the cemetery. Lyn lost sight of it behind a tree only to catch it further on its journey, joined by a second.

She watched the butterfly and its twin bob in and out of obstacles until they landed on a newer headstone and were joined by a third. They sat opening and closing their wings as if breathing.

Lyn matched her breath to theirs.

Scout stood up and followed her line of sight. "Do you want to go alone, or should we do it together?"

Lyn watched the tiny creatures' wings flap.

"Lyn?"

She reached her hand out to find his and started walking without saying a word.

CHAPTER ELEVEN

The warmth from her hand spread up his arm. His heart fluttered and he hoped she'd never let go, even though he knew she would. She wasn't his, but for now, in this quiet place, he could pretend.

Lyn slowed down as they reached the other side of the cemetery. She came to a stop two feet behind a pair of gravestones, her eyes glued to the back of the nearest one.

The pulse in her fingers drummed on his skin. He knew her well enough to know that she was fighting invisible demons. He squeezed her hand to lend his strength.

"Is this your mom's?" Scout asked, facing her. This pair was newer than the rest. Not the newest in the cemetery, but close. They had yet to develop the aged grey-green color rough stone takes on after years in the rain. He reached for her other hand and held both as he tried hard not to smile at her touch. Now was not the time for that either.

She didn't speak. Instead, she loosened her fingers without letting go of Scout's hand.

He took a step backward toward the front of the stone. He kept his eyes glued to hers, watching for any clues or warning signs that would tell him to stop. She followed, her hands still in his. He took another step but she planted her feet. Their arms stretched between them like a low bridge.

Lyn's eyes stayed glued to the curve of the headstone.

Scout looked away from her and read the carved surface of the stone. *Maria Davis; Beloved wife and mother.*

Scout took a deep breath and separated the smells. "Fresh cut grass, a tingle of lightning, rosemary, and a warm hug." He stepped back to Lyn and she folded herself into his arms. Scout felt like the luckiest guy on the planet, or would have if she hadn't started crying.

"She loved the smell of rosemary," Lyn said through ragged breaths. Lyn's eyes moved from the stone and seemed to flit around before settling back on the ground in front of the marker.

"Then she's in the perfect spot." Scout pointed past Lyn to the back fence where a large rosemary bush grew, despite the fence buried deep in its midst.

Lyn kept her eyes on the ground and Scout just held her. She relaxed into his embrace and he rested his chin on her head, glad that he could be here for her.

She pulled away. "What type of butterflies are those?" Lyn wiped her eyes with her hand. While they stood there, her hair had changed from white to brown. Curls licked her face and she brushed the flyaways behind her ear.

Scout followed her gaze. "What color are they?"

She turned to look at him, her brow knit in confusion. "White?"

"There are several white varieties. If it's a white with amber and brown bits, it's a Mestra. If it's all white, it's just called a White, sometimes Florida White, even though we're in Texas."

"What do you mean if?" she asked. Lyn's hand slipped out of his. She took a step back and tilted her head. "You can't see them?" The pitch of her voice increased with an edge of panic. She wrapped her arms around her middle

Scout took her face in his hands and looked into her eyes. "No, but I trust that you do."

Lyn looked away from Scout, and he released her even though he didn't want to. *She belongs to someone else.*

"There's at least 50 of them." Lyn's eyes flitted around the space. "I followed three to get here. The grave is my mom's? Maria's?"

Scout nodded and reached for her hand, hoping she'd let him hold on to her.

"So, they led me here and you can't see them?" Lyn's voice bordered on frantic. She pulled her hand away and her sharp nails raked against his palm.

He knew her tells almost as well as he knew his own. He needed to diffuse the situation before she lost control or he'd be facing down an angry wolf instead of a scared girl.

"Some cultures think butterflies represent our loved one bringing messages." Scout reached for her hand and for something to say that would keep her from bolting. Only short, frail nails touched his skin, but her grip was firm.

He realized the amped up music playing from his pocket was not helping and he wished he could change it to something more soothing without letting go of her hand. He settled for using his free hand to reach into his far back pocket for the volume down button.

She calmed a little, but not much. Something other than music was at play and he wasn't sure what it was. He sniffed without bringing attention to it. He smelled a touch of fear mixed in with Lyn's usual scent.

"Tell me about them?" he asked quietly. He stretched his wolf's senses out. He noticed wildlife and people walking along the street outside of the cemetery gates, but for the most part, he and Lyn were alone.

Lyn took a deep breath. "They are bright white, like a blank canvas or freshly fallen snow. No brown or amber bits." She held out her free hand.

A moment later, she looked at the tip of her finger. "This one is tiny, about the size of my fingernail, but some are larger. Not so large as to be odd, just normal sized, I guess." She lifted her finger slowly toward Scout's face.

Scout looked at the tip and for a split second saw what might have been the blur of movement. But his rational brain cut in to tell him he was imagining things.

"Nothing?" Lyn's green eyes locked onto his brown ones. They pleaded with him to see the things she saw.

"My eyes might have seen a blur, but my brain is telling me it didn't."

Lyn's head snapped away first, facing the back fence line. Her body followed and she took a step back, into Scout.

He put his hands on her arms to steady her, but her heart was racing and she was close to running. He knew it. He wrapped his arms around her, carefully and slowly, to keep her in place.

"What did you hear?" he asked near her ear. He breathed her in. He would have closed his eyes and enjoyed the closeness, but he didn't feel as relaxed as he would have liked at the moment. The hairs on his arms prickled with anxiety.

"My name." She pulled free of his embrace but kept a solid grip on his hand. She walked toward the fence and pulled Scout along with her.

"Can you see anything?" Scout asked, aware that her vision was more useful than his at the moment.

"The butterflies are going in the direction the sound came from. They are almost in a line, like they know where they are going. It's not like any butterfly flight pattern I have ever seen."

Scout sniffed and pushed past the smell of rosemary from

the bush at their side and tried to filter out Lyn's unique scent. "I smell winter snow and gardenias, with an undercurrent of ..." Scout shook his head and sniffed again, "summer afternoons, jasmine, and a game of hide and seek?" Scout sniffed again, but the scent shifted. "The scent changes each time I sniff. The only stable smells are your scent and that bush."

Lyn put her free hand through the bars and stepped so her shoulder was pressed against the fence. She picked up her foot to place it through as well.

"Don't even think about going through the bars," Scout demanded, before he thought better about it. "Please," he added more gently.

"You could find me." Lyn looked wistfully toward the edge of the tree line, as she tried to force her shoulder through the slightly too thin space.

"Maybe. But I'm already down my sight, and my nose can't stick to a scent." Scout put his hand up to her face and turned her cheek to look into her eyes. One silver, one amber. "I will go with you, if that's what you want. But we have to be smart and we need to tell someone, maybe three someones, where we are going."

"You're scared." Her eyes accused him.

Scout smiled. "A little," he admitted, "but I think that's allowed. You are ready to follow a phantom voice and a string of invisible to me butterflies into a dark wood, at dusk, without a thought about the consequences."

Lyn looked at the sky. "I didn't realize it was so late already."

"Time doesn't seem to follow the rules around you," Scout said. Most days he was content to lose time with her. Today was no exception.

"You know that sounds crazy, right?" Lyn asked.

"Are you sure that's the only thing that sounds crazy?"

Scout looked into her eyes and his lips curved up. He wished he were brave enough to kiss her.

She put her hand on her hip and gave him a sideways smile.

"Please say you won't go without me." Scout knew his smile faded into concern, but he couldn't help it. He gripped her hand. Fairies were just as much predators as wolves were, but they were far more sneaky about it. And this stunk of fairy.

"Okay. I won't go without you," Lyn agreed.

A spark jumped between their hands and spread across their palms.

They dropped the connection and shook it off.

"That is worse than a joy buzzer," Scout looked at his palm

Lyn looked from her palm to his face. Her eyes drooped and a pout spread across her lips. If Greg was right, that was not a static reaction, it was a fairy deal binding.

"I didn't…" Scout felt his cheeks redden. "I honestly forgot." He cast his eyes down to his feet. He didn't want to take the deal back, but he also didn't want her to think he used her fairy traits against her. He didn't want to treat her like Killian and Greg did, without regards to her feelings. "I'm sorry. I wouldn't have…"

"It's done." She reached her hand out, palm up. "But you took without giving. I want it fair."

Scout gave her his hand.

"Promise you won't say anything about this to anyone." Lyn demanded.

"I promise."

A tingle started in the center of their palms and radiated out.

"That wasn't nearly as jarring as the first one," Scout said.

"I barely felt anything." Lyn squeezed his hand. "I don't think it worked."

"Worked, or not. I will hold up my end, if you hold up yours."

Lyn nodded and let go of his hand.

Scout's heart sank. He had missed his chance and probably ruined future ones with his absent minded deal making. He stuck his hands in his pockets. They were cold without her touch.

CHAPTER TWELVE

*L*yn kicked at the dirt. The tip of her shoe turned a dusty brown from the impact. She heard the voice again. Her name was faint like a whisper on the breeze.

She sighed and turned away, "Are you hungry?" She wanted to follow the sound of her name, but she had made a deal and, according to Greg, it was binding. She wanted to believe Scout hadn't intended to trap her, but she wasn't sure. He had never tried to force her to do anything. Even during training, she always had a choice with him. Killian was another story.

"I could go for a bite." Scout replied, a little more subdued than usual. "Are you thinking fresh or grocery store?"

"Grocery store," Lyn said. She was not in the mood for a hunt.

"Cool. Do you have a grill at home?"

"Yeah, but it hasn't been used since before…" She stifled a yawn and realized that she explained her life in two parts. Before the only mother she'd ever known died and after. "Plus, Greg probably has my house under surveillance. I'm not ready to reappear."

Scout nodded. "Okay. In that case, we could go to my house, but my brother and mom are home." He paused for a moment.

Lyn thought she could hear gears whirring away as Scout formed a plan.

"I could reappear, field questions, and give scant answers. Per our deal." More whirring. "Or... You can change your hair and eye color, I wonder if you can change your features."

Lyn picked up the whirring. She closed her eyes and ran her fingers through her hair, picturing her mom's hair style as if looking in a mirror, but instead of stopping there, she continued. She turned her reflection into her mom's one detail at a time. The shape of her eyes with the slight creases at the edge of each one. Her thin eyebrows. The crook of her nose and the smile lines between her lips and cheeks. Essentially, Lyn, but two decades older.

When she opened her eyes, she knew it had worked. Scout lifted his phone and a bright light momentarily blinded her.

"Sorry about the flash." Scout handed her his phone.

Lyn looked at the picture of her mom. She flipped over to the camera app and put it in selfie mode. She moved the features of her face and watched as the features of Maria's face on the camera screen moved in response.

Lyn sank to the ground as the wind rushed out of her lungs. She started gasping for breath.

"You're okay," Scout said, sinking down with her. "It's cool. Really."

She turned her wide eyes on him and heaved in as much air as she could.

He sat on the ground and pulled her close, wrapping his arms around her and stroking her head. He sang to her. She couldn't make out his words, but she felt the vibration in his collarbone against her head.

Lyn steadied her breathing and willed her face to change once more. She lifted the selfie camera to see the results. This time her own face stared back at her. A tear formed in her eye and slid down her cheek. *What am I? why can I do these things?*

"Are you sure you don't want to go back?" Scout asked, his face visible in the photo screen.

She took a deep breath and shook her head. "Umiko will ask too many questions. She's already starting to plan her next mission." Lyn shook her head more quickly, a whine edged her words. "I don't want to be the mission this time. I want to figure out answers first. On my terms, in my way, and at my speed." Lyn sat up, forcing his arms to release her.

Scout nodded and opened the weather app on his phone. The storm that they noticed earlier was absent from the radar. "Let's go. I have an idea of how we can stay off grid for a little longer." He smiled. "Do you want anything from your house?" He offered her his hand.

She accepted but needed more than a hand to pull herself off the ground. "I think the…" she made a motion with her hand around her face, "…took a lot of energy. I'm tired." She stood up using Scout as a crutch.

"I'll make a phone call." Scout said and dialed a few numbers. "Jake, do you have a few minutes to drop the Rover and some food off at the cemetery?" He paused. "Dinner and breakfast, for now. For two. Camp ready." Scout paused again and listened. "Yeah, we can drop you off on the way. Thanks, bro. I owe you one."

"Jake?" Lyn asked.

"Yeah. He'll hook us up with everything we need for a night under the stars." Scout made it sound like the words were on a marquee.

The cemetery lighting slowly bloomed in the dim light, almost on cue.

Lyn looked up.

"Wow, that was really great timing on my part," Scout said with a chuckle.

Lyn chuckled and stood on weak legs beside him. She

took a step toward the front gate, but her legs felt like cement blocks.

Scout scooped her up and carried her. Lyn laid her head in the crook of his neck and closed her eyes. The long run from the creek to the cemetery caught up to her, she was exhausted. Not getting a good night's sleep in forever doesn't help.

CHAPTER THIRTEEN

"Not cool, bro. Are you seriously accusing me of drugging a girl?" Scout asked. He took the keys his brother dangled in front of his face.

Jake laughed. "Chill. I know you better than that, plus I'd be able to smell it." He took a deep breath. "She doesn't smell like drugs or alcohol, just rain, lightning, and fresh air, with a little of you mixed in." Jake turned his eyes to his brother, a smile played across his face.

Scout put the keys in his pocket. "I had to carry her from the back fence." Scout looked at Lyn. The trunk of an old oak tree just inside the cemetery gates held her in its exposed roots. Her eyes were closed and her breathing was steady.

"Should I check her out while I'm here?" Jake asked. He pulled a pin light out of his pocket.

"No, she's just tired. She tried to do too much. She had an emotional day, starting with Killian and ending with seeing her mom's grave." Scout leaned on the front quarter panel of his Land Rover. "Did you find a way in?"

Jake reached into his pocket. "Of course I did. It took me a bit, but I finally found her phone hidden in her bedspread."

Jake handed Scout the device which Scout powered off and shoved in his pocket.

"Why did you turn it off?" Jake asked. "If you don't want to use it, why get me to bring it in the first place?"

"I'm probably just being paranoid, but if my phone battery dies, I want a back up."

"There is a charger in your car and I filled the generator the last time I was out there. You should be fine on power."

Lyn stirred from beneath the tree. "Scout?" Her voice was low and tired.

"Right here," he called back. He took his weight off the car and stood straight. His eyes met hers in the dim light of the cemetery lamp posts.

"Hey, Lyn," Jake called to her. "You okay?"

She ran her fingers through her hair. "I don't need a paramedic if that's what you're asking. I'm just tired and hungry." Lyn used the tree to help her stand. "Did you bring chocolate?"

"Of course I did." Jake laughed. "What's camping without s'mores?"

Lyn walked toward them. "We're going camping?"

Jake turned to Scout and spoke softly. "Do you need a chaperone, little bro?"

"It's not like that." Scout felt his face pink.

"Why not?" Jake whispered. "Because Killian likes her? You need to stop playing second in everything. Especially to him."

"It's complicated," Scout whispered.

"Of course it is. But you have just as much right to that pack as he does. More even. Your father was the golden boy, after all. Not his."

"By three minutes."

Jake went quiet as Lyn stepped over.

"Camping?" she asked again.

"If that's alright with you," Scout said.

"As long as there's chocolate." Lyn stepped beside Scout. "Thanks for bringing food," Lyn said to Jake. She stifled a yawn. "Sorry. I haven't been sleeping well. I think it caught up to me."

"Don't worry," Scout said. He wrapped his arm around her shoulders and smiled at the way she fit perfectly.

"No problem. Will you be okay alone with this twerp or should I come along? I can call V and reschedule."

"I think I can take him," Lyn said. "After a nap. Please don't cancel your date."

Jake bellowed with laughter. "I do not doubt at all that you could wipe the floor with my little brother. I watched you take out that coyote mid leap." Jake used his hands to replay the coyote catch. "He was dead before you hit the ground. I don't think he saw you coming."

"I've had some good trainers." Lyn looked at Scout. She turned back to Jake and held out her hand for his. "Don't tell anyone where we're going, deal?"

He gripped her hand. "Deal." Jake said and pulled his hand back as a shock tingled up his arm.

"That must be the lightning I smelled. It's a little more real than I imagined." He looked at Lyn. "Anyway, I'm late for my date." Jake stepped around Lyn to open the backdoor of the Land Rover. "Get a move on, bro. V is waiting for me."

Scout walked Lyn to the passenger side and opened the door for her. He whispered as she stepped up into the SUV, "I saw what you did there."

She shrugged. "I might as well learn to use it to my advantage." She slid into the vehicle.

Scout closed the door and walked around to the driver's seat with a smirk on his face.

"First and Park, please chauffeur," Jake said from the back of the car, "and step on it."

CHAPTER FOURTEEN

*L*yn woke to a bump as the Land Rover's tires fell from paved road to gravel. "Where are we?" She looked out the window into the dark, tree lined, dirt road ahead. Shadows parted as their headlights attacked the darkness.

"Not too far from Colorado Bend State Park. A piece of property my dad bought for my mom when they were married." Scout turned down the radio and opened his window. The smell of cedar trees wafted through the window. A chill followed.

"It's a hundred acres of untamed Texas brush, complete with prickly pear cactus and too many cedar trees. If you come in January, you'll need a pollen mask, but if you have cedar allergies, I wouldn't recommend it. Jake and I usually skip pollen season, simply because everything gets covered in a thick layer of sticky yellow and green dust."

Scout pulled the SUV left off the gravel path into what looked like the perfect spot for a single vehicle. He rolled the window up before he cut the engine. "We have to pack it in from here." Scout turned and looked at Lyn in the interior lights from the car. Her hair was back to brown and curly. Her eyes green with a slight sparkle due to the light. "Are you rested enough to walk?"

"I think so," Lyn answered. "How much are we carrying?"

"Let's find out." Scout opened his door and stepped out. He opened the rear door before Lyn jumped down from her side of the off-road vehicle.

"I can fit most of this in my pack," Scout called.

Lyn closed her door and looked around. They were in the middle of a forest of sorts. The dirt road curved just out of sight and short trees covered the road with their branches. She didn't think anyone driving by would know they were out here. She walked to the back of the SUV, where Scout was.

He shoved a thin plastic grocery sack into one of two canvas packs. "You can carry the lighter of the two backpacks. I'll take the other one and the cooler." He finished packing groceries and gear into the bags and held them out at arm's length. He pulled one back and handed the other to Lyn. "Ready for a hike in the dark?" He put both arms through the straps of the backpack and shouldered the soft sided cooler.

Lyn shouldered her pack and stepped out of the way of the rear door as Scout closed it.

The glow of the interior lights dimmed, leaving them in semi-darkness. When the lights went out completely, sound slowly faded back in.

Lyn heard the skitter of tiny feet in the underbrush and the hoot of an owl not too far away. She breathed in a deep cedar filled breath.

"Do you think you can pull out your wolf's senses without the rest of her?"

Lyn considered. She wasn't as angry as she was this morning, and the fear from this evening was calmed. "If not, my trainer will be disappointed."

"Indeed, I will." Scout said from just behind her right shoulder. He stepped around her, and smiled. He settled his pack on his back and adjusted the straps.

Lyn pulled her straps tight and followed Scout into the woods. Her eyes adjusted quickly to the dim light and deep dark of the unfamiliar setting, even without her wolf's senses.

Scout led her through cedar trees and around prickly pear bushes to a small clearing.

The branches overhead broke and allowed a little light to seep onto their path. The stars above glowed brighter than Lyn had ever seen them. She stopped to take it all in and almost started counting. She'd never had the chance to see this many stars. When she went hunting at night with the pack, they stayed relatively close to the pervasive lights of the suburbs.

"Are you coming?" Scout called from a little farther ahead, where the trees opened into a clearing. He stood framed by complete darkness.

She shifted her senses to get a better feel for her surroundings and a good look at the void that loomed behind him. Her senses came into focus one at a time.

First, Lyn's ears picked up a trickle of water in the distance to add to the other night sounds she was hearing. Next, her nose was filled with an even stronger smell of cedar. She stifled a sneeze at the intensity of it.

The wind blew the hairs on her arms and a slight chill curled up her spine. It was cooler than she expected it to be, and all she had was the dress she'd stormed out in. No sleeves, no sweater, nothing to keep the evening chill at bay. She was dressed for hanging out with her friends, not camping. She shuddered and wrapped her arms closer to her chest.

When her eyes shifted, the void emerged as a box with a peaked top. A moment more and the lights of the stars bounced off the peak, showing where the metal roof line was. The sides lightened to a dull grey, possibly wood grained.

"It's not much more than a shelter," Scout said when she caught up to him. "There's no running water and the cell signal is weak, if you get any at all. However, there is a generator if we need power and it has walls if the weather turns bad. It is also stocked with everything we need for a night off grid, besides food. But Jake took care of that for us." Scout stopped at what Lyn now recognized as a door to a cabin and fumbled with his key ring until he found the right one. "After you." He unlocked the door and pushed it open.

Lyn stepped into the pitch black shadows of the cabin. There were no stars here to give shapes to the darkness.

"Watch your eyes," Scout said and a moment later a lantern flickered to life behind her.

Scout was right. It wasn't much. As far as amenities went, there were walls. Four of them. Folded camp chairs stood in a corner along with a folding table and plastic bins. Along another wall were floor to ceiling shelves holding more plastic bins and gallons of water.

Lyn took it all in. It was closer to a shack than a house. There was no designated kitchen space. No bathroom. Nothing but four walls, shelves, and plastic boxes.

"We can leave if you want," Scout said at her shoulder.

Lyn eyed the sparse, off the grid space. "Does Killian know about it?"

"Nope. Just Jake, my mom, and now, you. It's a family secret."

"Then it's perfect." Lyn smiled and slid the pack off her shoulder.

Scout took it from her and matched her smile. "Okay then." He set both packs on top of a plastic bin and turned to her. "I'll start a fire first, so we can eat. Feel free to look around and scrounge. Your pack has some protein bars that Jake threw in if you don't want to wait for the fire."

He looked at her with a huge grin on his face. She could tell he was happy she hadn't wanted to go back. That had been an easy decision.

Going back meant confronting her BFF, her bully, and her

almost boyfriend. She'd have to defend her actions or explain herself, either way, Lyn wasn't ready for that.

Out here, there were stars, the sound of crickets and owls, the smell of wide open spaces, and peace. No-one wanted anything from her. She didn't have to play a part. She just had to exist.

Scout grabbed a box of matches and walked to the back wall. He unlocked a second door and swung it open.

Lyn stepped to the doorframe and watched Scout stack logs in a metal lined fire pit as she leaned on the door frame. She listened to the sound of trickling water not too far away, and the louder sounds of night creatures at home in their habitats. It was peaceful and just what she needed. She looked up at the tiny pinpoints of light between the branches of trees.

She took a deep breath of fresh air and stepped back into the cabin. Lyn set up the folding table and dumped out her pack on the surface to sort.

She picked up a package of blueberry fig bars and opened it. She took a bite while she unpacked Scout's pack and peeked inside the cooler.

When Scout returned from lighting the fire, Lyn had discovered two steaks, a head of broccoli, a bag of baby carrots, and the ingredients for s'mores. Minus one chocolate square that had disappeared inside her mouth with the fig bar.

Scout walked past her for the chairs. "Fire pit is out back, if you want to sit, while I finish setting up camp." He took two chairs and opened them by the fire.

Lyn shook her head. "What can I do?"

"Count stars?" Scout offered.

"No, seriously." Lyn's hand went to her hip.

"Is that dinner?" Scout looked at the spread on the table.

"Yep. Broccoli and carrots, and two small steaks in the cooler." Lyn said.

"Breakfast?"

"Eggs and bacon." She pointed to the cooler.

"Great. Is the ice still good?"

"For now. Maybe not overnight."

"That's fine, we can plug in the generator to cool the mini-fridge." He pointed to the opposite wall where Lyn noticed a black dorm sized refrigerator. "I'm going to go to the spring and get a bucket of water for emergency fire maintenance, do you want to walk with me?"

"Sure."

"Great. Grab a bucket." He tossed her one and grabbed two of his own.

Scout led Lyn to a spring fed creek with only the moonlight and their preternatural senses to guide them. The creek was ankle deep at the spot they came to. She bent down to put her hand in the water. It was colder than she expected. She pulled her hand out, dried it on her dress, and followed Scout against the flow of water until the creek was little more than a trickle.

Scout bent down and moved some bricks out of the way to expose a PVC pipe with water coming out of it. He filled a bucket half way and handed it to her so he could fill the next.

They carried the three half buckets of water back to the cabin in a comfortable silence.

Lyn put her bucket by the fire as Scout indicated and sat in a camp chair looking at the stars overhead. She wrapped her arms around herself and closed her eyes.

"I've never been camping," she said when she heard Scout return to the fire pit from taking his buckets inside. "I've also never seen this many stars."

"Really?" He kneeled down and shifted the logs on the fire with a long set of tongs.

"Really."

Scout sat in the chair next to her and looked up. "My dad would bring us out here once a month when he was alive.

Mom too. She doesn't come out as often anymore, but Jake and I still do. It's our thing."

"My mom and I had a standing date of movies and junk food every Friday night," Lyn said. "It's not the same. This is…" She couldn't find the words. Her face began to heat up and she was afraid she might cry.

He put a hand on her arm. "I have a feeling your movie nights were a lot like our camping trips."

They sat in silence for a moment before Scout spoke again.

"So, do you want to sleep inside or outside for your first camping experience? Inside, means we need to sweep and set up the cots. Outside means we should set up the tent and sleeping bags." Scout waited for her answer.

"Outside." She looked back at the stars, happy that her voice didn't betray the sheen of tears that blurred her vision. "It's too pretty to be indoors."

Scout nodded. "There is a small tent in the green box, along with sleeping bags and blankets, if we need them." Scout stepped back inside and Lyn followed, eager to help.

She wiped her eyes with the hem of her skirt when Scout wasn't looking.

"I mean the tent isn't that small. It's meant for four, so it's plenty big enough for us to share…unless you want your own. There are two." Scout's words tripped over each other. "We could set up both if you want." Scout walked over to the wall of shelves and took down a folded blue plastic tarp. "I didn't want you to think…"

"One is fine." She located the green bin in the dim light of the lantern. "Is everything color organized?" She lifted the lid off the green bin and pulled out the tent bundle."

"Green is for sleeping. Grey is for gear. The black locked case has hunting gear. Blue is fishing, although the poles are hung up there." Scout pointed to exposed rafters. "Paper products are…" Scout turned around and pointed, "in the purple one, along with food prep items, including dishes, silverware and earth friendly soap. Do you want an entire inventory?"

Lyn looked around at the colorful selection of bins and laughed. "I think I'm good for now. You set up the tent and I'll wash some dishes for dinner. Purple, right?"

"Agreed and yes." Scout took the tent from her hands and carried it, the tarp, and another lantern outside. "The spring water is fine for putting out fires, but there are gallon jugs over there for dishes and drinking. You'll find reusable water bottles in the purple bin too. We can fill those up."

"I can figure it out." Lyn shooed Scout out of the cabin to tend to food. "Wait, can I borrow your phone?"

He pulled it out of his pocket and handed it over.

She set his phone to music, turned up the volume, and began domesticating.

CHAPTER FIFTEEN

When Scout finished setting up the tent far enough from the cast iron fire pit to avoid flying sparks, he sat tending the fire with one eye and watching Lyn dance through the open door with the other.

She glowed with the movement. Not a metaphysical, dewy skin glow. No, she physically shone as well as any lantern.

Scout didn't doubt her fae blood. No one who had been allowed to see her dance could deny it. He completely understood where Greg had gotten the idea. He did not, however, understand why he kept it from her. He also didn't understand their relationship at all, which meant he had no idea where he stood with Lyn. Her shifter trainer? A friend? How good a friend? Was there potential for more?

Scout sighed and let his head fall back as he stared into the sky.

He was playing with fire by liking the same girl that Greg and Killian were territorial about.

Scout's position in the pack might be assured politically, but if he went after something Killian wanted, he'd be hard pressed to keep his role as second. Killian would find a way to force him out of the pack or worse. Plus, Killian was only one side of the equation.

On the other side, was Greg. Scout had never personally crossed the warrior or any of his kind, but he had seen him hold his own against Killian and walk away bloodied, only to come back stronger and without a mark. He knew Killian didn't hold back. Killian viewed Greg as a threat and was out for blood with every confrontation. Scout didn't think it was too much different for Greg, although maybe he was less blood thirsty. Scout had no way of knowing, he wasn't privy to Greg's motivations like he was Killian's.

Scout leaned forward and looked down at his feet.

Lyn came through the door with a black plastic case under her arm and two metal bottles of water.

Scout pulled his head up and straightened his spine. He took the proffered bottle and case of grill tools.

Lyn moved the other chair closer to the warmth of the fire.

Scout stood. "I think the fire is ready. How do you like your steak cooked?"

"Medium rare to rare," Lyn said and unscrewed the lid to her water bottle.

"Me too." Scout disappeared inside the cabin and returned with butcher wrapped steaks. He unwrapped and placed them on a hot grill rack.

A fragrant sizzle rose up from the surface, mixed with burning wood and cedar scents

"Three or four minutes then we flip." Scout took the butcher paper back inside to start a trash bag.

While he had been walking the ledge of a pity party, Lyn had swept the cabin, washed two sets of dishes, and trimmed the vegetables.

He looked back out at her from the safety of the dim cabin. She was looking up at the stars. Her brown hair danced in the light breeze. He saw her wrap her arms around her body and kicked himself for forgetting that the only clothes she'd have would be her dress and though she looked nice in it, it wasn't enough to keep her warm. June nights could still get chilly, especially when the wind blew over the water.

He walked over to the shelf of bins and opened a clear one. He rummaged through his stash of clean clothes until he found what he was looking for. He walked back to his chair and handed Lyn a grey hoodie as he sat. "I should have asked Jake to bring you some clothes. I'm sorry."

Lyn took the jacket and slid it over her head. "This is great. Thanks." She wrapped herself in the oversized fabric and lifted the sleeves to her face.

Scout watched as she closed her eyes and breathed in the scent of the hoodie. He was glad it was clean. He saw a smile peek out from behind the long sleeves.

Maybe I do have a chance.

reg laid in his bed and looked up at his ceiling fan. He picked up his phone and began another text to Lyn.

Again he deleted it.

He threw the last pillow from the bed and pressed his head into the mattress with a stifled yell.

He tried several times to apologize by text, but never came up with anything that didn't sound lame. He had called twice, only to be sent to voicemail both times.

He wasn't sure what he had done. He had sided with Killian, that was probably part of it at least. He should have known that wouldn't go well, but if she needed to show her wolf to prove that she and her friends could handle the change, so be it. Greg didn't regret pushing her. Sometimes she needed to be pushed past her limits, for her own good.

She had been spending less time with him and Umiko, because she had too little time outside of school and training. It sucked, but she needed to learn to control her shifts. She almost killed someone. She wouldn't have been able to live with that.

He knew she wouldn't hurt anyone on purpose, that

wasn't who she was…even though she was a hybrid of two of the top three supernatural predators. She wanted to control her wolf side even more than Greg wanted her to.

No, it had to be that he sided with Killian.

He could think of a laundry list of ways Killian had screwed up and chased her away. The first of which was showing up at her house at all. Killian wasn't welcome there. Killian was and will always be a bully in Greg's eyes. Lyn's bully. Why had Umiko called him in the first place? He didn't need to be involved in Lyn's life, even if he was more like her than Greg was.

Greg, Umiko, and Clark. They were her friends. They could take care of her. They didn't need Killian's help or hindrance.

Greg cradled his head in his hands.

He had been the one to convince Lyn to accept Killian's offer of shifter training with the team. He thought it was a good idea at the time. She had no one else in her life that could teach her to control what she was.

Was that his mistake? Should he have found her a different teacher? One without the bullish attitude and history of being a jerk? Maybe, but that would have come up before now. Now was something different. Was the lack of sleep worse than he thought? The nightmares?

He lifted his phone and finger typed. Again he deleted his progress. "Ugh," he groaned to the fan.

It continued to rotate, unconcerned with his plight.

He wondered if Umiko had heard from her yet. He didn't know what Umiko had done to make Lyn storm out, probably nothing. Maybe Lyn only left because of him and Killian. Umiko had nothing to apologize for. Maybe Greg had nothing to apologize for either.

But he had better be prepared with an apology for something just in case and he needed to convince her to tell someone else about the nightmares.

He sighed.

At least he knew Scout had found her and that she was safe. Although, Killian tried to hinder that. too.

The four of them were still sitting in Lyn's living room waiting for her to come back when Scout's text arrived. Greg had to threaten Killian to get him to tell them what the message said and even then Killian only told them she was safe, he wouldn't offer any details.

Greg pounded his fist into the mattress.

He hated having to trust Killian, to depend on him for any information, but Greg didn't have Scout's number and neither did Umiko. He'd never thought he would need it before.

Greg tried to track her phone when the message came in, before Killian had told them anything, but the phone said she was at home, which they all knew she wasn't. There was no way she could have gotten by them and up the stairs without them noticing, not even as a wolf.

Greg drew in a breath and held it, at the last possible moment, he breathed out again. He rolled over and put his phone on the charger.

Scout was right. She just needed some space. He'd talk to her in person tomorrow. He'd take her coffee and donuts after his run. Maybe before. Maybe she would want to go for a run with him tomorrow morning.

He picked his phone up and tried again to compose a message. *I'm sorry. Run in the morning? 6am? We can get coffee after.*

He stared, waiting for the three dots to appear that meant she was typing, but the phone mocked him with its ambivalence.

~

*U*miko checked her phone again. She texted Lyn hours ago, but it didn't even show received.

She called but was sent directly to voicemail, which she knew Lyn never bothered to check, so she didn't bother to leave one.

Umiko began typing *MMQ*, the code she and Lyn had agreed to use when they needed to see each other in person. She deleted the letter from her screen. While not technically an SOS, a meet me quick would still be like crying wolf. Wolf. Umiko replayed Lyn's entire shift from this afternoon. She still ached at the sounds, and her pulse raced.

Lyn's anger was palpable earlier, and her wolf was scary. Umiko never wanted to be on the receiving end of that snarl again.

Umiko put her phone on the charger and pulled her blankets up to her chest. The clock read 12:04 a.m. but she couldn't sleep. Not while her best friend was mad at her.

She watched the numbers on the clock change and tried to think of how she would make it up to Lyn.

She could try to stop being bossy. Umiko knew she favored the trait and usually Lyn was okay with it, but something had changed. Not just Lyn learning her creature type, though that certainly played a part. Something else was putting their relationship on rocky ground. The nightmares?

Did Scout know about the nightmares? Did Lyn talk to him more than she did Umiko? They had been spending a lot of time together because of training twice a day every day for the past few months. Was he taking her place as Lyn's BFF?

Umiko sat up in her dark room.

Does Scout have feelings for Lyn? Does Lyn like him back? What about Greg?

Sure, he and Lyn had never been an official anything and things had gotten more awkward after she started training, but those first three months were going well, weren't they?

Why did Lyn and I not talk about any of this? What is going on with her?

Umiko braided her hair over her shoulder and considered.

"Does she not trust me?" Umiko wrapped a pony tail holder around the bottom of her braid. "Maybe she doesn't realize I'd want to know or maybe she's worried I would just tell her what to do."

Umiko chose Lyn's clothes, or more often, told her what not to wear. She chose which house they slept over in and what they had for dinner. She made plans for all four of them without consulting Lyn. She just assumed Lyn would go along with it because she always had. Umiko realized she never considered Lyn's opinions. But she hardly offered them, how was she to know what they were?

Umiko threw herself back onto her pillow. She had been a horrible friend exactly when Lyn needed one the most. Lyn wasn't sleeping because of those stupid nightmares and everything in her life had been changing. Umiko thought the changes were exciting, but did Lyn?

Umiko replayed Lyn's shift in her head. It had been terrifying to her. The sound of bones breaking or whatever they did. Lyn's pained screams. The anger her wolf radiated afterwards. She wondered where all of that anger had come from and if Lyn really would have hurt Greg or Killian.

Umiko hated that she didn't know. That she'd never thought to ask.

Killian made Umiko angry just thinking about him. She regretted calling the alpha now. She was happy to blame all of Lyn's anger on him, only she knew that wasn't where it all belonged. She had to shoulder some, and Greg too.

She picked up her phone and thumbed one more message. "Spa day?" She hit send and waited for a read notification to pop up under the message. None came.

Umiko considered her message. Did it count as controlling? Would it just make things worse. She typed a new message. "Let's just hang out, you can choose when and where." Umiko sent it and put her phone back on the charger before she rolled over and tried in vain to go to sleep.

~

*L*yn stood in the middle of her bedroom while Umiko stuffed clothing into a trash bag. The walls were too close, the bed took up the whole space, and the floor was littered with clothing and blanket scraps.

"These are no good," Umiko said. "They have to go." Umiko dropped the full bag out the window and moved on to the next.

Lyn's phone rang from somewhere on the bed. She reached around for it, as Umiko took the blanket and shoved it in a different trash bag. "This too. Your room is too dark. I think you need some color. Maybe pink. I like pink."

Umiko stripped the sheets and the phone rang again.

"Something fresh and cheery." Umiko said

Lyn answered the phone. "Hello?"

"Lyn, I'll be there in two minutes," Greg said and hung up.

A knock pounded on the door downstairs. Greg's cop knock. Either she opened it or the door would come crashing in. It sounded again and Lyn found herself standing in front of it.

"Lyn, I know you're in there. It's time to hunt." Killian's voice called from the door.

Lyn heard a growl and turned to find Killian in her living room, surrounded by wolves.

"Today, we're hunting you." Killian said and shifted into his wolf. His growl was louder than the knocking on the door.

"No!" Lyn shouted.

"Run, Lyn. You can't beat them all. You need to run." Greg said from her foyer.

Lyn ran out the back door and into the woods. Shadows loomed and clouds teased the moon. Branches creaked in the wind and growls followed her escape.

A cloud of white butterflies surrounded her and hid the sounds of the pack with their beating wings. They closed in on her and she couldn't move. She struggled but the white winged butterflies wrapped her in white threads, binding her in place.

They flew off as a twig broke and growls rose up all around her in the darkness. She was surrounded.

"You didn't run fast enough." Greg said in her ear as the wolves advanced on her.

"This is ugly, right?" Umiko held up Lyn's favorite T-shirt and wadded it up before she added it to the garbage bag at her side.

Jaws snapped at Lyn's knees and she turned to see two red eyes. Wolf breath heated her face.

She tried to lift her arms to protect her head, but she couldn't break the strings.

"It's okay." A voice said to her left and she turned to see Scout's smile. "You're okay." He wrapped his arms around her and the strings melted away, along with the rest of the world.

~

"No," Lyn mumbled in her sleep.

Scout rolled over in the dark to face her, immediately awake and on guard. He shifted his senses and tried to find the threat.

Lyn struggled in her sleeping bag. The thick fabric bunched up around her body.

"Lyn, are you awake?" he whispered.

She thrashed again. Was she trying to get out of it?

He pulled his arms out of his sleeping bag and moved closer. He put his arm over her and whispered into her ear. "It's okay." Scout unzipped her sleeping bag to free her arms. "You're okay. Shhhh."

Lyn relaxed under his arm and went still.

Scout stayed awake for a few more minutes and listened to her breathe. When he was sure she was sleeping peacefully, he let himself drift back to sleep with his arm around her.

CHAPTER SEVENTEEN

Scout woke first the next morning. He opened his eyes to find his nose inches from Lyn's forehead. Brown, curly hair flowed out on the ground behind her. He blinked to clear his vision. *Not a dream.*

Lyn was asleep next to him, peaceful and beautiful and showing no signs of last night's nightmare.

He relaxed, but he didn't dare move, instead he slowly breathed her in. He closed his eyes and picked apart the different smells in his mind. An exercise reminiscent of his mom's training.

"What do you smell this morning, bug?" he heard his mom's voice in his head.

A long run through a rain storm, lightning in the distance, and hickory smoke.

"Anything else?" his mom asked in his mind, leading him to go deeper.

A mix of unwashed bodies and fresh flowers. Another breath in. *Jasmine.*

Scout opened his eyes. "You smell amazing," he whispered and stared at the lines of Lyn's face. The cut of her cheekbones, the ridge of her nose.

Lyn blinked her eyes opened. She looked at him with two bright green eyes and smiled a barely awake smile.

Scout fought the flush on his skin. "Good morning," he said softly, and prayed she didn't hear his previous statement.

"You smell nice too," she said. "Like hickory smoke, and cedar, mixed with peace, new books, and..." Lyn cut off her statement and color rose on her cheeks.

Scout smiled. He couldn't hide his embarrassment at being caught, but when he saw it matched in her face he didn't care to.

"And what?" He smirked.

"I don't know, I lost it." She stretched her arms out of her sleeping bag and rolled onto her back.

Scout knew she was avoiding the question. He rolled onto his own back and tried to work the kinks from sleeping on the ground out of his body.

"Did you sleep okay?" he asked.

Worry creased Lyn's face. "Why? Did I wake you?" Her lips curled down.

"I didn't mind, but you...how long have you been having nightmares?"

Lyn looked away. "Too long." She gathered her sleeping bag around her. "But I normally wake up sweaty, confused, and fighting to slow my pulse so my wolf doesn't come out. I actually feel rested this morning. So, that's better."

"Have you told anyone?"

She burrowed further into her sleeping bag. "Umiko knows everything but the details. Greg knows something, but he thinks it's my wolf's influence. I haven't told anyone professional if that's what you mean."

He nodded. "Do you want to talk about it?"

"No." She shook her head.

He wanted to help her, but he wasn't going to push. He'd just have to wait for her to want to talk about it. In the meantime, he could distract her. "Do you feel like a hike this morning?"

"Yes. Please!" Lyn uncurled from her sleeping bag. "Before or after breakfast?"

"Your choice." Scout offered. "There are waterfalls not too far away and the Spicewoods Spring trail has some great views."

Lyn considered. "That sounds wonderful, but I'm hungry. Let's run after?" She shimmied out of her sleeping bag.

"Whatever you want."

"Right this moment, I want to pee." She pulled the skirt of her dress down as far as she could and pushed up the sleeves of his borrowed hoodie.

Scout watched her unzip and crawl out of the tent door. He listened to her retreating footfalls before he unzipped his own sleeping bag.

He laid back and smiled. Her scent lingered in the small space and he wanted nothing more than to lay here smelling it, but he also had a full bladder.

Scout stepped out of the tent and stretched his arms over his head. He heard her go left, so he went right and put the cabin between them.

"It's earlier than I thought. I'm not sure we should be up yet." Lyn called from her hiding place in the woods.

He heard a slight yawn follow her words.

The sky was a light shade of blue and purple, the sun only a hint on the horizon at the moment.

"Mornings come early when you're camping. I'm not sure why, but it happens to me every single time. It makes for better sunrises, though, and there's a peace to starting the day when your body tells you to, instead of your alarm clock. Do you want to sleep in a little more?" Scout would be happy to crawl back to bed with her, even for just a little while.

"I'm not sure I could get back to sleep." Lyn called,

coming back after her break. "But I'm also not awake until my coffee."

He zipped up his pants and walked back around the cabin to the fire pit. "Did Jake pack any…"

"I'm already on it," Lyn said from beside the fire where she had just placed a new log and a cast iron kettle. She blew across the few red smolders from last night's fire and her breath alighted a new flame.

Scout wanted to tell her she was amazing, but he managed to keep it to himself this time. "Eggs and bacon or bacon and eggs?"

"Ummm? Both." She giggled.

Scout wasn't sure he'd ever seen her this carefree. Not since before her life imploded. He hoped it would last long enough to clear out the nightmares. He hated the idea that sleep caused her distress.

CHAPTER EIGHTEEN

*I*n a comfortable silence, Scout and Lyn cleaned up after breakfast as nature woke up around them.

Scout turned to Lyn as he scrubbed stuck on egg from a small cast iron skillet. "Unfortunately, girl clothes did not magically appear in the night, but you still have choices. Mom, Jake, and I each have a clear bin of clothing inside on the shelf. You can scrounge through any of them for something that will fit you."

"How do I know whose is whose?" Lyn reached for the skillet as Scout finished washing it.

He laughed and touched his nose, leaving behind a collection of soap suds.

"Right." She grinned at the bubbles on the end of his nose.

"You can go look. I'll finish up here." Scout picked up the greasy bacon skillet.

Lyn used the towel to wipe the bubbles from the tip of his nose and walked inside to the clear bins. She lifted the lid off the first one and sniffed. She didn't recognize the scent. Laundry detergent, of course, but she didn't know what type, and it masked any other smell. "I haven't met your mom. I don't know what she smells like." She closed the lid and opened the next one. She took a deep breath. "Jake smells like oranges to me." She closed the lid and opened the last one.

Scout's familiar scent wafted out. Since he was the only one around to offer, she felt better starting here. She had yet to meet Scout's mom, and while Jake would probably be okay with her wearing his clothes, she preferred to have permission, if she could.

She rummaged in Scout's less than neat box but found nothing that would fit her well enough to hike in. His pants and shorts would dwarf her and there was no way they'd stay up. She grabbed a T-shirt before putting the lid back on Scout's box.

"Are you sure your mom won't mind?" Lyn called out to him. She hesitated to go through the neatly folded clothes, but she needed something to go over her legs. Scout's jeans were both too wide and too long, Jake's would be a little shorter, but not enough. "There is no way I can get things in and out of here without her knowing someone was in it."

"I'm more than sure. Go ahead," Scout said, stepping inside to stack the clean dishes on the folding table.

Lyn took the lid all the way off the box and scrounged inside for a pair of pants. She tried to leave things as neat and orderly as she could. She looked at the size on a pair of jeans and considered herself lucky. They would only be a little too big. She held them up to her waist to check the length. Determined to make them work, she put the lid back on the box and pulled the pants up under her dress to button them. She leaned down to roll up the cuffs. She wiggled her hips to see if they would fall down and they stayed put. She removed the hoodie and set it aside for later. She replaced her dress with the T-shirt from Scout's box, and put the hoodie over it. She'd have to take it off when the sun rose more, but for now, it felt cozy.

She went back outside to find Scout drying the last pan. He moved a large lid over the fire pit to smother the fire without water and picked up a full backpack before they set off on two legs for Colorado Bend State Park, the back way.

~

Scout led the way. When the path was wide enough to accommodate both of them, Lyn walked by his side.

"There's a fence coming up. Three feet tall, barbed wire. Jake and I usually run and jump it."

She motioned for him to lead the way and he picked up speed. She followed in his wake. She saw his muscle tense when he planted his foot and leaped. Moments later, she did the same thing and cleared the fence a little after him. She didn't even have to pull her borrowed pants up to do so.

"I do pay for my state parks pass, by the way," he said, "and we donate to the parks department. We could go through the front park entrance, but this is faster.

Lyn didn't care about logistics. She was too busy listening to all the nature sounds around her. Birds chirped overhead, calling back and forth from tree branches that gently rustled in the breeze. An occasional snake or lizard darted through the underbrush, pushing leaves from its path. Squirrels chittered from every tree, only to disappear when she and Scout approached.

They stayed off the main paths instead, they walked through brush and brambles. Lyn was glad for the thick pants. Her legs would have been scratched and Umiko's dress in shreds.

Lyn heard the sound of water falling before she saw it and took off running.

"It's slippery and not safe to jump from." Scout called after her. "Unless you can fly?" he teased.

Lyn found herself at the top of a ten foot tall low sloping

waterfall. She peered over the edge at the bubbling water below. She looked left and right for the best way down.

"Left," Scout said and started that way.

Lyn followed. Her shoes lost traction twice, each time Scout kept her from falling with a hand on her arm.

At the bottom, Scout jumped off a three foot ledge to get to the ground and put his hands up to offer her help, but she jumped down on her own and sat on a rough stone beside the water to remove her shoes and socks.

"I can get in, right? There's no posted sign?" She looked around.

Scout nodded. "You're good. There will be people later, I'm sure, but for now it's just us."

Lyn dipped a toe in the water. "It's a little chilly."

Scout kicked his shoes off and spread a towel on the rock she had vacated. "Too cold?"

Lyn put her foot back in and struggled to keep it there. "I wish it were a bit warmer."

Scout put his own foot in the water. "It's definitely brisk." He pulled it out and shook it dry before making himself comfortable on the towel.

Lyn put both feet in the water. She knew it was silly, but she had been hoping for warmer water, warm enough at least that she would want to submerge herself in it. She wanted a bath, a shower, something. She looked at the waterfall. She imagined sitting under it. The falling water massaging the tension out of her upper back and shoulders. "I'm going for it." She stepped out of the water and stood next to him and the rock. She unbuttoned and shimmied out of the borrowed jeans and tossed them and Scout's hoodie onto the towel with him.

In only her underthings, she carefully picked her way along slippery rocks to wade into the stream up to her waist. She turned and looked back at Scout still standing where she left him, a foot from the bank of the creek bed. "Are you coming?"

He shook his head. "It too cold for me."

Lyn inched further into the water. "It gets warmer as you get used to it. It practically feels like bathwater out here." Bathwater. She looked around at the water flowing past her torso.

"I did not picture you as a cold bath type of girl." Scout said.

"I'm not." She looked at Scout. "This is… It's…"

"Lyn, are you okay?" Scout took a step toward her until his bare feet were in the water.

"I am not in danger." She said, just as much to herself as to him, and closed her eyes.

Lyn counted her breaths and calmed her mind. *Just like the bathwater.* She told herself. She bent her knees and sunk into the water up to her neck, expecting a chill. What she got was warmth. A happy sigh nearly escaped her mouth. With her eyes closed, she could easily imagine sitting in a tub of warm water. She extended her legs and laid back on the surface of the water, letting her senses trick her.

"Lyn!" Scout shouted and moments later, water splashed over her face.

Scout put his hand out to touch her. "Are you doing that?"

She opened her eyes. "You feel it? It's not just in my head?" She pulled her legs back under her and faced him. The water pulled her curly brown hair straight against her back.

Scout nodded. "It's warmer right around you. Less than a foot away, it's ice cold." He shivered and stepped toward her warmth.

Lyn reached out behind him. "I can't feel any cold. Not that I want to. The warmth is so nice."

Scout sank up to his shoulders next to her. "That is a handy skill you have there."

"The first time I did it, I had no idea what was happening. It got too hot and I had to jump out of the bathtub." She pulled her arms in. "I didn't think I could warm a whole stream."

"You can't." Scout said as tremors danced over his muscles. "It's just the water around you that's warm."

Lyn reached her hands out in two directions. "But it all feels warm to me."

"Trust me. I am standing in cold water up to my armpits."

Lyn moved her arms closer to his body. "Better?"

Scout nodded. "Hold still."

Lyn held her arms out to either side of Scout's chest and watched him explore the water around them.

"Here it's warm," he said with his hand close to Lyn's body but moving away. "But here it's cold." He ran his hand along her arm. When he reached the tips of her finger, he sank his hand into the water. "A foot, give or take." Scout said, looking down at the top of her head.

Lyn heated up at Scout's closeness.

"It's getting warmer." Scout said and moved his hands in and out around her body without touching it. Scout stopped and looked at her.

Lyn breathed slowly and concentrated on keeping her temperature down under the gaze of his volcanic eyes.

"Every inch of my skin that is a foot or less away from you is warm. Which is an odd feeling, since my back is ice cold." Scout cocked his head slightly. "I'd say it's a good twenty degree or so difference."

Lyn wrapped her arms around his chest, but kept from touching him. She was afraid she might scald them both if she touched his bare skin. She looked up into his face.

Lyn saw his Adam's apple bob. He opened his mouth like he wanted to say something but he stopped. He was holding something back. She dropped her arms, planted her feet on the creek floor, and stood up. The wind brought goosebumps to her wet flesh.

"Lyn?" Scout stood too. "Are you okay?"

"Yeah, it's just weird," Lyn said while looking down at the surface of the water.

"Right," Scout said. Disappointment hung from his words.

Lyn turned to look into his face, to see if he thought her skill with water was weird too, but Scout turned and walked back to the bank with his shoulders hunched forward

She stood up to her middle in water that was quickly losing whatever warmth Lyn had given it. A shiver ran up Lyn's spine as another breeze blew through. She watched the water stream down Scout's back. His muscles glistened with the moisture in the early morning sunshine.

The water around her warmed again, but soon became hotter than she could handle. She closed her eyes and counted to two, then twenty. At thirty, the water stopped heating. She opened her eyes.

A white butterfly landed on Scout's head. Lyn looked at the butterfly and beyond it to the grouping on the water's edge.

"Don't move," Lyn said as all the heat left the water in a rush.

Scout froze with water up to his knees. He didn't turn around.

"Scout, can you see her?"

His head slowly lifted and his muscles tensed. "See who?" he asked.

CHAPTER NINETEEN

Scout watched as Lyn's eyes shifted from their usual green to her wolf's amber and silver.

He extended his wolf's senses and tried to find what had Lyn's attention. He could see nothing except trees and bushes. The sounds of birds and squirrels met his ears, but they were faint, as if they too were waiting. "Lyn?"

She was standing ab deep in water, staring past his shoulder. He turned while keeping track of the direction of her gaze. There was nothing there. He peered into the trees and as far beyond as he could, but he saw nothing.

He turned back to face Lyn. Her arms were wrapped around her in the water. Her body shuddered with a shiver. "Come here," he whispered.

Lyn walked toward him, her foot sure on the slippery stones, but she did not break gaze with whatever had her attention. Scout put his pants back on as she neared the shore.

"Tell me what you see, please," Scout asked softly so he wouldn't startle her as she stepped close enough for him to reach.

He took her hand and led her out of the water.

"White things flitting in a circle."

"The butterflies again?"

Lyn shook her head. "Not butterflies. Lights. And there's a woman. White hair, pale skin."

Scout stepped behind her. He kept a hand on her shoulder and looked around. He couldn't see anyone, and his wolf's senses weren't helping.

"What color are the woman's eyes?" Scout asked near her ear as he wrapped her in the towel and began drying her. He wanted to keep her talking.

Lyn spoke, her voice calm and quiet. "Silver. They're cold. Like ice."

Scout took a deep breath. "I smell gardenias and jasmine. I can feel something tickling my skin. Like a breeze," Scout said.

Lyn shook her head. "Wings."

"We need to get you dry," Scout said and took a step to pick up her clothes from the rock he had laid them on when he had gotten dressed. When he turned around, Lyn was already dry, including her hair. A puddle of water soaked into the ground at her feet. She just stood there, silent, and continued to stare into the trees beyond Scout.

He filed her turbo dry feature away for later. He had a feeling it was less important than whatever Lyn was seeing. He opened the shirt's bottom hem and placed it over her head to help her slip the sleeves on her arms. He slid the hoodie over her head next and she put her arms in the sleeves.

"Can you hear them?" Lyn asked.

"Wing flaps?" Scout guessed and held out the jeans for her to step into. She placed her hands on his shoulders and picked up her leg.

"No. They are trying to tell me something but the sounds are all wrong." Lyn cocked her head. "Like they're out of order." She finished pulling the borrowed pants up and buttoned them.

"Can you put the sounds in the right order?"

Lyn kept her eyes trained on the same spot of nothing. "Come." She took a step forward and Scout put a hand on her arm to hold her back.

"You should put your shoes back on before we follow butterflies." Scout picked up her shoes from the ground and handed her one.

"They aren't butterflies." Lyn took one of her shoes and slid her foot in without bothering with socks.

"And you want to follow them?" Scout folded the towel and shoved it into his pack along with her socks.

"I think she's waiting for me." Lyn turned her eyes toward his face and blinked several times as if trying to focus on him. "But we have a deal."

Scout nodded. "We do. If you're going then I'm going and we're telling someone." He zipped up the pack.

"Tell Jake," she said.

"No." Scout shook his head. "We need to tell someone you haven't compelled to silence. If something happens to us, I want someone to be able to talk about it. Call for help, if necessary."

Lyn nodded and tuned her face back to whatever she was seeing that Scout was not.

He pulled out his phone and waited longer than he wanted for it to power up. He dialed and held the phone to his ear while he reached for Lyn's hand.

She let him take it. A tremor vibrated in her muscles. Her hand flexed and her arm tensed. She sank on her thighs.

Scout squeezed her hand. He didn't have a lot of time. She wanted to run, but this time it was toward danger, not away from it.

"Umiko, be quiet," Scout commanded when the phone connected. "We're fine. She's fine. Listen. She sees something I don't." Scout's spine tensed. "Lyn, did you say, 'not butterflies' earlier?"

She nodded. "Tiny figures with wings."

"Umiko, get Greg. Text me what he thinks I need to know about fairies."

"I think the woman is my mom," Lyn said.

Scout moved the phone away from his ear. "How do you know?" he asked Lyn.

"She just changed from woman to wolf."

Scout nearly dropped the phone, but he recovered. "Yes. That's what I said. And her mom is here. I can't see her, but Lyn is certain. Colorado Bend State Park, but I'm not sure we'll be here long." He paused. "Jake's a great tracker. Tell him to start on the Spicewoods Springs Trail, by the waterfall." Scout looked at Lyn and nodded his head. "I promise I won't let her out of my sight, but I've never dealt with fairies, so I need that info. All I have is what I know from stories."

He hung up the phone and turned Lyn's face to meet his with a finger under her chin. She reluctantly moved her eyes to his. "Are you sure about this?"

"No." She broke eye contact and stepped away, pulling him with her.

"That makes two of us," Scout mumbled and followed Lyn and the trail of fairies.

CHAPTER TWENTY

Umiko stared at her phone like it was a bomb. She took a breath and texted Greg first. "I need to know fairy lore. Fast. Anything helpful. Meet me at the skate park."

She started to message her next contact, but decided to call instead. He picked up on the second ring.

"What?" the brusk voice on the end of the line said.

"Killian, I need to know Scout's brother's cell phone number." She paused. "What do you mean you don't know it?" Umiko yelled. "Fine, just give me that one." She paused again.

"No? What the hell Killian? This is not a game. Lyn and Scout need us. He told me to call Jake, but I don't have the number." Umiko stomped her foot. "Fine. Meet us at the skate park. I'm headed there now. Just give me the number."

She recited numbers as Killian gave them to her then disconnected the phone and dialed as she repeated them again.

The phone rang once. Twice. On the third ring a tired voice answered the phone.

"Jake, I need your nose," Umiko said.

"Who is this?" The voice on the other end yawned.

"It's Umiko. Lyn's friend. Jake, wake up and listen." Umiko shouted while she gathered her purse and rooted around on her floor for something of Lyn's. She found the dress she had borrowed from Lyn yesterday and flung it over her shoulder.

"Mom," she yelled, "I'm going to meet Lyn."

"Okay, dear." Her mother's voice called from the kitchen "Do you want breakfast first?"

"Not this morning, mom. I have to hurry, I'm already late." Umiko reached the bottom of the stairs. Umiko locked the front door behind her. She didn't need her mom getting worried. Not yet.

"Jake, are you listening?" Umiko asked into the phone once she was outside. "Meet me at the skate park."

She listened and pulled the phone away from her ear. She gave it a dirty look and moved it back.

"Because Scout told me to call you. I think he and Lyn might be in trouble. They're at …"

Umiko looked at the phone again. Jake had disconnected without a word. She hoped that meant that he would meet her, but if not she would just have to do her best without him. Maybe Killian could track Lyn and Scout.

Umiko shoved her phone in her pocket and put her purse strap across her body. She folded the dress in half and half again. She clutched it in her hand as she ran to the end of the street.

An engine roared behind her.

"Hop on." Greg said as he handed her a helmet and shifted his backpack to his front.

Umiko did as she was instructed and Greg pulled her arms around his stomach. "Hold on tight." When she was settled, he sped off to the skate park.

Umiko held on and hid behind Greg with her eyes squeezed shut. She hoped her mother would never ask her about this.

Greg cut the engine and Umiko opened her eyes.

"Spill it. Why here? Why do you need fairy lore?" He looked around. "Where's Lyn?"

Umiko got down from the bike and unclipped the helmet. "Jake will be here soon I hope, and Killian," she said.

He looked at her with a severe and disapproving look.

"He wouldn't give me Jake's number otherwise." Umiko defended herself. "Scout specifically asked for him."

A black Toyota Tundra pulled up beside them in the parking lot and the driver's window rolled down.

Jake blinked at them, his hair still wild up from sleeping.

"What's up, Sunshine? This better not be a joke. Why would my brother call you instead of me and why isn't he answering his phone?"

"Scout said Lyn sees something he can't and she's following it. He said you're our best bet at finding them." Umiko held out the dress.

"He's not wrong. What's this?" Jake asked as he took the folded up fabric.

"Lyn's dress. For her scent," Umiko said.

He took it with a shake of his head. "Let's go," he grumbled and unlocked the car doors.

Greg opened the rear door for Umiko to step up as the rumble of a third engine roared into the parking lot.

"Killian," Jake and Greg groused at the same time.

"What's the deal, Umiko?" Killian asked without turning off his engine.

"We're fine. You can go back home. I can take care of my brother." Jake started to pull out of the parking lot.

Greg raced around and jumped in the passenger side while the car was moving. "Are you really going to leave him?" He placed his backpack at his feet.

"Yes, but don't get too excited. He'll follow us all the way and he'll be pissed when we get there, which suits me fine."

"Get where?" Greg asked.

"Colorado Bend State Park," Jake and Umiko said in unison and shared a glance in the rearview mirror.

"How did you know?" Umiko asked Jake.

"How did you not?" Jake countered.

Umiko clamped her mouth shut and sat in the backseat, alone. Her best friend hadn't told her she was going out of town. She crossed her arms at her chest and sat back in her seat.

She wondered when Jake had found out. "What did Scout say when you talked to him this morning? Did he call you before or after me?"

"I didn't talk to him this morning. The last time I saw him was last night."

"Lyn was with him?" Umiko asked, looking at him in the mirror. *Jake knew where she was this whole time?*

"Focus! What did Scout say to you, Umiko?" Jake asked instead of answering her question.

Umiko looked at the phone in her hand. "He said that they were fine. Lyn saw something he didn't. Fairies, maybe? They were following it. You would be able to track him from some waterfall."

"Why are they in Colorado Bend?" Greg looked at Jake before he started thumbing something on his phone.

"Training?" Jake shrugged and pulled onto the main road.

Umiko heard him laugh and looked into the rearview to figure out why.

"You don't like him either," she said after she looked back over her shoulder to see Killian's open sided black Jeep following them.

"Let's just say, he and I have some irreconcilable differences," Jake said and flipped his blinker on to signal his next turn.

"What kind?" Umiko asked.

Jake put his hand up. "That was not an invitation to ask for more details."

Umiko turned her head down to look at the phone in her lap. She texted Lyn.

"Are you okay?" She paused the send button. "Are we okay?" She hit send again.

She thought that she and Lyn agreed on no secrets, but apparently there were things going on with Lyn that other people knew more about than she did. She would be mad if she weren't so worried.

"Faster, Jake."

"Quiet, Sunshine. It's a long drive and I'm not going to risk getting pulled over. That would just delay us more." Jake said without looking at her. "I can drop you off somewhere if you have a problem with that." He turned to the mirror.

Umiko caught his eye. She didn't doubt he'd drop her off so she stayed quiet. She turned to look out the window and kept her comments to herself. Her phone vibrated with a message from Greg.

CHAPTER TWENTY-ONE

Scout ran through what he knew, while keeping his hand wrapped around Lyn's. He would use the information he was provided until it no longer fit, even if it was acquired in a crummy way.

Scout didn't like his choice, but he was forced to call Umiko over his brother because Jake had made a deal with Lyn and Greg was sure enough that deals with Lyn were binding to risk pissing her off in a crowded room just to prove a point.

If Jake couldn't help Scout, he'd have to trust Umiko to run the play to the end. He was certain she'd call Clark and Greg on her own, and Jake because Scout told her to. Would Umiko call Killian? She called the alpha yesterday for less.

The deal Lyn suckered his brother into meant that Jake couldn't tell anyone where Lyn and Scout had gone. He tried to play back the deal in his head to make sure that was the only thing his older brother had agreed to and realized that Jake actually hadn't agreed to anything other than keeping the cabin location a secret. Jake never would have divulged that anyway.

Scout could and probably should have called Jake instead of calling Umiko and involving the whole posse, but it was too late now. Plus, he still didn't know what he and Lyn were walking into. Maybe a posse was a good idea?

Scout stepped over a fallen log and helped Lyn over behind him. She let him without focusing on what was happening. Her eyes, amber and silver, were trained ahead of them, almost in a trance, and that worried him. Almost enough to be glad he called in the cavalry.

He was following blindly toward who knew what and as much as he trusted Lyn, he wanted someone else at his back, someone thinking rationally. Because he admitted to himself, he and Lyn were not.

Scout adjusted the grip of Lyn's hand in his. He was going to hold onto her, if only to make sure he wouldn't lose her. He might have been able to follow her scent trail, but every time a fairy had been involved in the past two days, the scents had been jumbled. Like there were far too many things around for his nose to filter.

Scout thought quickly. He rubbed his free hand over a branch that stuck across the unmarked path they were following. *Keep hold of Lyn with one hand, leave a trail to follow back with the other.* He snapped a branch on the next tree. He wanted Jake to know exactly which way they had gone, in case he had trouble scent tracking too.

Lyn tugged on his arm and pulled ahead of him. He picked up his pace. "Lyn, you have to be my eyes." Scout squeezed her hand to keep it from slipping in his grasp. He didn't bother to whisper. He didn't know if the thing or things they were following were close or far and he needed to be sure Lyn heard him.

Lyn startled, like she had forgotten he was with her. He took larger steps until he was walking slightly in front of her. He looked at her face and caught a glimpse of her eyes. The amber and silver orbs didn't bother to focus on him.

Amber was for her wolf, he was certain. Was the silver the reason she could see something he couldn't? If she was part fae, like Greg thought, she would presumably be able to see fae. Whereas, he would only be able to see what they wanted him to see, which, in this case, was nothing more than his natural surroundings. He looked down at his feet and racked his brain for a solution to his blindness. He noticed a white ribbon trailing behind one of her feet.

"Lyn, your shoe is untied," Scout said.

She stopped and looked down at her shoe as if the sight was unfamiliar to her. A moment later, she stooped to tie it and he let go of her hand reluctantly.

"Lyn, I need to try something." He stood behind her as she stood up and put his hands over her eyes.

"What are you doing, Scout?" Lyn's hand flew up to grab his wrists.

"If I am right, this is what I see." He uncovered only the amber eye.

"Where did she go? Scout, did you see what way she went." Scout heard the panic in her voice and it notched his own up a level.

"I don't think she left." He switched eyes.

Lyn sighed with what Scout imagined was relief, which meant the mysterious, and invisible to him, fairy lady was still there. Not that Scout thought she'd go, but it would have been nice.

He turned Lyn to look at him. "I will follow you, but you needed to see how blind I am. My scent tracking is the best in the pack, but it's not a replacement for sight and my sense of smell is off kilter. All I smell right now are flowers that shouldn't be here, you, and…" he sniffed, "so many conflicting smells that I don't think I could find you if you weren't standing right in front of me."

Lyn looked from his face to something he couldn't see and back again before she nodded.

She planted her feet, took his hand in hers and called into the woods. "I've gone far enough."

Scout felt the wind tickle the hair on his arms, only he was no longer sure if it was a simple breeze or invisible butterfly wings.

"I won't keep following if my friend can't see you," Lyn said and turned her head this way and that, as if she was trying to catch a distant tune. "What?" Lyn's eyes looked at something around his head. "Why?" A pink flush rose in her cheeks as she took his head in her hands and pressed down with her toes to give herself more height. "Close your eyes."

It was then that he knew he'd walk headlong into a fairy trap for her. He sighed and closed his eyes. He felt her soft lips and warm breath on an eyelid. His skin tingled over every inch and his breath caught for a moment. A moment that lingered far longer than her lips did, but nowhere near long enough.

"Open," Lyn moved to stand at his shoulder. "Can you see them now? They said it would work. That all it took was a kiss."

Maybe Scout could learn to like the invisible butterflies. At least he could if they weren't tricky fairies.

Scout opened his eyes to see Lyn standing in a blurred swirl of white butterflies. He closed the eye she had kissed and they were gone. They reappeared when he switched eyes. He squinted at the closest, and realized his brain was telling him one thing, his eye another. Tiny legs dangled from between the white wings.

"Hurry," she said and took his hand.

He heard the rustle of wings and Lyn pulled him along behind the scent of gardenias and jasmine. Now that he could see the tiny creatures, maybe he could start to get a handle on their smell, but the gardenia and jasmine scent didn't seem to be coming from them. They smelled like flowers, maybe candy. There were too many, and each scent was different, but the overall gardenia and jasmine belonged to something bigger.

Before he could follow the scent further down the trail, Scout's phone vibrated in his pocket. He pulled it out and unlocked it with his thumb as messages blew up his notification screen.

He waited for the digital flood to abate and opened his messages. He scrolled to the first one and began reading Umiko's texts.

"From Greg: 6 rules. 1) no gifts, 2) don't eat anything offered, 3) don't tell them your full name, 4) be extremely polite, but DON'T say 'thank you', 5) don't lie, 6) don't let her listen to the music!! If they ask what eye you can see them with, don't tell them. I pray to every god ever believed in by anyone that you can see them. Bro is on his way. Sunshine called Alpha. Help is coming. Be careful."

Scout put his phone back in his pocket and started to tell Lyn the rules, but she was back to not paying attention to anything but the trail of butterflies. *Fairies, not butterflies.* He needed to rewire his brain, but at least he could see them. Things were a little less scary with his vision working again. He watched as they bobbed to and fro along an obscure path. He still didn't see a woman or a wolf. "Is she still there?" he asked in a low voice.

Lyn didn't answer

"Lyn, what can you hear?" Scout asked, straining his own ears.

"I don't know. It's too faint now. It was louder before, but we're getting farther from it, I think." Lyn pulled him forward.

Scout pulled his phone out and looked at the battery bar. Scout took a breath to suppress a growl and chose a playlist at random before he stuck his phone in the pocket closest to

Lyn's ear on a medium volume. He didn't know how he was supposed to counter a song he couldn't hear, especially with a battery in desperate need of a charge, but he had to try.

CHAPTER TWENTY-TWO

*S*cout recited the list of rules under his breath and cursed Greg for not telling any of them about the fairy angle, especially her.

Beside him, Lyn stopped walking.

Scout unfolded and stretched his fingers. He snapped out of his frustration to see the figure Lyn had been following for the first time. He watched as the snowy white wolf jumped from the bank of the stream to an elevated section of rock in the middle. He would have sworn it was Lyn's, except for the ice white eyes and a tuft of black fur at the tip of its tail.

The wolf laid down with its belly on the damp rock near one side and the trail of butterfly fairies scattered. Some landed on the rock, some on the wolf, but most flitted free, no longer needed as breadcrumbs.

"Together," Lyn said and prepared her foot to push off from the bank.

Scout looked at the wolf, who turned her head slightly to bare her throat.

"That side." He pointed. "On three."

"1, 2, 3." Lyn counted and pushed off.

The pair landed on the rock opposite the wolf. The white

wings flew up at their landing, but gradually settled again, unconcerned about him and Lyn in their midst.

Scout kept his eyes on the largest of the predators, preparing himself in case she leapt at Lyn, but the wolf stayed low. Its ears down and back. Signs Scout recognized as submissive. Despite her posture, Scout didn't trust the creature that had led them here. She smelled of the same gardenia and jasmine scent that had changed on him in the cemetery. The same scent that had tried to lure Lyn from his side and forced him into a deal to keep her safe.

The wolf rose from her prone position and stood on all fours. In moments, a woman with white hair down to her waist and pale skin stood in its place. The woman's eyes were more like ice than Lyn's and made Scout shiver.

She drew a sparkling elongated pendant out of her shirt and jerked the cord free of her neck. She pointed to the center of the rock and slowly stepped forward. She maintained eye contact with Scout as she kneeled to place it on the ground. She stood and lifted her foot to stomp on the pendant.

Scout covered Lyn's body with his own, turning his back on the flying debris from whatever had just shattered and the consequences that came from breaking it. His ears popped, but nothing hit him. He straightened his back from curving around Lyn's body and looked over his shoulder.

"You have questions and I had a stolen moment," the pale woman said, only her voice was a deep bass. The woman with a man's voice backed away from the center of the rock formation.

Scout looked down at the spot she vacated. There was no sign of the item she had broken. No glass, no cord, no crater. It was as if it never happened.

Scout whispered Greg's rules on dealing with fairy to Lyn, while keeping his eyes on the threat. "And I think semantics is important," he added. "If you want answers, you have to ask the right questions."

"How long does a stolen moment last?" Lyn asked across the empty space.

Scout decided to stand on Lyn's wolf's eye side, just in case. He held her hand and looked around them.

The once gurgling stream was still. A motionless snake lay partially in and out of the water to their right. An immobile bird with wings fully extended hung in the sky above.

"As long as it needs to, but they are as rare as our kind," the male voice said from the woman's mouth.

"Are you my mother?" Lyn asked.

"No," the deep voice said. "Females are less threatening, on the outside. But I know her, she allowed me to take her shape."

"Are you…" Scout started, but thought better of his question. He didn't like the phrase the predator in front of them had used. To his ears it sounded like a trap. "Is Lyn in danger?"

"Yes. Both Winter and Summer want to claim her as their own. But her mother and I did not want that for her."

Scout tried to parse the answer. He knew a little fairy lore from books. Most Fae were divided into Summer and Winter courts. A much smaller subset avoided the choice.

"Are you my father, then?" Lyn asked.

"No."

Lyn was silent for a moment. "Where is my mother?" Lyn asked.

"Claimed by Summer. In exchange for my safety." The woman's shoulders slouched. "She had very few options."

"What type of creature is Lyn?" Scout asked and squeezed her hand.

"Do not say her name a third time, wolf," the creature barked and stood at her full height, shoulders down and back. "We are unheard while the moment is up, but names are power. Do not give hers up so easily." She glared at Scout.

Scout mentally kicked himself for not thinking. Greg had

told him not to use names and Scout had relayed that message to Lyn. Even so, it had slipped his mind and he needed to be more careful.

"We are called Mimics. What you are looking at is her mother's neutral form. Though her mother once looked like the wolf you followed, as well as many other things."

"Shapeshifters," Scout said with an inaudible snort.

The woman nodded. "We prefer the distinction."

"I've done it, but I don't know how it works." Lyn said.

The figure nodded.

Lyn sighed. "How does it work?"

"The first time, by contact. Once you have taken the form, you simply remember what it was like to be that thing." The figure of the woman shifted to one of a young male child, maybe six years old, Scout estimated. "But our scent never changes." The male voice almost fit the figure, although it was too low for a boy of that size and age. "Changing voices can be done." His voice changed to a higher lilt, more feminine than before. "But takes more effort to learn, to remember, and to mimic."

Scout sniffed. The creature still smelled of gardenias and jasmine, but he could now smell a touch of freshly fallen snow. "What's the catch?" Scout asked. "There's always a negative with a power like that."

"Besides the fact that both courts want to use us as weapons against the other?" The female voice said. The young boy puffed out his chest. "The change drains us of energy. The larger the difference, the larger the energy loss." The creature shifted from young boy to a large male with white hair, pale skin, and ice for eyes. "With practice, we can build stamina," the bass voice returned, "but unconsciousness or shock reverts us to our natural blank slate." The voice matched his appearance for the first time. "Passion, fear, and other intense emotions make us lose control of our shape.

During a fight, or when coupling, control is not something easily maintained."

"What do you mean by…"Scout started

"… contact." Lyn finished.

Scout bit his cheek. That wasn't what he had been about to ask, but her question was more relevant.

"Do you trust her?" The mimic made eye contact with Scout.

Scout looked at Lyn. "With my life."

Lyn's two colored eyes met his and a smile bloomed across her face.

"Child," the bass voice called to get her attention.

She turned to his voice and Scout bit his tongue.

His mind automatically began reciting the rules, even though he was no longer sure they were in danger. It was as if this creature wanted to help Lyn, or at least give her more information about her creature type, which is more than he could say for her boyfriend. He didn't want Greg or Killian to interrupt Lyn finally getting answers she should have had years ago.

He pulled out his phone to tell Jake to abort. *Crap.* The phone screen remained black. The battery was dead.

"Once you choose to take a form, it will always be within you to do it again. If you do not maintain control, it can happen at inopportune times, putting you at a disadvantage." The mimic turned to Scout. "I do not usually caution humans."

Scout waited for more, but apparently he was still not going to caution humans.

"Touch him. The more points of contact the better. Touch him and think of looking in a mirror. His form is your form reflected."

Scout's knees wobbled as Lyn held her hands up, palms facing out. His hands rose to meet them as if pressed against opposite sides of a mirror.

"What about the clothes?" Lyn asked without looking at her benefactor.

"Harder, but doable. Anything touching your skin or immediately surrounding you can be mimicked," he said. "But once it leaves your space, it reverts."

That's how she had changed the water temperature.

Lyn stared at Scout. Not just his eyes, but everything. His hair, his face, his shoulders.

Scout felt a trickle of electricity along his skin as her eyes took him in. It was nothing like the lightning shock of a bound deal. It wasn't coming from her at all. He wanted to step closer, take her in his arms, hold her gaze with his own and...

When she started changing, Scout fought the urge to step back. Her mimic was disconcerting, but it was a part of her, and he wanted to know every part of her.

A few moments later, Lyn's knees buckled. Scout reached out to catch himself. "Stay awake, please." He said to his face on top of his body dressed in Lyn's borrowed clothes.

"How does she reset?" Scout asked the other Mimic, a touch of worry in his voice. He should be watching their companion. He knew this would be the perfect moment for an ambush or a double-cross or a myriad of other traps to spring, but he let his guard down and concentrated on the girl in his arms. *This is why we needed back up. You are my weakness.*

"She simply remembers herself. Or forgets her current form. Coming back to herself costs nothing."

"Why do the courts want her?" Scout asked as Lyn's eyes closed and her hair began to revert to white.

"Do you not see how useful she could be in the wrong hands?" The mimic shifted from pale with white hair to dark skinned with black hair. His white eyes a spooky contrast to the rest of the image.

Scout looked down at the near prone girl in his arms. He did see it. Humans and fairies alike would kill to get her skill on their side. She could be anyone, go anywhere. "Will they come for her?"

"They are already on their way."

The man sounded sad to Scout, almost resigned. Scout turned to the figure. "How have you managed to stay neutral?"

"Carefully." The figure looked up and Scout followed his gaze. The bird caught in mid-flight, resumed his wing flap in slow motion. "Our moment is almost gone. Any last questions?"

"Where's the real child?" Lyn asked from the ground, her voice weak. Her eyes flickered open but threatened to close again. "The one I was swapped with?"

"She is safe for now, but if they know you want her, that will change." The Mimic shifted from the ashen skinned male to a white tailed deer and leaped from the middle of the stream back to the shore. Another leap and the deer disappeared into the woods. The butterfly fairies dispersed in all directions so quickly that it seemed they just blinked out of existence.

Scout looked down at the girl in his arms. They now knew what she was, and they could not let anyone else find out.

"Lyn, before you sleep, I want you to remember what it was like to be the Lyn from before your mom died. The frizzy hair. The green eyes. The whole thing. Head to toes."

Her eyes drifted closed.

"Please, Lyn. It's important," he pleaded.

Lyn must have passed out remembering because her white hair turned brown and frizzy as Scout lifted her dead weight off the damp rock and carried her through the stream. The current tugged the bottom of his jeans while his shoes filled with water.

When the moment passed, all sound returned, and a stiff breeze pulled at their clothing. A sound like thunder rumbled in the distance.

Scout's tennis shoes squelched with stream water and his legs were heavy with the added weight. He took in a deep breath and smelled rain mixed with faint traces of desert heat and ice.

A storm was coming.

CHAPTER TWENTY-THREE

*J*ake pulled up to the State Park's ranger station. He left Greg and Umiko in his truck with the engine running and went inside the small building. He flashed his Texas Parks Pass to the rangers and took pleasure in knowing that Killian would have to pay the daily use fee. It was only $5 but each little dig was worth it.

Killian stepped up to the thin counter beside Jake. "I'm with him."

"You still have to pay for entry," Jake said and walked out of the building with his parking pass.

Jake taped the white slip of paper to the inside of his windshield and drove into the park, leaving Killian to catch up or not. Jake hoped it was not, but knew it wouldn't be that easy. He didn't need Killian's drama, he already had Umiko's and Greg's.

You owe me big time, little bro.

Jake thumbed open his phone on the short walk back to the truck and opened his tracker app. Scout's location read 'not available' which was not unheard of this far from town. He sent Scout a quick text and put his phone back in his pocket. If it went through, great. If not, well, he was going to find his brother, so it didn't matter.

Jake parked the car in the first parking lot and jumped down.

Greg opened the rear door for Umiko and helped her down.

"Where's the waterfall?" Umiko asked.

Killian's jeep pulled into the parking space in front of Jake. He sneered as he jumped out of the open sided vehicle.

Jake smiled back, happy to have inconvenienced the shifter.

"Gorman falls is a three mile hike, roundtrip." Jake answered. "And be warned, this is a challenging trail and I am not going to go slow. If we get separated, come back here and wait. You'll want to carry water with you. I don't want to have to treat any of you for dehydration." He handed out plastic bottles, making sure to hold Killian's a little longer than necessary so the alpha had to rip it from his hands.

"Is that where they are?" Umiko asked.

He squinted at Umiko. "You got the call. You said Scout told you to start at the waterfall. That's what I'm doing. Gorman is the best waterfall in the park. Sixty-five feet tall and the formations are still growing. Scout would have taken her there." Jake looked at Greg. He wasn't sure what type of relationship the boy had with Lyn, but he was sure jealousy just flitted across the guy's face.

"If they did go to Gorman, they won't be there anymore," Greg said.

"True, but we have to start somewhere."

Greg looked around the parking lot and Jake hurriedly came up with an excuse why his brother's Range Rover wasn't there.

"What kind of car does he drive?" Greg asked.

"There are six or seven different parking areas in the park.

Just because you don't see his car, doesn't mean it's not on the property."

"But it's not here, so maybe they didn't start here. Why don't we check out the other lots and find where they started."

Because they didn't come by car. Jake opened the back driver's door and pulled out a backpack. He unzipped it to make sure he had his paramedic's kit and a few more bottles of water.

"Suit yourself. The next lot is down that way." Jake pointed.

Jake closed the door and locked his truck. "I'm going to Gorman unless Umiko has any details she didn't share earlier."

Umiko shook her head. "Just what I told you. Colorado Bend. Spicewoods Trail. Waterfall."

Jake glared at the girl. His hand formed a fist at his side. Why did Scout call her of all people? Even Killian would have been a better choice. He would at least know that details were important. "That's not what you said earlier. Gorman is not on the Spicewood Springs Trail." His voice didn't hide his frustration. Jake unlocked his car and tossed his pack in the back. "Anything else?" he asked Umiko. "Think carefully. Word for word would be preferred."

She shook her head.

"Umiko, are you sure." Greg's voice was softer than Jake's own.

He let the warrior handle the girl, maybe he could get more out of her by being nice. Jake had passed nice when he'd been woken before his alarm by the drama.

Jake checked his phone but there was no message from Scout. He flipped over to the tracker app and tried to reload Scout's location. Still no luck.

"I think so," Umiko said.

Jake huffed. His patience was wearing thin. He'd be faster

and more accurate if his information wasn't going through inept trackers. "Back into the truck unless you're walking to the right trail head." Jake stepped up into his truck and started the engine.

Everyone hurried to pile into the Tundra, including Killian, who jumped into the truck bed.

"Why did he call her?" Killian voiced Jake's own question.

Jake didn't respond.

CHAPTER TWENTY-FOUR

he wind picked up speed after the moment ended. Tree branches tossed and creaked in the increased pressure. Loose or dried branches broke off and fell from above. Scents of all kinds came and went, but the gardenia and jasmine smell was absent, along with the light aroma of sweets.

With Lyn's intoxicating scent so close to him, and the shifting winds, it was hard to follow his own breadcrumbs.

Scout wondered how Jake was doing at finding their scent.

"Crap. The cavalry." Scout stopped walking. He needed to get to his phone.

"Lyn?" he called softly.

She was still asleep or unconscious, either way, she wouldn't be any help to him at the moment.

He propped his foot on a rock and shifted Lyn's weight so that he could reach into his front pocket. He pulled out his phone and pressed his thumb to the home button. Nothing happened. He held the power button for a few seconds but still the black screen taunted him. Then he remembered the battery. A low growl grew in his chest and he switched his phone for hers.

Scout waited for what seemed like way too long for her phone to boot up. When it finally did, he used her limp thumb to unlock the screen. He was immediately inundated with text message and voicemail notifications. Her battery read thirty-six percent.

He skipped all the clutter and began a new message to Jake. He tried to be succinct since he had only one free hand, while also being cryptic, just in case someone else read it. He placed the phone in Lyn's lap with the screen up and pecked for the keys. "New plan. Tired. 3 for camping. Bring food. - Vs." He hit send, grateful that he had picked her phone up at the last minute.

He turned it back off to preserve the limited battery and stuck it in his hip pocket with his dead one.

"We will need to charge both phones tonight," he said to himself, just to hear something familiar.

The hairs on the back of his neck were standing up and he had a sinking suspicion that the Mimic and his fairy entourage had gotten far away as fast as they could.

Lyn didn't stir at his voice, or when he repositioned his arms under her. Scout reallocated her weight for faster movement and set off, circling back several times as he made slow progress back to the cabin.

If Jake didn't get his text message, maybe he'd catch on to the trail fakes and abort. Scout was sure his brother wouldn't lead anyone back to the cabin. He was equally sure he'd get a lecture about how he mishandled things, especially after Jake had been forced to spend his morning with people he wouldn't normally choose to spend time with.

Scout looked down at the girl sleeping in his arms. Her curly brown hair flew around her face in the strong wind. "You're worth it."

CHAPTER TWENTY-FIVE

*J*ake's phone vibrated in his pocket. He stopped between two emaciated trees and lifted it to his face.

"Is that Scout?" Umiko asked. She craned her neck to see Jake's phone screen.

He read the brief notification. It was a text from an unknown number. "No." He clicked the screen off before she moved any closer. He'd figure out why his girlfriend was texting him from an unknown number later. Veronica would understand that he needed to find his brother and his brother's crush. If she knew Scout was in trouble, she'd insist on Jake staying focused.

Unfortunately, the wind made finding a scent trail nearly impossible. One moment he had Scout's little league smell, the next it was gone, replaced by the fleeting scent of candy and flowers that weren't in bloom during the summer.

Jake shook his head. Something was messing with his ability to scent track. There was no reason his nose should be playing tricks on him. He was better than this. His mom's intensive training had made sure of it.

He stood at the base of the sad little waterfall and looked

around the swimming hole. "I need a minute. Stay here." The wind picked up and scattered leaves at his feet.

Jake walked around the wide open space. *Why would you bring her here and not to Gorman? Gorman is far more impressive and a much better backdrop to finally tell the girl you love her. I thought I taught you better.* He took in a nose full of air and tried to find Scout's or Lyn's scent.

The wind frustrated his efforts. It kept changing directions and obscuring what he thought he found almost as soon as he found it.

Another nose full and he caught a faint trace of rain, but it was hard to tell if that was Lyn's scent or the gathering storm. He needed to find them before the rain wiped out their tracks.

Jake climbed closer to the low peak of the waterfall and thought through the facts. He knew which way they had come to the falls, and it wasn't on any trail map. He also knew where they had stayed the night, but he wouldn't go there with an entourage, especially with this collection of annoyances.

He and Scout had made a pact never to tell anyone outside of family about the cabin in the woods. Although, Scout told Lyn, which meant his crush was a big one. Outside of Jake and Scout's immediate family, she was the only person to set foot on the land.

Jake had not even told Veronica where the cabin was. She only knew that it existed and that he and Scout would go there to camp and to do all the nature things she detested.

Jake's brow wrinkled. He pulled out his phone and read the message again. From V? V camping? That's amusing. She'd never... He read the message a third time. This time he picked up on the subtle wording and the tiny 's' at the end.

"Son of a..." Jake thrust his phone in his pocket and walked away from the pitiful excuse for a waterfall. He finally noticed broken branches just off the trail and he knew where they'd gone even without a scent trail to follow.

Getting rid of this crew is easier said than done, little bro. Jake looked back at the group standing by the stream. Their eyes were watching him like hawks, ready to move the moment Jake gave the word. *I can't follow you with this row of ducks on my tail.*

Should he tell them Scout and Lyn were safe? The text didn't exactly say they were safe. Just to meet them at the cabin. He doubted this group would believe him and go home without proof. Not after driving all this way. Umiko at the very least would demand to see Lyn with her own eyes.

Jake shook his head and growled under his breath. *This is a mess.* "I'm having trouble picking out his scent. The wind is throwing it," Jake called back to the group.

"Would he have left more than one way to track him?" Greg asked, making his way over to the older boy.

Jake hurried to meet Greg before the warrior could see what Jake had already noticed. *Of course he would have.* Jake thought, not looking at the broken branch. *My brother is not an idiot.*

Jake knew that if Scout wanted these people to know where he was or what had happened, he wouldn't have been so cryptic. A single call from Lyn would more easily send them home than the same from Scout or a second hand message from Jake.

"It depends on when the wind started," Killian said. "He might not have anticipated something masking his scent trail." Killian took a deep inhale.

Jake suppressed an eye roll. Killian might not have thought to double his trail, but his brother was smarter than his alpha and Killian's nose had nothing on his and Scout's. Their mother made sure of it with scent training everyday since their first shift.

Jake remembered the feeling of the silk blindfold over his eyes. The utter darkness behind it. The barrage of scents to dissect that followed.

"What do we do now?" Umiko broke him from his memory. "The weather is getting worse."

"I can keep looking for the scent, but when your scents get mixed in, it's harder," Jake lied. He could easily filter out Sunshine's salty air scent. The difficulty was the weather that came out of nowhere and the conflicting nonsense smells. But that didn't matter anymore, he knew where his brother was headed and he could get there fast if he could just lose his tail.

"GPS." Greg pulled his phone out of his pocket and unlocked the screen. He held the phone up and away from him. "The signal is weak." He crouched down and pulled a larger black square out of his pack.

"A satellite phone?" Jake asked. "Really?" He hoped his brother was smart enough to turn off the phone after he used it, but he'd need to buy him time.

"If you don't have a signal, why would Scout and Lyn? Their phones are probably just as useless." Jake floundered.

"I didn't say I don't have one. It's just weak." Greg countered and dialed a number. "Trace a GPS signal for me. Lyn's phone." Greg held the phone to his ear but added no more to the demand.

Jake's eyes widened. "Don't you at least need to give whoever is on the other side of your magic black box her number?"

"He already has it." Greg ran his hand through his hair while he waited. "I just hope she came home last night to get her phone."

He stared at Greg and made a note to never give him or any of the rest of them his cell number.

Jake took a deep whiff of fresh air, and acted interested. "I got something." He set off at a quick jog, not giving anyone time to think before they followed.

Jake weaved in and out of trees and underbrush on a fake trail with Greg, Umiko, and Killian following closely on his heels, while he tried to come up with some immediate reason they needed to go home.

Greg caught up to Jake, the black phone in his hand. "Nothing. The phone is either off, or disabled in another way. Give me Scout's number."

"So, you can keep tabs on my brother? No way," Jake said, still running. "I'll find him myself."

"This is not about privacy! This is about Lyn and fairies," Greg demanded.

Killian laughed from his position at their heels.

"And about the fact that you're not in control," Killian said to Greg.

Jake got a brief whiff of Scout and turned the trail away before Killian could pick up on it. His brain searched for a way to rid himself of three annoying tagalongs.

If I can turn Greg and Killian against each other…

"Stop fighting." Umiko wheezed from the end of the line of runners.

Jake pulled up short and looked back at the girl.

Umiko placed her hands on her thighs and struggled to deepen her shallow breathing.

Rain began to fall, slowly at first. He couldn't have asked for better timing.

"Umiko is tired," Jake said. "She needs to rest. One of you stay with her," Jake said. He took another couple of steps away from her and pretended to follow a scent trail.

He turned back to see Greg and Killian eying each other.

"No. I can keep going," Umiko said. "I just need to sit for a moment." She opened her water bottle and took a sip."

"We don't have a moment. The rain is going to wash everything away." Jake said. "You're not a runner and you have the wrong shoes for this terrain, especially when it's wet."

"In other words, you're slowing us down," Killian said

bluntly. "Greg will take you back to the parking lot. You can wait for us there."

"I will do no such thing," Greg said puffing out his chest and squaring off with Killian.

"Well, I can't take her." Jake said. "My nose is the only one capable of finding their scents on this wind."

A crack of lightning illuminated the sky. Umiko jumped at the crash of thunder that followed.

"Then Killian can take Umiko back," Greg said. "I'm going with you to find Lyn."

"I could take her back, but I won't. I'm built for running in the woods, rain or no rain." Killian stepped to Greg. "Besides, Scout is my second and Lyn is…"

"What? What is she to you?" Greg yelled at Killian. "She'll never choose you over me."

"Why? Because you're her knight in shining armor?" Killian said with a scoff and pushed his hair from his face.

"Because you're a predator," Greg shouted.

Killian laughed. The sound echoed around them under the trees. "So is she. And if she's part fae, that's another mark in the predator column. How will you reconcile that with your hero complex?" Killian taunted. "You save people, while she hunts them and toys with them for her amusement."

Greg swung first. His hand formed a fist and was halfway to Killian's face before Jake registered the movement. Killian caught Greg's fist in his hand, but was forced to take a step back with the impact.

Jake chased away a smile and ignored the fighting. He made a show of trying to find a scent, then he made his way back to Umiko.

He put a hand on her wrist and confirmed her heart was racing. "Can you make your way back to the parking lot on your own?" he asked. "All you have to do is follow the trail."

Umiko shook her head, water trailed down her face.. "Lyn needs me. I should be able to do this. I'm a swimmer. I have great lungs. My legs are strong." Umiko looked down and stomped her black flats on a root at her feet.

"I'll take you back, come on." Jake held out his hand to help her up.

"But Lyn..." Umiko started to argue.

"Is more able to take care of herself than you give her credit for." Jake said softly. Umiko was nice enough, a little controlling and extra nosy, but otherwise pleasant. "I'm also not worried about my brother. He's scrappy."

Umiko did not look convinced. The lines on her face suggested worry. "But he called for our help."

Jake sighed. "If you took the two of them home, I might be able to find some faint trail, if the wind and rain don't obscure it while we're deciding." He looked down at her. "I promise to find them and let you know when I do." Jake turned on his charm. Girls liked his charm. He smiled and tilted his head to the side. "They are okay. I know they are. Scout would not let anything happen to her."

Umiko nodded once and accepted his hand. She stood and faced Killian and Greg still trading punches. "STOP!" she yelled. Her voice was punctuated by a crash of thunder. When it passed, she continued. "Jake will stay. Greg, take me home. Killian, you're driving."

"What about..." Greg started to ask but Killian's fist connected with his cheek bone and words failed.

Greg closed the gap and drove Killian to the ground.

Jake tried to hide his amusement.

"STOP IT." Umiko shouted and the sounds in the immediate vicinity stopped. Birds flew away, squirrels hid, even the wind died down a little. The only sound that remained was the patter of rain hitting the ground.

Greg paused with his fist inches from Killian's nose. His eyes didn't leave the target. His muscles were still tense, but the momentum was long gone.

Jake followed the invisible line of impact to its natural

end. If Greg had not held back on Umiko's command, Killian's nose would be broken by now. Jake silently cursed Umiko's timing.

"I said," Umiko took a breath and spoke slowly, "Jake will find them." Umiko lowered her voice. "You two are wasting time and messing up the scent with your sweat and blood. Even I can smell you."

Jake knew that wasn't true, but he was content to let her manipulate them any way she wanted if it furthered his cause.

Greg pushed off of Killian and stood up. "I'm not leaving without them, and I'm not going anywhere with him." A layer of mud stuck to the knees of his jeans.

"Then we are at an impasse." Jake stood. "Because I've lost the scent and Umiko could use an escort, unless you trust Killian to have her best interest in mind."

Greg was silent and Jake knew he had the boy. Greg wouldn't trust Killian with a pet rock. He was surprised that Greg had allowed Killian to train Lyn all this time. He must really be bothered by her shifter traits to let her walk into what he viewed as the enemy's camp in order to learn to control her wolf.

Killian took a sniff and stood up from the ground. He swiped at the leaves and dirt on his clothes, but all that accomplished was getting his hands muddy. "You smell like locker rooms and motor grease, with a slight hint of getting your ass kicked." Killian planted his feet prepared for a rush by Greg.

Jake rolled his eyes. He really didn't like Killian, but the boy had almost nailed Greg's gym, sweat, and motor oil scent.

Greg looked at Umiko. "Are you sure?"

She looked at Jake before she nodded at Greg. Her voice came out small and laced with worry. "We are in the way here. Let Jake find his brother. Lyn will be with him."

"But what about…" Greg began again as a bolt of lightning flared.

"Either you trust her to take care of herself, or you don't," Jake said.

"It's not that easy." Greg met Jake's eyes.

"It is for me," Umiko said and began walking through the underbrush.

"Umiko!" Jake called. "That's the wrong way." He turned to the two fighters glaring at each other. "Which of you knows the way back to the cars?"

Greg looked around. Killian just stared at Jake, menace in his eyes.

Jake knew that both of them would be able to do it, but he needed to get back to his car anyway. "Great job, guys." He sighed and stepped toward the main trail. "I'll get you back to the parking lot." This way he could time his own exit from the park, and avoid getting caught leaving without Scout and Lyn.

"The trail is this way," Greg said to Umiko before he turned to Jake. "I can make sure Umiko gets home. You find Lyn."

And Scout. Jake lifted his hand in surrender and turned to the girl at his side. "Umiko, go home. I will text you when I know something, but do not give Greg my phone number or Scout's. If you do, we will never speak again. Do you understand?"

Umiko nodded and Greg waited for her to catch up to him.

Jake pretended to retrace his steps, his nose in the air, his breaths deep and strong as if hunting for a fresh trail.

Scout was going to get an earful.

CHAPTER TWENTY-SIX

Scout heard the sound of his brother's truck engine cut off in the distance and he waited near the cabin's front door. A few moments longer and he made out his brother's voice, grumbling something unintelligible, mixed with a light step on the gravel as Jake walked up the thin, dry footpath to the break in the trees.

The rain had not come this far. The only sign of the recent blip in weather was the occasional strong wind through the treetops.

"It took you long enough." Scout met him in the middle of the clearing.

"Hold up." Jake stopped walking and looked at Scout. "Do you know how hard it is to put three alphas off the scent of their potential mate?" Jake asked. "That is no small feat, little bro. Give me the credit I deserve."

"Umiko's not…"

"Seriously, word choice is where we're staring?" Jake held out several grocery bags.

Scout took them and walked back toward the cabin.

"Food for three." Jake said. "By the way, thanks for the invitation, 'V.' Whose phone? Lyn's?"

"Yeah, mine died. She's out by the fire pit. Come on." Scout walked Jake inside and sorted food onto the folding table. He focused less on his task and more on the pile of blankets beside the fire outside.

"Ask me how I lost them." Jake said. He elbowed Scout in the ribs as he took the cold items to the small dorm fridge and tossed them inside.

Scout humored him. "How did you lose them?" he sighed.

"I started a fight. Umiko helped, but she doesn't know it. Dude, Greg got in the first punch, but Killian grabbed it mid flight. Those two are pretty well matched. Greg slammed Killian into the ground at the end. After Killian gave Greg a black eye, for sure. It was nice to see that cocky asshole go down. Greg was this close," Jake held his fingers a pinch apart, "to breaking that asshole's nose when Umiko interfered. That girl's timing was terrible. What is Greg? Do you know? Some warrior breed, but what exactly?"

"His mother is Amazonian. His father is Gargarean. The male counterpart." Scout said peering into one of the bags.

"There are male Wonder Women?"

"How do you think Wonder Women are created?"

"Fair point."

"So, you started a fight. That's how you distracted them?" Scout closed the front door to the cabin.

"I didn't have a lot of options. You called in the cavalry and they weren't going to be easily swayed. I had to use Umiko's poor choice of footwear to seal the deal with her, and promise to let her know when I found you. After that I used Greg's mistrust of Killian against him and managed to get him to play hero and take Umiko home. Thanks for turning off your phones, by the way. That almost blew it. Greg is an ass. That storm was a great help, too."

"Did you check the forecast before you drove in? How bad is it going to be?" Scout asked. "I can't get enough signal to check the radar." He pushed open the back cabin door. "Is it going around us?"

Jake followed and propped the door open with a large limestone rock to let in some light.

"There was and is no storm in the forecast. Whatever that was, it came out of nowhere and disappeared the same way. I thought it might have been you guys. Maybe Lyn has weather skills? I don't know. I guess the wind was a fluke. Clear skies and sunny weather expected for the rest of the week." Jake looked around the fire. "Where's the girl?"

"Under there." Scout pointed to a person sized lump under a thin blanket on a blue tarp by the fire. "Lyn hasn't woken up yet. She's just sleeping, so don't start up with that whole thing, again."

"I was just kidding. Jeez. Let it go already." Jake slapped his brother on the back. "I brought my medic bag." He hefted his shoulder and his backpack thunked on his back. "I didn't know what shape you two would be in when I found you."

"Thanks." Scout pushed wood around in the fire pit. "We're fine. Physically. Lyn's exhausted. I'm tense and sore from carrying her this far, but otherwise okay. Nothing your bag can fix."

"Anything you want to tell me? Greg seems to think she's been taken by fairies. All three of them are on edge. Under normal circumstances, I wouldn't care, but I got woken up in the early hours by a frantic best friend to come hunt you down, then I got called off again before lunch. I had better ways to spend my morning." Jake reached inside the back door to grab another camp chair and unfolded it across the fire from Lyn.

"I don't blame them."

"I do! I blame you, too."

"No," Scout said. "I don't blame them for being worried. I'm sorry you got called in for what turned out to be nothing."

Jake leaned forward in his seat. "Are you going to deny the fairy angle?"

Scout didn't reply, he pushed around another log.

Lyn rolled over on top of a canvas tarp near the fire and tossed the blanket off. She had gone through cycles of being hot and cold since Scout brought her back to camp, but she slept through both, albeit fitfully.

"That girl changes her hair a lot." Jake said.

"You have no idea." Scout left the fire and sat on the tarp by her head. He brushed the frizzy brown hair from her face.

"I want to," Jake said softly. "Especially since I ticked off two and a half people for you today."

"Half?" Scout looked up.

Jake shrugged. "Umiko might have been swayed by my charms," Jake crooned, "but I don't know for sure. Actually, I don't care if she is or not. Are you hungry? I'm hungry. For some reason I was forced to skip breakfast this morning."

"Yeah, sorry. What did you bring?" Scout hadn't paid attention when he'd unpacked the grocery sacks.

"Sausages and cheese." Jake shook his head. "How many do you want?" Jake said. He walked back inside the cabin.

"Two, and toss two on for Lyn," Scout shouted as Jake was swallowed by the cabin. He looked down at the girl sleeping next to his lap. "She'll be hungry when she wakes up." He smiled. "She's usually hungry."

CHAPTER TWENTY-SEVEN

*L*yn's eyes opened as her nose woke her to the aroma of bratwursts. "Is one of those for me?" She turned her green eyes up to Scout's face. "I'm starving." She tried to blink the sun away and Scout shifted to block the patch of light from her face.

His brown eyes smiled back. "You can have two." Scout said, wrapping a sausage in a bun and holding it out for her to take.

Lyn sat up. "Mustard?"

"Heads up." Jake said from the door of the cabin. He tossed a yellow plastic bottle at Lyn and she caught it in her free hand. Jake smiled and disappeared back inside.

Lyn squeezed the condiment bottle and a thin line of yellow appeared between her sausage and bun. She took a bite and closed her eyes as the warmth of the sausage juice trickled over her tongue. "Thank you," she mumbled.

"You can have more than one if you want. I bought enough for a few meals." Jake shouted from around the corner of the cabin. His voice was followed by the thunk of something hitting the ground.

"Jake's putting a second tent up around front," Scout said

to Lyn. "I've told him nothing. But he's put some things together on his own."

"We're alone otherwise?" She took another bite of her sausage, unconcerned with the new arrival.

"The only creatures, human or otherwise, that I smell are you and him. Plus the ones that live here, squirrels, birds, and such. The wind quit. I'm not sure if that was related, but it was eerie enough that I'm glad it's gone." Scout said. "A group of deer passed through, but I doubt they're a threat."

"I don't remember any wind," she said and then lowered her voice a little more, "I don't remember much after I tried to mimic you. How long was I asleep?"

"A couple of hours." He matched her volume. "It zapped your energy. I tried to keep you awake, but couldn't." Scout paused. "I'll catch you up in a bit. For now, keep looking like this Lyn." He handed her a camp sized shaving mirror.

Lyn wasn't sure what that meant, but took the mirror and checked her reflection. Curly brown hair, the way her mother used to style it, and green eyes looked back. This is what she looked like before the binding started wearing off. "Why?" she asked.

"Camouflage." He winked.

Lyn creased her eyebrows. She wanted to know what he meant by that and what she missed in the two hours she was passed out. But before she could ask, another voice cut in.

"Hey. We have three sleeping bags, right? Where is the third one?" Jake came around the corner. "Feeling better, sleeping beauty?" He smiled at Lyn.

"Thanks for the food." Lyn took another bite of her sausage and smoothed out the worry lines on her face.

"You're welcome."

"We used all three last night. They're still in the tent." Scout pointed with his head in the direction of the tent he and Lyn shared last night and took another sausage off the fire. He put it in a bun with cheese and took a bite.

"Hey, how come you get cheese?" Lyn asked.

"Because I cooked?" Scout took an exaggerated bite of his fancy hotdog while looking at her.

"Jake," Lyn whined, "Scout won't give me any cheese." She slit her eyes and stared at Scout.

Scout scoffed but a huge grin spread across his face.

"I'm not here to be a babysitter. Also, I'm not going to find anything in there I don't want to see, am I?" Jake's gaze moved between the tent and Scout's face with a slight arch to his brow.

"Just get your sleeping bag and be quiet," Scout handed Lyn a slice of the coveted cheese.

She opened her bun and slid the cheese under the sausage before taking a bite.

Jake unzipped the tent flap and pulled out the bottom layer of sleeping bag. He tossed it over his shoulder and walked back to his tent.

"You said I could have two sausages?" Lyn held her last bite of sausage in her fingers.

Scout smiled and handed her the skewer he was cooking with and the package of unheated bratwursts.

CHAPTER TWENTY-EIGHT

"Now that you're awake, spill it." Jake leaned back in his seat, a bottle of water in one hand, the other resting on his crossed knee. "I got a call from Umiko telling me you and Scout found your mother, whom I thought was dead, by the way." He looked at Lyn but there wasn't pity in his eyes. He was just stating a fact. "She didn't make much sense after that. To be honest, she didn't make sense to me at that point either. Did I mention it was way too early for phone calls? Anyway, Greg was worried about some fairy threat that Scout, here, hasn't outright denied."

Jake looked at her like he was daring her to do what Scout hadn't. She just didn't know if that was to deny it, or tell the truth.

Lyn looked at Scout, then at Jake. "My biological mother is a ..."

"Fairy. Type unknown." Scout finished for her.

She looked at him. Why would he lie to his brother?

"So, you followed her into the woods." Jake shook his head. "Not smart. Fairies are tricky predators. Present company notwithstanding. It's a good thing Scout called someone. I just wished it had been me instead of the whole annoying gang. They are a handful. How do you put up with those three and their colossal control issues?"

"I couldn't take a chance that you wouldn't be able to tell anyone." Scout defended himself before Lyn could answer. "You made a deal with Lyn not to tell anyone where we were."

"I've broken plenty of deals for worse reasons than your safety." Jake waved him off.

"Those deals didn't smell like lightning." Scout lifted his eyebrows and stared at Jake with his head tilted on his shoulders.

Jake stared back. His eyes narrowed. "She got me?"

"She did."

"Fool me once." Jake shook his head. "But why did you call off the search? Umiko and those two idiots are going nuts. Not that I don't enjoy Killian being frustrated in pursuit of a pretty girl."

Lyn looked at Jake like he had sprouted wings. "What are you talking about?"

"Seriously? You don't know? Lyn, I love you like a sister, but you are oblivious if you don't already know that Killian has a thing for you. One which makes things difficult on my baby brother."

"Jake, can you get Lyn a bottle of water?" Scout asked.

Lyn picked up a slight tremor in his voice.

Jake shifted in his seat about to get up. "Sure. Hey Lyn, you know those stories where the boy doesn't get the girl until the end because he's too much of a coward to talk to her in the beginning." He stood.

"Yeah?" Lyn answered, not sure where he was going with his question.

"I'm not a fan. I prefer the stories where the girl has all the details and makes her own decisions. What about you, Scout? Which ones do you like most?" Jake walked away from the fire and into the building, a smirk on his face.

Scout rolled back into the grass beside where Lyn was curled up earlier and closed his eyes. The sun played over his face as it moved between sparse clouds and billowing branches.

Lyn watched him.

"Look," Scout started.

"If you're going to say it's complicated, don't."

"Okay." He sighed and remained quiet.

Lyn laid back and turned on her side to face his profile. "My life is complicated enough. I don't want more of the same."

Scout nodded, keeping his face turned toward the sun and his eyes closed.

"You are the only person in my life besides Clark that doesn't try to control me," she paused, "usually"

"I'm sorry about the other day. Killian is…"

"Complicated?"

"A jerk." Scout laughed once and stopped. "And the deal was an accident, I swear. I was just scared you would run off without me."

"Do you think you need to protect me?"

Scout was quiet for a moment and she wasn't sure he was going to answer.

"I wasn't scared for you." Scout whispered.

Lyn watched his chest rise and fall in a deep breath. He rolled over to face her.

"You are the strongest person I know," he said. "Maybe not with your brawn, but with your will to live on your own terms, most of the time. I admire that and wish I had an ounce of it to call my own."

Most of the time? What did that mean? When did she not live on her own terms? Lyn saved her questions for later, she didn't want to fight with him. Not right now, well, not about that.

"Then take it," she snapped. "Take some of mine, or take

Killian's. I took mine from Greg. I was standing on the porch at my… at Maria's husband's house and I was over my head in complications. I took Greg's steady and calm and made it mine. And when I knocked on Ms. Evan's house after she had taken Umiko, it wasn't my weak and scared little knock. It was Greg's take no shit knock. I walked into that house with all the confidence Greg had mixed with Killian's pride. I didn't make them mine until after. When the world slowed down and I decided I wanted to be those things I didn't give them back."

Scout smiled. "You've been mimicking since before you knew what you were."

"I think I've been mimicking since I was born, with the help of the binding. But that's beside the point. This is not about what type of creature my genes come from. It's about who I want to be." Lyn smiled. "Who do you want to be, Scout?"

"Am I interrupting anything?" Jake said as he walked out of the cabin and held full water bottles down to Lyn and Scout.

Lyn sat up as Jake took his seat. "How does Killian make things difficult for Scout?" If Scout was being bullied, she wanted to help. She opened the bottle and took a sip.

Jake looked from Lyn to Scout, who was still laying on the ground with his face turned to the sky. "If Scout tells you what he wants to tell you, he'll have challenged his alpha."

"Not yours?"

"I run with the big boys. Killian's god complex means nothing to me."

"I don't think so." Lyn shook her head. "Try again."

"Fine, it does. It pisses me off." Jake admitted. "One day, Killian will take over the big dogs and my mom and my little brother will be under his thumb."

"Why does that matter?" Lyn asked. "One king complex versus another. It's all the same."

"Killian's dad killed Scout's," Jake said.

"You can't prove that." Scout rolled up to sitting. "It was a hunting accident."

"Maybe. Yet, you never fight by Killian's side when it matters," Jake said. "Why else would you do that unless you thought it was possible that his dad had something to do with your dad's death. And don't say it's never crossed your mind that Killian might…"

Scout growled.

Lyn startled at the ferocity and turned to him, expecting to see signs of his wolf. They were absent, but the rage in Scout's face was like nothing she'd seen on him before.

Lyn let everything sink in. Scout's anger. Jake's words. She thought back to the only fight she had been in with Killian and his pack. Jake was right. The day Lyn faced Ms. Evans, Scout had gathered intel, but was not included in the plans, or the actual confrontation. Lyn didn't think anything of it until now. Another question demanded her attention. "Not your father?" Lyn eyed Jake.

"My dad died when I was too young to remember his face. Scout's dad claimed me as his own and raised me as such, but I am not a Jacobs' by blood. Killian and Scout, on the other hand, might as well be twins."

"He's exaggerating." Scout twisted the lid off his water bottle and took a sip.

"Wait," Lyn said. "Why do you follow Killian's dad, if you think he killed Scout's?"

Jake sneered but didn't answer.

"My dad and Killian's dad were twins." Scout filled in the silence. "My dad was older by three minutes. He would have been alpha had he survived past my grandfather's death. Killian and I were born to different parents on the same day."

"Scout's older," Jake said.

"By seventeen minutes." Scout clarified.

"Whatever." Jake waved the detail off. "The pack was

ready to split until Killian's dad forced Killian to take Scout as his second. It settled the rift but there are still a few members that would follow Scout if he wanted to claim alpha."

"But you don't want to be alpha, either." Lyn looked at Scout.

"It's…" Scout started but paused when he saw her green eyes sparkle in the sunlight.

"Complicated." Lyn finished.

Scout shut his mouth.

"Then there's the hero. We can't forget him, if we're talking complications." Jake broke the silence. "Did you know he has Lyn's phone tracked?"

"He what?" Lyn growled and rounded on Jake. She felt her wolf rise to the surface.

Jake dropped his water bottle and it splashed the fire, causing a sizzle that bloomed smoke. "I'll take that as a no." Jake reached for his bottle. He picked it up without looking instead of turning from her anger. "I'm not the bad guy." He put his hands up in surrender, sloshing water onto his jeans. "I'm telling you, so you will know. As soon as you turn your phone back on, he'll know where to find you."

"My phone is at home. In my bed."

Jake and Scout traded a look.

Lyn looked at Scout. "Isn't it?"

Scout held out the device. "I had Jake bring it yesterday when he picked us up at the cemetery. I turned it off when he handed it to me. I should have given it to you, but you fell asleep shortly after I got you in the car." He hung his head. "Then I had to use yours to text Jake earlier, because mine died. Plus, I didn't want them to know it was me, and I knew it would show up as unknown on Jake's phone. I turned it off immediately after. It's been powered off the entire time we've been here." He lifted his head. "I'm sorry. I should have told you."

She took the device and removed the case. "I need a pin or

a needle. Something thin and strong." She looked at Scout. "A fishing hook maybe?"

Jake reached into his pocket and pulled out a small safety pin. "It's truly amazing what ends up in a boyfriend's pocket. I still don't know why Veronica wanted me to hold onto this." He tossed it across the fire to Lyn, who caught it like it was a baseball and not a tiny bit of flying metal.

She opened the safety pin, popped out the sim card from her phone and flicked it into the fire.

Scout leaned forward in his chair and caught it before it landed. He waved off the heat from his hand.

"Why did you do that?" Lyn's anger was palpable.

"You might want the data from this when you get a new number." Scout slid the small thin rectangle of plastic into his pocket.

"Fine." She nodded. "Can they track you?" She asked Jake.

Jake shook his head. "Sunshine called me on the house phone. I also threatened Umiko if she gave him mine or Scout's number, but I powered it off just to be sure."

She turned to Scout.

"Umiko has my number for sure. I'm almost certain Greg has it too."

She reached out for his phone.

He reached toward her with an empty palm. "I'll take out the sim card for now, but I think we need to have one working phone between us. I'll take you to the store when we get back and we'll both change our numbers after this fairy business is figured out."

She placed the open safety pin in his hand and sat back down.

Jake sat back and smirked. "Fairy business. Please, tell me more."

Scout and Lyn exchanged a glance and silence.

"First things first, brother." Scout said. "You will keep

Lyn's creature type and everything you learn today to yourself." Scout nodded at Lyn.

Lyn stood and extended her hand across the fire. As the heated air from the open flame rose into the air and licked at her skin, she remembered what it was like to be cold

"Wait." Jake hesitated. "Fool me once, shame on me. Fool me twice…"

"Shake on the deal or leave," Scout said. "No hard feelings."

"I thought we trusted each other." Jake met Scout's eyes.

"I trust you with my life, Jake." Scout agreed.

"But not with hers." Jake looked at Lyn.

"Shake and you'll find out why," Scout said.

Lyn kept her hand in the hot air above the banked fire, sure that it made her look more hardcore than she was. She smiled at the effect. Now that she knew how it worked, she thought her mimic skill was kind of awesome.

Jake looked at his brother and Lyn waited for him to come to a decision on his own.

"You could just walk away, Jake. No questions, no answers. Just leave it alone."

Lyn heard the conviction in Scout's voice. Whatever he knew, he wasn't going to back down. She hoped Jake agreed, because she desperately wanted to know what it was that Scout knew. What had happened after she passed out in the middle of the stream?

Jake met Lyn's eyes.

She found herself curious whose eyes looked back at him. Her green ones, her heterochromia, or Scout's brown eyes, had she picked up any other colors on accident? Could that kind of accident happen?

"I'll admit, you have me intrigued, Lyn Davis." He grasped her hand. "Are you a good fairy or a bad fairy?"

Lyn saw a flicker of curiosity as his hand expected heat, but met chill air instead.

"Interesting. So, what's in it for me? If we're going full on fairy manners, let's do it right. What's my boon?"

"What do you want?" Lyn kept his gaze and his hand.

"I will keep your creature type and everything I learn here today to myself and in exchange I get to claim you as my sister."

"What? No!" Scout stood up to object. "Relationships and fairy deals do not mix."

"Done." Lyn agreed before Jake could change his mind. "You can claim me as a sister in exchange for all my secrets kept." A shock spread from the center of her palm to every finger tip and up her arm. She held Jake's hand and his gaze until the shock dissipated. Then she dropped her hand and the heat returned to the space above the fire.

Jake pulled his hand away from the heat. "Is that heat trick on the agenda?" Jake said and sat back down. "Because that was awesome."

"It is, brother." Lyn said with a smile.

"Wait just a moment." Scout stood up and pulled Lyn aside. "Lyn, can I speak to you? Alone."

"Don't keep my sister long." Jake called to their retreating bodies.

Lyn let herself be led away from the fire and out of earshot of Jake, even so Scout whispered.

"That deal…"

"…is all about semantics right?"

"Well, yes." Scout stood baffled.

"Then he will keep my secrets in exchange for a title. He can claim me as a sister without it being anything more than a nickname. Just because he claims me as a sister…"

"…doesn't mean you are."

"Unless you want it to be true." Lyn turned and walked back to the fire before he processed her answer.

"Wait, what?" Scout asked, following her.

CHAPTER TWENTY-NINE

"So," Jake said, "in addition to being a wolf shifter, she's some sort of fairy shifter."

"Essentially," Scout agreed.

"And this somehow makes her a weapon that both fairy courts want?" Jake scoffed. "I don't buy it."

"Not just the courts." Scout looked at Lyn.

She sat with her eyes closed.

Scout worried that she would be overwhelmed by the implications of being a weapon. He watched as her chest rose and fell, silently counting the duration of her inhale and exhale. Four seconds in. Four seconds out. She was eerily calm.

He moved his chair closer and put a hand on her knee. She didn't so much as twitch.

Scout looked back to Jake. "If anyone found out what she is, they'd want to use her as a spy, possibly even an assassin." He tried to calm his own racing pulse. "Think about it. She can be anyone, go anywhere. She could get close to politicians, military leaders. She could infiltrate corporations, regimes, you name it. She can eventually get to anyone without being challenged. She could trick someone and take their form, force them not to tell anyone, and get up close and personal with her target. Then…" Scout wasn't going to say it, not in front of her, but he knew Jake would follow his thought to the end.

"Is it really that easy? Wouldn't someone be able to tell you weren't who you said you were?" Jake asked Lyn, but she didn't respond. "Surely someone would be able to tell the difference?"

Scout squeezed the fleshy part just above her knee. "Are you okay?"

She opened her eyes and nodded, but there was no emotion in them.

Her pulse was normal and her breath steady. Her non-reaction almost worried him more than if her wolf was fighting to get to the surface. He'd prefer her pulse to race, for her to show some sign that she understood what he was saying, but it was like she was in a fog. He wondered when the information would catch up to her, and if he would be able to help her process.

He knew that she had trouble coming to grips with the scary side of her shifter and now she finds out that she is essentially a deadly tool, doubly so, since she carries her weapons with her. She could kill anybody, anywhere.

"You tell us," Lyn said. "Close your eyes, and wait to open them until Scout says you can." Lyn stood up.

Scout stood by her side, their hands pressed together between them, a smile on his face. "Are you sure?"

She took a deep breath and looked at Scout.

Lyn's frizzy brown hair straightened and shortened. Her green eyes went brown. Her weight shifted from her chest to her torso. She even managed to mimic Scout's clothing this time.

A strong gust of wind blew in from the trees at their back.

Scout watched Lyn shift, painlessly, jealous of how

effortless it seemed, but he knew better. He was prepared to catch her if she fell.

She swayed on her feet, but this time she stayed upright. She opened her eyes and Scout saw his own brown orbs blink at him.

They turned toward Jake, still sitting in his camp chair across the fire pit with his eyes closed.

"Open." Lyn said with Scout's voice.

Scout waited patiently for his brother's jaw to close. He kept the smile from his face, but just barely. It was nice to see his older brother speechless. To be fair, he was impressed with how thorough her mimic was also.

"So, she can look like anyone?" Jake asked. He stood up and walked around the campfire to get a better look.

The light from the sun was dimming as it made its way to dusk. The air was again still.

"Anyone that trusts her." Lyn said in Scout's voice.

"She's a hot shifter chick, who wouldn't trust her?"

"I'd trust her." Scout said. He was impressed that she had gotten him down perfectly without collapsing. Plus, he really enjoyed the baffled look on Jake's face. "Can you tell a difference?"

"Not with my eyes." Jake took a deep breath. "But she smells a ton better than you." He said and stepped away from his brother's swinging arm.

Lyn shifted her features from Scout's back to the old Lyn with perfectly curled hair and plopped down into her camp chair.

"Are you sure you're okay?" Scout asked her.

She nodded. "Water?"

Scout handed her his bottle, even though hers was on the ground next to the chair.

"So her scent?" Jake asked.

"Won't change. At least that's what Mimic man said. But how many people have shifter noses and of those how many are as fine tuned as ours?" Scout asked and sat down. "It would be a calculated risk to send her anywhere deep undercover, but plenty of people wouldn't think twice about sending her into a dangerous situation for the right outcome."

"And the fire thing?" Jake asked.

"Parlor trick. I just remember what my arm felt like cold," she said through droopy eyes and leaned back in the camp chair.

Scout heard the tiredness in her voice before she yawned. He watched her eyes droop closed and open again. He sat next to her and put his hand back on her knee.

"I can't feel a limitation, but Scout says it's about a foot away from my skin." Lyn gave in to her heavy eyelids and sat with them closed.

"So you can share some of these feelings with someone who is close enough to kiss you." Jake turned on his charm.

Lyn opened one eye. "But if someone gets that close, brother, they are also close enough to kill." She closed her eye back, her face didn't give her nerves away, but Scout felt the tremor in her leg.

"So you could take out Killian and leave the pack minus an alpha just by picking the right face. Hell, you could take his place as alpha and most of the juniors wouldn't be able to tell." Jake whistled. "Nice weapon." He sat back in his chair with his arms crossed. "So, Summer has one, and Winter wants one. Your kind must be rare."

"We don't know that." Scout said.

"Trust me, if these Mimics were common, everyone and their brother would have one. There would be militia. Better yet, governments wouldn't need armies. They'd have carefully placed Fairy Mimic Assassins." He leaned his elbows on his knees and looked at Lyn across the fire. "Why haven't they come after you, yet? Surely, not just because you've lived as a human for all these years."

Lyn spoke without opening her eyes. "The binding hid me

in plain sight. I'm assuming my Mimic mother never met my human mother so she couldn't give my hiding place away. The witch was a calculated risk, I guess. I won't know everything until I find my mother."

Scout spewed water across the fire. The overheated wood sizzled where the drops landed. He turned his face to Lyn, chin dropped.

"Until you what?" Jake barked. "Are you serious?"

Scout agreed with Jake's incredulity. He fought to find words, but couldn't. Would she really go that far? *Yes. Yes, she probably would.*

Jake found his words first. "You want to mimic your way into Summer and find a woman you have never met."

"Okay, this conversation is over." Scout snapped when he had control over his vocal cords again. "We do not know who or what could overhear us." Scout's pulse quickened and the hair on his arms stood up.

"We'd see if a fairy was near." Lyn defended.

"Would you, sitting there with your eyes closed, half asleep?" Scout's heart hammered against his chest. "Can you see through walls? Does your vision have a better range than their hearing? Does that green eye still work if it's not ice white?"

"Well, no and I don't know. I haven't met a lot of fairies." Lyn opened her eyes and glanced around from where she was still curled in her chair. She remembered her heterochromia and felt a tingle as her eyes shifted. She looked around the circle again. "But it's all clear. Plus, I gave you fairy sight. You'd have seen something even if my green eyes didn't work." She leaned back and closed her eyes again.

"Not through walls."

"Point of fact." Jake interrupted. "Fairy sight, when given, is only temporary. If I'm not mistaken, most fae will even take your eye if they find out you have fairy sight. I don't know about the whole green eye vs ice eye thing, but if you keep your scent when you change, maybe you could keep your sight too, but it's not guaranteed." Jake nodded at Scout. "Even so, I agree with him. No planning out loud unless you know who is whom. That goes for everyone. Smell them first. Myself and Scout included. What did I smell like when we first met?" Jake asked. He relaxed back into his chair.

Scout watched as Lyn took a deep breath. He tried to calm his racing pulse. Jake had changed the subject for now, but he still didn't want her to race off to rescue her mother without him. Could he chance another ill begotten deal with Lyn? He glanced at her, then around the campfire and the surrounding area, or as much of it as he could that was not obscured by things or shadows. He didn't enjoy feeling that something could be just out of his enhanced sight range. He was used to having better vision than the human population and most of the creature one as well, but now, he felt blind.

"Oranges, cloves, and hospital sheets." Lyn recalled, smiling.

"And now?" Jake asked.

She took a deep breath. "Oranges, cloves, clean sheets dried in the sunshine and…" Lyn sniffed again. "There's something else." She opened her eyes and took in another deep breath.

Scout imagined her trying to filter out his scent and the lingering smell from the fire. He stayed quiet and watched. He tried to train her like his mother had trained them, only without the blindfold and the constant barrage of scents.

"Like Scout, but not. There's a hint of lightning too, and safety." She sat up and faced him.

Jake nodded at her. "What do I smell like, sis?"

Lyn hesitated to answer. "I'm not sure, something familiar."

Jake nodded and took a sip of his water.. "People's scents change over time, but not fast and not drastically. You've taken on a peculiar scent. One that's hard to explain because loyalty and trust aren't usually associated with scents. But it's the best words for what I smell. Maybe pack would be a better term for it, or family."

"I don't smell it." Scout said sniffing the air around her. She smelled the same to him. Like a long run in a rainstorm.

"You didn't make the deal, little bro. She's not your family." Jake smiled and spoke to Lyn in his teacher voice. "People smell different to different noses. What I smell like to you is definitely not what I smell like to Scout?"

Lyn turned to Scout. "What does Jake smell like to you?"

"Baseball games, pillow forts, and gym socks." Scout answered. "Scent is as much memory as it is actual smells." He recited the lesson his mother had drilled into them both in the early years of their training. "Killian doesn't understand that. He wasn't trained the way we were."

"He will never have our nose for scents." Jake eyed Lyn. "But you, I think you will. If my mother trained you, you'd be as good, if not better than the two of us."

"Pillow forts and clean sheets are very similar." Scout shrugged at Jake.

"What about the oranges and the cloves?" Lyn asked.

"I almost always have orange oil under my nails. I love mandarins. But Scout filters that scent out as trivial. He looks for the right mix of smells that reminds him of just me."

"It's why the pack couldn't figure out your scent when Killian challenged them to in September. We can only match new scents to old ones, and no one had ever smelled anything like you before, not even me. Most people will pick out your shampoos or soaps you use. They confuse those with your scent, but lots of people use those. They can't filter through to your unique scent."

"Which is?" Lyn asked.

"Loosely controlled lightning." Scout and Jake said in unison. The brothers laughed.

"Mixed with other things, depending on our memories." Jake snickered.

"But Scout smells like…" Lyn paused.

Scout turned to her, interested in what she associated with his scent.

As he watched, she took a deep breath, "…things I haven't experienced."

Scout looked at her and cocked his head. "Like what?" What couldn't or wouldn't she label.

Jake smiled. "Then you've just given them a place holder name and when you do experience them, you'll either know you named it right, or change the label in your head." He shrugged. "It's getting late, and I'm assuming this deal thing will wear off at midnight, so anything else you want me to know and not share?"

"I admire you, big bro." Scout said.

"You were not part of the deal, I can still tell people you said that." Jake stuck out his tongue.

Lyn stepped over to Jake and whispered in his ear.

Scout wondered what she said for Jake's ears only.

"Well played, little sis." Jake smirked at Scout. "I have a secret." He taunted Scout.

"What?" Scout looked between Lyn and Jake.

"Can't share, won't share." Jake looked at Lyn. "Okay, it's been a while since I departed company with the calvary, I should tell the trio something, even though they are a pain in the ass. I can get them a message without giving up my cell number, but only if you want me to. I owe them nothing."

"How?" Scout asked.

"I'll call mom, and tell her to call Umiko from a landline. They can trace that to a stationary house and knock on mom's door if they want to, but she's faced worse than Killian, Greg, and Umiko."

Lyn nodded her agreement to Jake and he walked off, phone in hand.

"Scout, start the fire back up, unless that's in Lyn's skillset now." Jake called over his shoulder. "Either way. I'm ready for dinner." He moved the phone to his ear.

"What did you whisper to Jake?" Scout said after his brother walked off.

Lyn smiled. "None of your business." She pointed at the fire. "You stack the logs, I'll remember the flame."

He did as she asked and afterwards she knelt down with her face close to the dying embers and breathed life back into the fire.

"Do we have sausages left?"

"We've got better," Scout said. He stood up and walked to the cabin's back door. "The fridge is fully stocked for now. Dinner is chicken, caesar salads, zucchini, and mushrooms that do not smell like ammonia."

"Maybe Jake should plan all of my meals." she joked.

"Not me?" Scout teased back.

Lyn shrugged. "It's a family thing."

He chuckled and left her sitting by the fire.

CHAPTER THIRTY

*L*yn made whimpering sounds twice in the middle of the night, but didn't wake up. The third time, she sat bolt upright and frantically crawled out of her sleeping bag.

"Lyn?" Scout whispered in the dark. "Are you okay?" He heard her labored breathing and unzipped his sleeping bag so he could reach her. "It's okay. We're camping. You, me, and Jake.

She turned and buried her face in his chest. "I'm sorry I woke you," she said.

A thin line of water trickled down his chest. "Don't be sorry." Scout put his arms around her. "Do you want to talk about it?"

Her face rubbed against his chest. "I just… I couldn't…"

Scout held her tight around the shoulders and stayed quiet. If she was going to talk, he had to leave the silence for her to fill.

She finally spoke. "It's silly, but I felt trapped in the sleeping bag."

"Your feelings are not silly." He loosened slightly, so she

wouldn't feel trapped by him. He didn't want to make her pull away, not when she felt so nice next to his skin.

Scout felt her face pout against his chest. "Except I'm cold," she whined, "and the thought of crawling back into the sleeping bag… I don't like feeling confined."

"That is definitely not silly," Scout said into her hair. "We can solve cold other ways. There's still my hoodie somewhere in here, and sleeping bags can be unzipped to be blankets."

Lyn pulled away and Scout blindly searched for his hoodie.

"Here's this." He found the thick fabric and handed it to her.

She slid it over her head while he unzipped his sleeping bag and hers.

"The ground is a bit hard without the padding of the sleeping bag, but we can put one down and the other on top," Scout said. "I promise to sleep on my side." He lifted his hand and folded in his pinkie and thumb. "Scout's honor." He couldn't see her face, but he hoped she at least smiled. He wished he could do more than comfort her. He wanted to scare away her nightmares, to help her sleep peacefully in his arms.

"Is it okay if we sleep with our backs together?"

"Of course." Scout settled back down and turned away from her.

He felt Lyn settle in, her back as close to his as she could get. He pulled the sleeping bag over his arm, making sure it didn't cover her head. He would happily deal with the chill, but she'd generate enough heat touching his skin for it to not matter.

Before he had finished settling in and fluffing his pillow, she was back to sleep.

It took him much longer.

CHAPTER THIRTY-ONE

The next morning, the smell of coffee drifted through the thin sides of the tent along with the chirping of birds.

Scout opened his eyes, but didn't dare move. He wanted this morning to last forever. He wanted to hold on to her as long as he could. He wanted to forget about everything happening around them and just hold her, and kiss the top of her head. He wanted to claim her as his. It irked him that Jake could because of a deal, but he wanted more than the deal offered anyway. He wanted more than a sister.

He took a deep breath and the scent of jasmine and lighting tickled his nose, so did the frizzy hairs on the top of her head. He stifled the urge to rub them away and prayed they wouldn't make him sneeze. He wiggled his nose to move them, but that made things worse.

"Do I smell coffee?" Lyn's barely awake voice asked as she stirred from sleeping.

"Yeah," Scout whispered over her head. "Jake is good at mornings. At least when we're camping. At home, in his bed, he would sleep to noon. Of course, he usually works the night shift. He finds it's more exciting."

"Is Jake donut good?" Lyn asked.

Scout laughed. "I doubt it. But he is coffee, bacon, and eggs good."

"I don't want to leave. I like it here. It's peaceful and quiet."

Scout smiled. "I feel the same." He closed his eyes and drew her closer, folding his body around her.

"I think I should talk to Umiko and Greg."

Scout sighed and his smile faded. He unfolded his arms from around Lyn and rolled over onto his back, where a rock was hiding under then tent floor to make him uncomfortable. He moved farther away from her. He needed to get his emotions in check. He counted his breath and repeated it several more times to dull the ache at her missing touch and her need to talk to Greg. *Her boyfriend!* He yelled inside his head.

"Can we go for a run this morning?" Lyn stretched.

He took a deep breath so he wouldn't raise his voice when he spoke next. "Two legs or four?"

"Four. With Jake."

"You got it." Scout stretched. *A chaperon for a run. This is going well, I think.* He stifled a groan and turned it into a yawn and a stretch. Sarcasm wasn't going to help.

"Are you two lo...awake," Jake called from outside the tent.

"Having trouble with your words there, bro?" Scout called back. "Do we need to call the paramedics? Make sure it wasn't a stroke?"

There was a long pause while Lyn and Scout waited for a response, but nothing came. Silence settled inside and outside the tent.

Scout whispered, "Smell him when you get out. Just to be sure."

Lyn nodded.

Scout pulled his shirt on over his head and ran his fingers through his hair.

Lyn sat on her knees. "Jake, is the coffee ready?"

"Yeah. The bacon is cooking now. Eggs soon." Jake's voice said through the thin fabric, but Lyn had proven that mimicking a voice wasn't that difficult.

Scout nodded, unzipped the tent flap, and took a deep breath.

"I can present my backside for a better scent if you want, little bro."

"Don't be rude," Scout snapped. "It was your idea, anyway."

"So it was. Did I pass?"

"Yes, but why did your words fail earlier? It's not like you."

"Yeah, it caught me off guard too. I have a feeling that was Lyn's doing. That whole electricity thing." Jake wiggled his fingers in the air then shrugged, "Never mind that. Anyway, I ran the fence line this morning and I didn't smell anything unusual. No one has been here but us."

"Did you smell white flowers? Our friend from yesterday smelled like white flowers. Gardenias and jasmine to be exact." Scout turned to Lyn. She had smelled strongly of jasmine this morning. He shook his head. He'd know if she was kidnapped and replaced while they were sleeping. After all he'd held her most of the night. "Also, be wary if you see a swarm of white butterflies," Scout paused and considered, "although that probably won't happen because I couldn't see them until Lyn kissed me."

Jake's eyebrow lifted.

Scout pointed at his eye. "My eye," he clarified and enunciated, "until she kissed my eye."

Jake shrugged.

"I'll do it again, but I want coffee first." Lyn crawled out of the tent.

Scout reached a hand to help her stand. Behind her back, he mouthed to Jake, 'smell her,' and pointed to Lyn's head.

Jake handed her a mug when she sat down next to the fire. He squinted at Scout over her shoulder but picked up his own cup and took a deep breath of coffee.

Scout knew he'd catch Lyn's scent through the powerful aroma.

Scout watched as Jake feigned obsession with his coffee's smell.

"Sit, Scout. It's a wonderful morning, and we have chores to do. Your favorite."

Scout sat and took his own deep inhale of coffee and Lyn. She smelled like a long run, a rainstorm, lightning and now jasmine. Still enough of Lyn to be sure she was Lyn, just a new layer. A new understanding of who she was.

He felt silly for being paranoid, but fairies made him twitchy and he felt like they were just waiting like prey for the courts to find her instead of going on the offensive. Mimic said they were coming, but what did that really mean? Today? Next week? A year from now? How badly did they want her? Was his idea of keeping her in this form really keeping them from finding her?

"There's a section of fence down in the east corner," Jake said. "We have the stuff to fix it and there is gas in the four wheeler. It might not keep…things out, but we should spend some time on it anyway. It won't hurt to have it whole."

"Fence repair, and wearing the same clothes three days in a row." Scout looked at Lyn over his mug. "It's a glamorous life I've brought you to."

"Oh, speaking of clothing, Umiko gave me a dress of yours yesterday. She thought I could get your scent from it. Like I was a trained dog or something. Anyway, it's in my truck." Jake reached into his pocket and tossed Scout his keys.

Scout and Jake exchanged a glance.

"I promise to not let her out of my sight while you are

gone." Jake crossed his heart with his finger. "I did a perimeter search, but thought you might like to do your own. Since you don't trust me with her life and all." Jake teased.

Scout looked at Lyn who was curled up in a camp chair with a hot cup of coffee steaming her face. "You don't have to watch her that closely. She's capable of taking care of herself." He knew it was true, but it was hard to remember that fact when she spoke of running straight into the Summer Court to rescue her mom. When she talked about doing dangerous stuff, he couldn't help but want to protect her. From herself.

He pocketed the keys and ran past the cabin, down the trail and to the cars.

CHAPTER THIRTY-TWO

"Can a brother ask a sister a serious question?" Jake sat in the chair across from Lyn and sipped from his mug while he watched the bacon sizzle.

Lyn took a sip of her coffee and cooed quietly.

Jake took the absence of an answer as permission. "Are you and Greg a thing?" Jake got right to the point.

Lyn choked on her coffee, but recovered without intervention. "Serious question, huh?"

"Yeah. As a brother."

"Do sisters tell brothers everything?"

"Yeah, probably not, but I'm hoping we have a different kind of relationship."

Lyn sighed. "The first few weeks," Lyn took a breath. "After I almost killed an old lady, I wasn't in a good place. He tried to convince me I wasn't a monster."

Jake sat up to say something, but Lyn held up her hand for him to wait.

"I tried to convince him I was. We fought about it a lot, but it wasn't bad until one day I got so angry and my wolf was so close to the surface, I was going to shift right then if I didn't run. So I did. I found a safe spot before she took over, but I don't remember anything about the rest of that night. When I came back to myself, I was far from home." She took a sip of coffee. "The next week, Greg talked me into training with Killian and the team." She stopped abruptly.

Jake watched her eyes widen.

"He tricked me." She lowered her mug from her face. "He used my fairy deal thing against me. He must have known even then." Her shoulders sank and a growl started in her belly.

"So you trained with Killian against your will?" Jake tried to distract her. Scout would be pissed if Jake set Lyn's wolf off.

She forced an exhale. "Not really against my will per se. It's... well the deal complicated the issue, I guess. But I knew he had a point. I could have hurt someone that night and not remembered anything. I might have agreed without the deal. I want to control her. I guess that's why I kept going back even after Killian pissed me off." Lyn stared into her mug. "That stupid deal."

"So, Greg is or isn't your boyfriend?" Jake flipped a piece of bacon in the middle of the pan that cooked faster than the rest.

Lyn focused back on Jake and shook her head. She shrugged. "We hang out a lot. Mainly with Clark and Umiko. Never alone. Maybe we're both afraid we'd end up fighting again. I don't know what it is. It's just complicated."

"I thought you didn't like that word." He flipped another slice of bacon.

She nodded and took a sip of coffee. "That's part of the reason." Lyn breathed in the warm steam from her mug.

Jake nodded. "Do you want more with Greg?"

Lyn lowered the cup to her lap. "Does he seriously track me?"

Jake frowned. She was avoiding the question. "Yeah. He made a call to... his people, I guess, and he didn't have to give them anything. He just told them your name and to find your GPS location."

"Do you always know where Veronica is?" Lyn took great interest in the dwindling contents of her mug.

"Not unless she tells me." Jake sat up and reached to flip the rest of the bacon with the long handled grill fork.

"Does she know where you are now?"

"I told her I was camping with you and Scout. She's fine with it. She's got her own life separate from mine. We split up and do our own things sometimes, then we come back together. It's healthy."

"So, as a brother, Greg tracking me..." Lyn looked at Jake.

"Is not healthy, in my opinion." He frowned at her. "Paranoid even. It's like he doesn't trust you to be okay on your own." Jake looked at her. "Since you asked, as a bother, I want to kick your stalker's teeth in."

It was Lyn's turn to nod. "Thanks, but I'll handle it."

Jake nodded. "Fair enough, but it's a standing offer."

She sat in silence for a while.

"What about Scout?" Jake pushed. He had nothing to lose and everything to gain, for Scout, who had been falling for this girl for months and afraid to say anything.

"I feel like a real person with your brother. He challenges me in training, just enough to push my limits. Like he's trying to see if I have any."

"Or show you that you don't." Jake smiled. He would do the same. Lyn had potential, lots of it. She just needed the right teachers and the confidence.

"Maybe." Lyn nodded. "To Killian, I'm either a prize to be won or a battle to conquer. I don't know which."

"If you've refused to submit to his alpha status, you're definitely a battle to be conquered," Jake watched her. "But I think he also has this territorial thing going on with Greg, so I can see the prize angle too."

"He doesn't treat me like he loves me though, so I think

you're both off base there." She paused. "Except that first night, right after he forced me to shift for the first time. I have never seen him that caring, before or after. He carried me to bed and made me breakfast the next morning. It was weird."

Jake's eye's lifted.

Lyn shook her head. "Exactly as I said, bro. Nothing more. I don't know if he slept there or not at all. When I woke up the next morning, breakfast was already made."

"Scout was there for that shift right?"

"He was, but I don't know how long he stayed."

Jake would have to ask his brother why he left a vulnerable girl with a jerk like Killian. Overnight.

"Stop that look. Nothing happened. I was asleep, not unconscious."

Jake's face must have registered his growing anger at the situation. He tried to relax. He couldn't change the past, but he could make sure the future was different. Killian would not be left alone with his sister again.

"Why do you want Scout to be alpha of the juniors?" Lyn took a sip of her coffee and settled into her chair.

"Killian is a thug." Jake spit the words. "His dad isn't much better. They both have an authority complex for sure. I'm pack, for now, because throwing me out would be bad for pack morale. My mom and Scout's dad were really happy and he treated me like his own son. The pack knows it and they'll make sure Killian's dad continues to respect it, but he couldn't care less if I moved on." Jake added more bacon to the pan and a fresh round of sizzles started. "If Scout were alpha, the thuggery would stop in a heartbeat. He wouldn't stand for it. As second, he keeps those boys on a tighter leash than Killian would, but he can't stop it altogether. He has a fine line to walk to be seen as submissive without being submissive. If that make sense."

Lyn heard a branch snap.

She and Jake traded looks.

"I know, sniff first, ask questions later." She lowered her mug.

Jake smiled. "Hey, Scout. The bacon is almost done. How do you want your eggs?"

"Cooked," Scout said as he came around the corner of the cabin with a black and white dress in his hands. "This doesn't even smell like you, not anymore. It smells like Umiko."

"Right? I don't know how people live without our noses." Jake stood up and smelled his brother. "You pass, go get plates."

Scout handed Lyn the dress and went inside the cabin.

"So what does he smell like to you?" Lyn asked Jake after Scout had gone inside.

"Little league, mischief, and super fresh newborn baby. As in before they wash them." Jake smiled. It was not an ew gross kind of smile like the one that crossed Lyn's face. It was a genuine loving smile. "I was the third person to hold him. He didn't have a lot of other smells around him yet, which was good, because I was four."

"Your mom started training you to be a tracker before your first shift?" Lyn asked over her coffee mug.

"She didn't see a reason not to." Jake shrugged. "She knew we'd both be shifters. There was no way around that one. She married shifters. We can't all be super awesome half-breeds like yourself." Jake winked at her.

"Your dad must have died when you were really young."

"Yeah. He didn't make it to my second birthday. Scout's dad was the only dad I remember. I lost my dad's scent a long time ago. I could still recall it for a while. It might still be buried deep, but I used to be able describe it to my mom and she knew exactly who I was thinking about, even though I couldn't tell her what he looked like." He paused, trying to remember the scent. He shook the failure away. "Scout's dad was a great stepfather. He would have been a great alpha too."

Scout came back out with plates. "Breakfast first, then a run, followed by fencing."

Everyone nodded.

Lyn took the last sip of her coffee and set the mug by the fire. Jake pulled off the bacon and put it on a plate covered in paper towels to let the oil drain off. He cracked several eggs into a clean preheated skillet and watched as the whites changed from transparent to cloudy.

Lyn took a sip from a water bottle and held out her plate for Jake to slide an egg onto. She picked up two pieces of bacon and sat back in her chair. "At some point we need to discuss strategy."

"What?" Scout teased, "You don't want to just run headlong into the problem and hope for the best?"

"My favorite trainer would boot me back to the beginner class if I pulled that...again." Lyn sipped her water through a smile.

CHAPTER THIRTY-THREE

*L*yn sat on the seat of the ATV with a battered notebook in her hands and a pencil pressed to her lips while Scout and Jake sweated in the heat, repairing a section of fence that a tree had taken out.

She jotted down notes as Jake leaned on the post hole digger and Scout wiped sweat from his face with his shirt.

It had taken them about thirty minutes to cut the fallen tree down enough to get it off the fence. The posts for this section were salvageable, but unearthed. Jake cleared out the old concrete from the holes and knocked as much as he could from the posts while Scout cut the rest of the tree up into moveable sections.

"Do you think the tree fell in the wind yesterday, or before that?" Scout asked, tossing his shirt over a secure post. "When was the last time you were out here?"

"Same as you," Jake said and lifted the post hole digger as high as his arms would stretch. "The split in the trunk is new, so I'd blame the wind." He slammed the metal end down in to the ground with a grunt and pinched dirt between the blades. He added the contents to a slowly growing pile to his right.

"I'm glad we had a chain saw. This would have been a bear if we'd had to do it with an axe." Scout stacked the last of the fallen tree logs into the small trailer attached to the ATV. "At least we'll get some firewood out of it."

"1, 2, 3..." Jake started.

"Not it," Lyn and Jake said at the same time and shared a smile. Jake lifted his hand to high five Lyn and the sound momentarily startled the nearby birds.

"Not it for what?" Scout stared at the pair, as he tried to puzzle out what just happened.

"I don't know." Lyn shrugged and went back to her list.

Jake laughed. "You get to split the logs for firewood. Also, I like her." He lifted the post hole digger and cut into the hard ground again.

Jake and Scout righted both posts and used buckets of spring water they had brought with them to mix concrete and secure the posts in the ground.

They talked about trivial things and loaded old concrete into the trailer while they waited for the new concrete to set enough to continue with the repair. Lyn tried to get them to plan out loud with her, but they both shut her down. Either they didn't want to think about the supposed fairy threat or they were paranoid about being overheard. Probably both, but she really wanted their help. Strategy was not her thing. She totally would just run headlong into Summer to rescue her mom if she knew where either of those things were. But only because she didn't know another way.

Jake and Scout reinforced the dirt around the bases of the posts after the concrete was dry enough and stretched new barbed wire between four posts, the two newly sunk and one to each side of those, to take up the slack created by the tree.

"I'll need headphones and my music. Do you think the phones will be charged by the time we get back?"

"Absolutely," Jake said and stretched another length of barbed wire between the posts.

"What else then?" Lyn asked.

"I'll want to be able to see what we're dealing with." Scout attached the other end of a section of wire to the wooden post on the far side before Jake pulled it tight to his.

Lyn made a note on her list to kiss both brothers' eyelids.

"What are the rules again?" Jake asked as he clipped the last strand of barbed wire from the spool.

Lyn recited the list of six rules from memory, "and semantics is of utmost importance," she added as a 7th.

"Good. Are we sure we don't want to call in backup?" Jake asked Lyn from his position crouched by the spool of wire.

"We need finesse, not vigilantes and a pack of wild dogs." Lyn said.

"Plus, we don't want anyone to know where we are," Scout added.

"We can pick and choose our allies. Mom for example," Jake said. "She's good in a fight, smart too."

"We do not need any more people knowing what Lyn is, not even mom. It will get out eventually, even with Lyn's deal making skills," Scout said. "We need to keep the risk minimized."

Minimize the risk. Would she have to pretend to be something she's not for the rest of her life? She didn't want that. It was just another cage she didn't want to live in. She was tired of living under other people's thumbs. First Ms. Evans' from the day she was born. Then Killian tried to make her submit to his alpha status. Umiko made all of Lyn's decisions and Greg had her under surveillance. Now, fairy queens? They all wanted her to be something she wasn't.

Jake hefted the spool of wire into the trailer. "Fine, but when we get a whiff of wings, we stay close to each other."

"Two legs or four?" Scout asked Jake.

"I can take out more threats faster on four," Jake said. "Will the sight thing survive the shift?"

"I don't know," Lyn looked up from her notebook with a line of worry across her brow.

"I guess we should find out." Jake shrugged. "Pick one. Me or him."

"What?" she asked.

"I'd rather know now, before we need the information."

Lyn looked between the brothers. Color rose on her cheeks as she thought about kissing Scout again.

"How is this going to help if there are no fairies around to see?"

"Good point." Jake conceded. He looked at Lyn. "Are there any fairies around?"

She shook her head.

Jake pointed at his eyes and Lyn shifted hers from whatever they were now to silver and amber and looked around.

She shook her head again and Jake picked up the post hole digger.

"How are your semantics coming?" Scout took off his gloves and put them and his wire cutters in a bag then tossed the bag into the trailer.

The boys worked together to make sure everything they brought was packed back into the four wheeler's trailer. Scout picked up his shirt and tossed the sweat soaked cloth into the back of the trailer after giving it a dirty look.

"Good, I think. I've used a whole page trying to close up loopholes." She held the page up.

Jake looked away. "I'd rather not know the details, in case they can make me give them up."

"Fair point," Scout said. "I wish we were going in with more than theories. None of us have dealt with fairies before, much less the courts themselves."

"When do you think they'll come for her?" Jake asked. He placed the post hole digger in the trailer and leaned on the edge. He drank from a gallon jug of water before he passed it to Scout.

"I'm not a hundred percent sure why they haven't already and that makes me nervous." Scout admitted after drinking his fill. He placed the jug back in the trailer and stepped to the ATV.

"But you have a theory." Jake said.

Scout nodded. "Camouflage."

Lyn crinkled her brow. "You think I'm keeping them from finding me? With this?" She waved a hand up and down her body.

"Not exactly. I think you mimicked the binding along with that look. That's the important bit. So, if you don't mind keeping them off our trail for a little longer, I'm tired and could use bit of a break before we confront fairy queens."

"And lunch?" Lyn turned around to face forward and scooted back on the ATV to allow Scout at the handlebars.

Jake hopped up onto the back rack of the ATV and braced himself for bumps. "We're going to need a grocery run if we stay out here passed breakfast tomorrow. As it is, we should think about fresh fish for dinner."

"At some point, I have to go back and deal with my friends." Lyn frowned.

Jake looked at Lyn. "Which would you rather deal with first? Summer and Winter, or your friends?"

Scout cranked the engine and kept Lyn from having to answer the question on the spot. She tucked the notebook under her thigh and put her hands on Scout's hips.

She wasn't sure she could decide between the two. Both wanted to control her, in their own messed up ways. Summer and Winter for what she was and what they wanted her to become. Her friends because up until now, she had let them. She wasn't sure when or how she had become a hypocrite. Slowly, she guessed. Slow enough she didn't realize it. Or maybe she only thought she took control after Ms. Evans.

Maybe she let her friends control her because it was easier. Suddenly, she understood why Scout didn't want to challenge Killian for alpha, or at least she thought she did.

She considered Jake's question as Scout weaved the ATV and the full trailer slowly through trees and underbrush. She could probably talk to Umiko, tell her how she felt. Her best friend would listen and try to change, maybe. Lyn didn't think Killian would care about her feelings. He hadn't up to this point, why would he start now. Greg could go either way. He wasn't unreasonable, he just suffocated her and kept secrets. Secrets that she could have used months ago.

All three of them reminded her of her nightmares, a hold over from her brush with the witch that bound her creature traits. They put her in a cage, albeit a gilded one, but she was tired of feeling trapped. She was ready to be wholly herself, but first she had to tell them and somehow extricate herself from two fairy queens.

Lyn sighed and pressed her forehead to Scout's back. *No big deal*, she thought.

Scout rubbed her knee as they broke though the tree line to the clearing and approached the cabin.

CHAPTER THIRTY-FOUR

$\mathcal{L}$yn folded the notebook closed and dropped it by her chair. She tilted her head back and looked at the sky. The blue was fading to navy and stars were starting to wink into existence in the dim light. The smell of fresh fish wafted over the fire and crickets and lightning bugs were making themselves known.

Scout leaned forward in his chair and used two forks to try to open the foil packet. He pulled his hands back from the heat several times before he got the foil opened enough to peek.

"I checked in with mom," Jake said, stepping around the cabin. "She said no one had come looking for Lyn yet. But she's gathered a few items from Lyn's front porch so that it doesn't look like she's gone." He shook his head as Scout put a singed finger in his mouth. "Why don't you let Lyn do that?"

"Oh, my grocery delivery." Lyn said. "I forgot that was coming."

"Well, mom took care of the delivery, and the rest."

"The rest?" She wasn't expecting anything else.

Jake looked at Scout and shook his head. "Two flower

arrangements. A box of chocolates. I think the chocolate is why she took everything to our house, if she left it they'd be melted by the time we got home, or you'd have a bug or a rodent problem to deal with. There was also a letter with a wax seal. I think that was all. I'll bring everything over when we go home."

"What type of flowers?" Lyn asked.

Jake smiled at her. "You think I don't know this, right? You think I wouldn't hear details. Oh, but I live with a woman who has a nose for things." He touched his nose and winked. "Mom said they were death flowers. I'm guessing that means lilies and mums."

"Who would sent Lyn dead flowers?" Scout tensed.

"Clark," Lyn answered, "and they aren't dead flowers. They are death flowers. Flowers the living bring to the hospital rooms of their dying relatives because they don't know what else to do. Your mom probably meant they smell like death, which they do. Clark brings them home from the hospital, but normally for Umiko."

"Okay. There's that explained. There was also a bouquet of white roses." Jake looked at his brother. "Those did not smell like death."

Lyn examined her fingers in her lap and Scout went back to the fire.

Jake filled the silence. "Nice work with the pole, sis. Did you just remember what it felt like to have a fish on the line?" Jake's lips quirked up at the edges.

"Funny." Lyn returned his smirk. "That was actually my first time fishing and before you look at me weird, I offered to cook the fish, but Scout insisted on burning his fingers.

He shrugged. "Then let him. He'll learn." Jake smiled. "I guess that means dinner is brought to us by beginner's luck."

"Thankfully we have that, otherwise, we would be eating sausages again," Scout said with a laugh. "I can't believe neither of us got a single nibble."

"Half a sausage. We only have two brats left." Jake shrugged. "You were too distracted. You moved too much for any fish to take your hook seriously."

"What's your excuse?"

"My pole was broken, of course." Jake smiled and they all laughed.

"So, camping trip is over tomorrow, like it or not." Lyn pouted on the inside. She liked spending time with her new brother and Scout, alone. She felt oddly relaxed, even with Summer and Winter hanging over her head.

"You can come back any time," Jake said. "If Scout won't bring you, give me a call." He winked at her.

"What about Veronica?" Lyn asked.

"Nah, she doesn't like camping," Jake said. "Hey, let's do that sparky deal thing." Jake stood up and held his hand out to Lyn.

"Okay…" Lyn stood slowly. She wondered what Jake had up his sleeve. "What's the deal part?" She slowly lifted her hand to his, cautious of any traps that might hide in his next few words

"It's simple. I won't tell anyone your secret identity, ever, and you don't share the location of our secret base," Jake said.

"We need a binding deal for that?" Lyn cocked her head. She hadn't intended to tell anyone anyway. She liked having a secret place she could get away to and hoped she'd be allowed to enjoy it from time to time. Truth be told, she had very little idea of how to get back on her own.

"It couldn't hurt, and I just want to hold your hand like Scout gets to do." Jake's toothy smile glinted in the firelight.

Scout threw his shoe across the fire and it bounced off of Jake's thigh, barely missing the flames on the rebound.

Jake laughed.

"Deal." Lyn clutched his hand. "I won't share the secret base location…"

"And I will never share your secret identity with anyone." Jake nodded his head once and pumped her arm.

The shock of a buzzer flowed through their palms, like an elbow hit on a corner that makes the whole arm tingle for what feels like an eternity.

"That is a trippy feeling." Jake looked at Scout. "You've felt it, right?"

"Only once, on accident." Scout lowered his face and his voice trailed off at the end.

Lyn smiled at him, but he wasn't looking. She forgave him, but he had yet to forgive himself.

"What was your deal?" Jake asked.

"That I wouldn't follow phantom voices or invisible butterflies without him and that he wouldn't tell anyone," Lyn said. "Will you both humor me one more time?"

Scout lifted his head to look at her.

Jake eyed her like he was trying to figure out what she was up to this time.

"Come on. Get up." She waved Scout over to the fireside. "It's a little archaic. Almost Arthurian, but don't laugh." Lyn looked from face to face. "For as long as it is wanted, you both have my loyalty."

"I don't think it's necessary," Jake said. "My loyalty is family before pack. I already claimed you as my sister."

"I don't think she's questioning *our* loyalty," Scout said.

"Do you see a problem with what I'm offering?" Lyn looked at Scout.

Scout shook his head and they both turned to Jake.

"I'd rather have you on my side than against me." Jake shrugged his shoulders and lifted his hand.

Lyn clutched Scout's wrist in her palm. Scout took Jake's wrist, and Jake formed the last side of the triangle.

"My loyalty for yours," Scout said first.

Jake echoed his brother's words.

"I give my loyalty to you both. Unconditionally and

without bounds," Lyn said formally and felt the familiar electric tingle spread across the three palms and through their wrists.

"To loyalty and family secrets." Jake lifted his bottle of water and the sound of metal crashed between them as the spark faded.

Family secrets. Lyn thought and looked at her new chosen family. It was even better than the last. She felt more valued. Free to be herself.

Jake pulled the fish that she had caught off of the fire and Scout plated them. She sat back in her canvas chair with a plate of food in her lap and hoped that the trouble Summer, Winter, and her friends would bring could stay away just a little longer.

CHAPTER THIRTY-FIVE

Scout woke to a tremor at his back and heard Lyn mumble.

He blinked and looked around at the darkness. The moonlight barely seeped through the fabric of the tent. He thought it was close to midnight, but didn't bother to check.

"Cold," she mumbled again, but it registered with his brain this time and he opened his arms to pull her close. Happy at how comfortable that movement had become.

She shivered again and the cold on his arms woke him completely. His eyes shot open. Even after dark in the woods, it shouldn't be this cold.

Lyn's white hair forced him awake. With the camouflage gone... He let out a breath and it was as if he breathed out smoke. His breath hung in the chill air as if it were January, not June.

"Wake up, sis." That moniker left a bad taste in his mouth, but they had all agreed to avoid using real names when the time came. "What are the rules again?" Scout rummaged in a tent pocket for Lyn's earbuds and phone.

"Coffee first, quiz later," Lyn mumbled. "What's that

sound?" She turned her head to listen better, but her eyes stayed closed.

"No quiz. This is the mother of all tests." Scout closed the distance between his face and hers. "Kiss my eyes, please." He lowered his lids to her lips.

"If I do, will you let me sleep," Lyn begged.

"I don't think I can. Come on, wake up."

Lyn placed her lips on one of his eye lids then squirmed back down in her sleeping bag. "Done." Her voice betrayed her tiredness. "Now, five more hours, please." She stopped moving and cracked open an eye. "What's that music? Is it Jake? Why would he be playing music in the middle of the night? And why is it so cold?" Lyn shifted her arms to wrap around her chest and rubbed her biceps with her hands.

"Surprise," Scout said without excitement. "Winter is here." He slid Lyn's earbuds into her ears and pressed play.

CHAPTER THIRTY-SIX

*S*cout dimmed the flashlight on his phone and set it to the side of the tent to keep it from shining in either of their faces.

Lyn confirmed that the earbuds were secure and checked the time. Her phone's clock said it was just after midnight. She had only been asleep for an hour. *Wonderful.* She looked down at her thin dress and shivered. The fabric, decently suited to afternoons hanging with friends inside warm houses, or being used as pajamas in a warm sleeping bag while camping in the summer, was wholly inadequate for freezing temperatures. She wrapped her arms around herself. "Do I smell snow?"

"Yes."

"It almost never snows in Texas."

Scout handed her his shirt. "Nope."

"Winter?"

Scout nodded.

She pulled the shirt over her head and tried not to let her emotions get a foothold. She shut out her desire to stare at Scout's chest, her wish to crawl under the blankets and hide, and her urge to cry. Her emotions were too close to the surface and this did not bode well for her first meeting with a fairy queen.

Scout's shirt almost fit, but Lyn preferred a looser neck and some semblance of a fitted torso. She tugged at the shirt and tried to figure out how to be comfortable in the borrowed top. She shook her head at the idea. Less than a year ago, baggy shirts were her clothing of choice along with jeans that didn't match her shape.

Scout held out his hoodie. "Problem?" His eyes searched hers, worry etched in his face.

She shook her head. "It's just your shirt. It's big on me." She looked at him and then looked down at the shirt. She hated herself for the shallow words. They were about to face Winter and Lyn was worried about her clothes. She looked down at the sleeping bag spread across the hard ground and would give anything to curl back up and forget this was happening.

"I kind of like it." Scout smiled and held out his hoodie. "Do you want my jeans too? I won't be using them."

Lyn looked down at her bare legs. "I should probably say yes." Her lips turned down at the corners. She could just imagine being warm, but that would cost her energy that she might need for other things. Fairy things. Besides, how vain was she?

Scout stripped down to his dark blue boxers and handed over his pants.

Lyn's body began to warm under the thin layers of clothing she was wearing, but her breath still hung in the cold air. She looked away and slid the wide legged denim over her skinny legs. She stood as tall as she could in the center of the tent. She sighed, closed her eyes, and focused on her breath.

She yawned, involuntarily, and covered her mouth with her hand. When she opened her eyes, she saw Scout looking at her with a sparkle in his eye from the phone light and a curve to his lips.

"What?" Lyn asked. She shifted her weight to one hip and cocked her head to the side. *If he makes fun of the way I'm dressed.* A tear bloomed in her eye. "I look silly." She shoved her hands into the large pockets of his jeans.

Lyn wished she had not been chased out of her own home by well-intentioned and misguided friends or that she had packed a bag of her own clothes. Anything was better than facing Winter in clothes that made her feel like a child playing dress-up. Lyn felt the lone tear slide down her cheek. *I've got this. These clothes are better than freezing, and they don't fit too bad.* Just a little long. A little extra room in the butt. She could handle both those things. Lyn took a long, deep breath and let the tension she was holding flow away. *These clothes are perfectly fine for facing whatever is out there.* Besides, she was going to do this on her terms and no one else's. That meant jeans and a T-shirt.

When she opened her eyes, Scout was looking at her with his jaw slack and one eyebrow raised. "I don't think those jeans will ever fit me again."

Lyn wrinkled her own brow and looked down. She could make out her curves underneath the borrowed clothing. She rubbed her hand down the front of the fitted shirt. "Is this why everything in my mom's and Umiko's closet fits me?"

Scout shrugged and handed her his hoodie. "Focus. Last layer."

He was right. She could ponder the fashion side of her mimicry another time. She slid his hoodie over her head.

"I don't know if I can do this," Lyn said. Another tear threatened to follow the first. She shook, not with cold, but with nerves.

He put his hands on her arms. "Then trust me. I know you can do anything you put your mind to. You prove that everyday," Scout said.

The weight of his hands bolstered her confidence somewhat. Lyn brushed the tear away and stifled the rest. All she wanted to do was curl back up into her sleeping bag and sleep for a week, but since that wasn't going to happen, she had to get through this without cracking.

Lyn saw Scout twitch as he shifted, almost silently. She grimaced at the memory of her own shift. The popping of joints, the elongation, and shortening of bones. The excruciating pain of knees turning forward to back.

Lyn closed her eyes and took a breath to slow her rising anxiety. She had a fairy queen to outsmart and she couldn't do that with her pulse hammering in her ear and her wolf pawing to be in control.

"I'm never buying women's jeans again." Lyn said to the wolf at her side. She leaned down and kissed the eye she had not kissed earlier. They wanted to know if the sight transferred, but didn't want to risk Scout being blinded to whatever fairy glamours were in store outside the tent flap.

Lyn stepped out of the thin shelter with her wolf companion to snow covering the ground.

The landscape was stunning in the slight light of the moon. Unmarred by footsteps, the snowy ground looked more like a blanket than an act of nature. The stark white of her surroundings memorized her. A thick layer of snow lay everywhere except over the fire. In another time and another place, she would have enjoyed it. Texas was not known for its abundance of wintery landscapes, not even during winter. The most they ever got was an inch and that usually melted by noon.

Scout, as wolf, stepped forward and lifted his nose to the air. His brown gray fur stood out among the white of the world outside their tent. His dark paws sank into the plush ground. He lifted his snout higher and sniffed.

Lyn was glad Scout brought her running shoes instead of

the thinner white ones she had intended to wear the day she ran away. These were so worn in that she didn't have to bother with the laces. She slid her foot in and stomped once. Then reached down and picked up a handful of the frozen moisture. She formed it into some semblance of a ball and considered throwing it at Scout. She'd give anything to have a snowball fight, right now, with Scout and Jake. *Jake?*

The ball slipped from Lyn's grasp and landed on her shoe.

"Big Bad Wolf, where are you?" Lyn whispered. She felt silly calling Jake by his self proclaimed code name, but names were power and she wouldn't be the one to give them away.

The snow crunched near the corner of the cabin nearest Jake's tent as his blonde wolf stood with his light colored feet sunk in the snow. He all but blended into his surroundings. Lyn wondered how long he had been standing there, waiting on her while she fangirl-ed over the weather. She needed to get her head in the game. Lyn stepped closer and breathed him in. "What's out there, brother? Can you see anything?"

The wolf rubbed a front paw by his nose and cocked his head at her.

Lyn leaned down to nuzzle his face and her white hair fell around them. She kissed one furry wolf eyelid and then the other. "Thank you for being here." She stood up and pushed her hair behind her ear.

The wolf's tongue hung out of his jaws in a big puppy smile before he stood sentinel again and peered out at the clearing from his spot by the cabin.

Jake's wolf stifled a growl and the fur on Scout's wolf's neck stood up. Lyn placed her hand in the ruffled mane. "I've got this," she said into his eyes. As much for her benefit as his.

Scout didn't relax, but then again, neither did she.

She took in a deep calming breath, adjusted the volume on her phone, and checked her clothes.

Jake stepped forward and Lyn realized she could no longer stall.

"I guess it's time to meet Winter." Lyn stepped out from around the back of the cabin with a wolf on each hip and remembered what it was like to be well rested.

CHAPTER THIRTY-SEVEN

*L*yn's white hair and pale skin camouflaged into the soft white glow of the scenery. Only the darker colors of her borrowed clothing made her stand out from the snow surrounding them.

She suppressed a shiver as the earlier dropped snowball melted into her shoe. She quickly dispelled the chill and dampness thanks to her special skill with mimicry and what she'd learned from meeting her mother's…husband?

How come she never knew what to call the men in her life? Was Killian a bully, a friend, a leader, some guy that had feelings for her and a horrible way to show it? And Greg, was he her friend or boyfriend? Lyn had no clue. Jonathan was just some name on her birth certificate that she had met once before he died and left everything he owned in her possession, which basically meant boxes full of a life she was never part of.

Every single male relationship in her life was complicated. She looked from Jake to Scout. Maybe not every one.

She stomped her now dry shoe in the snow and the cold snow pricked at her bare ankles.

She was sick of complicated. She was sick of living by

someone else's rules. She was sick of being told what to do and where to do it. She was sick and tired of being controlled by other people. Her hands formed fists at her hips. There was no way she was going to let Winter or Summer own her. Lyn's nails extended and dug into her palms.

Scout's wolf pushed his muzzle into her side.

Lyn took a deep breath. "I got it. Don't wolf out. But I'm tired and cranky and that's really hard right now." Her voice shook with her near tantrum.

Scout lifted his head, which was already close to her hip and leaned against her.

She looked down into his eyes. Volcanoes looked back at her, intense brown and amber volcanoes. Volcanoes she could fall into and never catch herself. Then his tongue fell between his jaws and those dark brown volcanoes rolled around in their sockets. She giggled at the sight of a shifted wolf rolling its eyes and some of the building tension ran off at the sound of her laugh.

Lyn straightened her posture, shifted her shoulders back, and lifted her chin. She took a moment to remember what it felt like to be warm. Really warm, like the summer sun beating down against her skin warm.

The snow melted beneath her feet and left her standing in a lukewarm puddle which quickly soaked into the ground. Lyn pulled the dark hood over her white hair and took a step forward.

Despite the better fit of the clothes she wore, she still felt like a toddler going to fight dragons in her mom's high heeled shoes and fancy oversized dresses. Except, imaginary dragons were more predictable than fairy queens. Dragons would eat you. Fairies would play with your first and make you want to be eaten.

Both wolves bristled at her side, wary of the stranger watching them. Lyn tamped down her own frayed nerves and took in the threat.

Standing in the center of the snow covered glade, lit by moonlight, was a woman in a thick green dress with white fur trim. Her skin had a warm glow and her brown hair, like fresh flame-licked wood on a fire, blew in the gentle breeze.

Thanks to movies, Lyn expected an Ice Queen, pale from head to toe with icicles hanging from her eyelashes, but the woman in the center was far less threatening than movies made her out to be.

She looked friendly, her smile was warm and inviting. When she opened her arms Lyn was tempted to run to them and let them fold around her, welcoming her home.

Lyn blinked. *That is stupid and makes no sense.* Lyn peeled her eyes away from what she was sure was the Queen of Winter.

Behind the woman stood a collection of both some of the prettiest and ugliest creatures Lyn had ever seen. Ephemeral wings graced the backs of some, others wore faces marred by bumps and green skin. Some were mostly human looking except for the exaggerated height, or lack thereof.

"We've been looking for you." The woman's voice was sweet as honey. Far from the sound of crumbling glaciers Lyn had expected.

She fought the urge to go to her. To stop being strong and proud and let Winter take care of her, mother her. Lyn allowed a single wolf's claw to extend, just enough to pierce the skin on her palm. She focused on the pain and came back to her senses. This time Jake's wolf whimpered and nudged her hand.

"I didn't intend to be hard to find." Lyn meant it. *Rule number six: Do not lie to fairies.* Lyn reevaluated her expectations. She forced herself to remember that she was facing the Queen of manipulating predators, not the sweet welcoming mother figure she saw in front of her.

"I know, child. That was someone else's intention, but I've found you now." The woman smiled with perfect white teeth.

Her voice reminded Lyn of a soothing hug. "I'm Winter, in case it wasn't obvious." She waved her hand in front and around herself.

The crowd behind the lady giggled, but Lyn thought it sounded forced as if on an audio track in a TV Studio. She wasn't sure if it was amusement at the lady's words, or something done out of obligation or fear. She assumed the latter, since every creature present stood tensed and their eyes skittered between Winter and Lyn.

"How may I help you?" Lyn asked, sidestepping the swapping of names.

"I came to make you a job offer." The woman lifted her arms and several of the uglier creatures carried forward a small table and two seats, one more elaborate than the other, all made from bright white wicker. A small girl with iridescent wings and a blemish free face laid a cloth and a selection of edibles. "But you already surround yourself with Summer." Winter motioned to Lyn as she took her own chair.

Lyn walked to the table, leaving a trail of melted snow and dry grass in her wake. She tried to think of something to say but nothing came. Her brain was running on the fumes of only an hour's sleep. She took a seat across from Winter on a cold white wicker stool, flanked by her wolves. Jake on her left, Scout on her right, while the woman sat in a high-backed seat more akin to a throne. "I assure you this is my own influence, and no one else's," Lyn said. Her mind was starting to get the clue that sleep would not be coming, no matter how much it protested.

"Would you like a bite to eat?" Winter asked.

"I don't usually eat while the sky is still dark," Lyn pulled her eyes away from the delectable treats. "I'm used to human eating patterns." *Rule number 2: Don't eat Fairy food.*

"So you are." Winter waved the winged girl over and she cleared the table of the delicious assortment.

Lyn noted the smile plastered to the fairy girl's face as she took the plate from in front of Lyn. It wasn't genuine. It looked like it could have been once, but now it was frozen to her face, like mothers told children all over the world would happen if they made terrible faces. Looking at that fairy girl, she believed her mom, now.

When the girl finished, a male, dressed in the same green and white as the lady but with a face more akin to the Ice Queen persona she had expected, laid a paper and pen in front of Lyn and stepped away from the table. He remained close enough to remove the papers when instructed, but far enough to provide the illusion of privacy.

Lyn didn't look down. She kept her eyes focused on the predator she knew sat across from her even if her eyes were telling her otherwise.

"Aren't you even a little bit curious?" Winter smiled. Her teeth were more perfect than Greg's toothpaste ad smile. The moon glinted off the enamel surface. How could you not trust it and her? Lyn would do anything to earn the affection that smile promised.

Her claw pressed further into her palm and Lyn took a steadying breath before speaking. "Why you chose paper? Yes. What's written on it? No." Lyn said. "I am not looking for a job. I have two more years of school. After those, I'm committed to a nursing program."

"How very human." Winter's voice dripped with contempt. A crack showing in the otherwise friendly facade.

"It's how I was raised."

"Against my sister's wishes." Winter smiled, the crack concealed behind the glow of humor radiating from her face.

Lyn was silent. She maintained eye contact with the lady across from her but forced herself to blink several times. Something she never would have considered doing with Killian. She didn't want to challenge the queen of Winter. Lyn would rather avoid a fight if she could help it. She wanted to get out of this without making an enemy. It wasn't just her neck on the line. Jake and Scout were depending on her too. Lyn set her right hand into the dark fur around Scout's wolf's neck and stroked it, giving herself something to hold her focus besides the illusion of affection in front of her.

"Summer has tipped the balance in her favor for too long. With you by my side, the balance is restored." Winter announced like it was a done deal.

"If my joining Winter would bring balance, so would removing something from Summer. Something equal to my involvement." Lyn fought hard to remember the hours she spent grueling over the wording in the salvaged notebook. The one that now sat discarded by her camp chair covered in snow.

"Summer is not going to part with your mother, child." An air of condescension hung from her words.

Lyn hated being patronized. She held on to that anger, a low rumble in her belly. She fought the emotions warring inside her. She needed to keep a balance that would allow her to be free of Winter's influence and her wolf's. She wrapped her hands around each other and held them in her lap.

"On the contrary," the Winter Lady spoke, when Lyn did not. "Summer enjoys sending your mother to needle away at my court, one member at a time. She has nothing to lose by doing so. If your mother is caught and tortured, Summer is no more disadvantaged than she was before she gained the boon and she has weakened me in the process." Winter folded her hands into her lap. "My sister would have been stupid not to make a deal with your mother for loyalty, and my dear sister is far from stupid. Your mother can no more swap sides than I can."

"My mother has not been caught, I take it."

"She is elusive, as of yet." Winter sat back in her chair and glared at the man in green. He paled further than his already pale complexion.

Lyn took a breath and steadied her nerves. *Do I do it now?*

Is it time to offer a deal? Did I think of all the possible loop holes? Will Winter even consider the arrangement I'm offering?

Scout's wolf nosed her arm.

Lyn came back to herself and spoke before she spiraled into overthinking. "I'd like to make a counter offer. I will render my mother useless to Summer in exchange for my continued neutrality."

Winter laughed.

The gathered crowd of winter loyal fairies laughed with her, their postures stiff.

Winter silenced them with a look that Lyn was glad didn't include her, but did wonders to quell the illusion that she was safe here. She briefly wondered how the fairy Queen would choose to end her if things did not go Lyn's way. Would it be swift like a successful hunt, or would the fairy queen prefer to toy with her? Lyn couldn't allow the latter. She would have to be decisive if her ploy failed. Could Lyn take her own life if it came to that? Would that be preferable to being a play thing to a manipulative predator?

"You'd rush Summer and rescue your mother?" Winter laughed. "Summer will have two boons if you fail, or you'll be useless to me by being dead. Your deal serves me no purpose."

Lyn let the laughter wash over her, but she did not let it sway her resolve. "I will sweeten the deal with my promise to never fight for Summer."

"You'll never fight for Summer even without a deal," Winter said, turning her icy disapproval toward Lyn this time. Her eyes crackled like fissures on a frozen lake.

Lyn registered the threat but stayed quiet. Partially because her brain was sputtering, and partially because in the deep recesses of her mind, she remembered that most negotiations were about the awkward silences and who would succumb to the pressure first. Lyn refused to crack with Killian staring her down, she wasn't going to crack now.

The smile returned to Winter's face. "I will humor you. Proclaim your loyalty to me, and I will stop hunting your kind," Winter said.

Lyn exhaled slowly. "My loyalty lies elsewhere. It can not be rebound."

Winter's eyes shifted to slits. A frigid wind blew Lyn's hood from her face, her white hair loosened in the gale. "Who have you bound your loyalty to if not myself, or my sister." Winter demanded.

"Family," Lyn stated.

Winter leaned forward. "You haven't seen your mother since your birth. Your father is on the run, hiding from my people, but we will find him soon. Your human surrogates do not deserve your loyalty. I offer you more than they could ever give you. A home with your kind, the safety of Winter, a place by my side as my weapon."

Lyn sat motionless. She reached inside herself for Killian's alpha pride and Greg's take no shit knock. She mixed in Umiko's my way or the highway and her wolf's stubbornness. She found some of Jake's family loyalty and Scout's resolute belief in her abilities and sat up straighter in her chair. She faced the Queen of Winter.

"My loyalty lies with those that value my worth as I am, not as who they want me to be, or for what I could do for them," Lyn said. "We need a new deal before the sun comes up. My offer stands. I will promise never to fight on Summer's behalf, and to return balance by taking my mother out of the equation."

"I tire of this," Winter stood and the male fairy that had delivered the contract and pen removed it from the table and stood at her side, "if you fail, you will slit your own throat and that of your mother."

Lyn heard the grumble in Scout's throat. She stroked his head and stood. "I need time to consider."

"I will return before the sun threatens the horizon."

Winter stood, her height towered over Lyn and her cold eyes glared at Lyn.

Lyn froze in that gaze. No one had told her how to walk away from a Queen. She held eye contact. She wasn't going to let this creature control her, even if she was a Queen of Fairy. Lyn didn't care. She had had enough of bullies. She would finally be the one to come out on top.

Scout nipped her hand.

Lyn wouldn't look away from Winter just like she wouldn't look away from Killian.

Scout bit harder and began to drag her away.

Lyn's anger bubbled closer to the surface. The rumble built in her chest and threatened to break free.

Scout pulled again and she turned. With the knowledge that Scout and Jake had her back, Lyn walked toward the cabin with her head held high.

CHAPTER THIRTY-EIGHT

The melting snow and warmer winds blowing from the creek bed signaled Winter's temporary reprieve.

"She could have just said 'dawn.' She didn't need to be so…" Lyn made a face and stuck out her tongue. She stomped her foot and held out a blanket for Scout.

"You can't make that deal," Scout completed his shift and yanked the blanket from her hands.

"I can," Lyn stepped back and planted her feet. She tensed for a fight. Her annoyance at Winter, her anger at being told what to do, and her fear of what failure meant poured together and fed her wolf. A rumble made it to her throat unbidden.

"Alright," Scout lifted his arm in surrender "you are able, but I'm begging you not to." Scout sat down in a camp chair. The blanket wrapped around his lower half. His chest exposed above his crossed arms.

"Why?"

"Because…" Scout's words faltered. He looked up into her face, "because I don't want you to die."

Lyn saw the sadness there. The near damp shine of his eyes in the moonlight. She looked away before the sight fed her fears more. "Then I just have to succeed. Next objection." Lyn looked back at him with renewed determination. "Go on, no objection is too small. I need to think all the way through this."

Scout looked at her. He sat forward in the chair and lifted his fingers to count. "You can only mimic three forms besides your own, none of which will get you past Summer undetected."

"Okay." She lifted her pointer finger to count along.

"You're new to this. The last time you tried to change forms fully, you passed out in my arms. I had to carry you from the stream, and the cemetery before that."

"You forgot the mimic I did for Jake, but I'm not strong enough, got it." She lifted a second finger.

Scout stood up, barely keeping the blanket around himself. "I'm not saying that." Scout ran his fingers through his hair.

"You are and you're right. No judgements. What else do you have?"

"You don't know where she is," Jake walked up dressed in pants and pulling his shirt over his head. "You don't know what Summer's defenses are like. You have no idea if your mother will know who you are or if she'll kill you on sight." He stepped into the cabin and returned with his backpack.

"Okay. That's a good start." Lyn held up her hands to stop the onslaught of negatives. She walked over to the fire. She knelt down beside it, blew across the embers, and coaxed the fire into remembering how to be hot. "Now, what do I have in my favor?" She stared into the growing flames.

"Your loyalty is protected, for now," Jake said. "Smart, by the way." He moved a chair closer to her. "Sit and give me your hand."

"Thank you." She sat in the proffered chair, her exhaustion catching up to her. "I also don't think they know I'm not full blooded." She held up her right hand like Jake asked, expecting to make a deal.

"Not that one, the other hand." Jake unzipped his backpack and drew out a pin light and a roll of gauze.

"That thing about your father being on the run?" Scout asked.

Jake shined his light on her hand and rubbed it with dampened gauze from the outside in.

"Yeah, I think she was talking about the butterfly man," Lyn said, ignoring Jake. Her eyes were on Scout. "Jonathan is dead. I have no idea who my biological father is, and no way to start looking." Lyn turned to look at Jake. "She had to be talking about the butterfly man, right?"

"Ouch." Lyn looked down at her hand in Jake's. Her pale flesh was tinted with streams of red.

"Shit." Jake said. "This is worse than I thought."

"What the hell happened?" Scout asked and moved closer so he could see better.

Jake shook his head. "Lyn, this needs stitches. You went too deep."

Lyn looked at her hand for the first time. Jake held a dry piece of gauze on the still bleeding cut.

"You can do it. You've dealt with worse injuries." Scout told his brother.

Jake applied pressure with a clean piece of gauze and shook his head. "I can, but I've had less sleep that she has. I'm not sure how fine I could make the stitches." He looked at Lyn. "Can you do it?"

Lyn stared at him then looked at her hand where her blood had soaked through the thin layer of gauze.

"She can not." A voice said from behind Jake.

Jake kept pressure on her wound as he stood and turned toward the voice.

Scout put his hand on Lyn's shoulder. He flanked her with his brother as if they were knights and she were their queen.

Lyn peered into the darkness and the brothers stepped in front of her to face the threat in her place.

A figure stepped from the shadows of the tree line. "Well met, Lyn." The dark skinned, dark hair man lifted his palms face up. "I mean no harm to you and yours." He lowered his head. "Please forgive my manners. In the heat of the moment a trade was not reciprocated. My name is Nix," said a voice she recognized. "I trust you'll keep it safe, as I will yours."

Lyn stood and stepped between Jake and Scout. Jake had to shift his hold on her hand to allow her the movement. "Aren't you hiding from Winter? Won't she find you here?" Lyn took a deep breath and noticed the boys remained tense, on guard. Jake's fingers increased their pressure on her wound.

"Jasmine and gardenias?" Jake asked.

Scout nodded his head.

"Now is no longer for running." He reached into his pocket and drew out a bauble that swirled blue and yellow in the firelight. "May I?"

Lyn nodded.

Nix moved to the side and tossed the stone onto the fire. As it met the heat of the fire, it disintegrated.

The same shockwave as in the middle of the stream rushed over her. This time she watched as a wave of barely registered pressure swept through and around them. The fire trembled as it brushed past.

"Where do you get those?" Scout asked.

"Each moment is precious," Nix said.

"Each what?" Jake asked.

"Later, boys." Lyn said. "Relevant questions and planning only. Moments don't last forever."

Nix nodded. "But for now, we are unheard and unwatched."

"Fine, but this needs to be dealt with now." Jake indicated Lyn's hand. "You have to wait." Jake looked at Lyn. He reached down for a new piece of gauze and traded it out for the old one. "You hold pressure and keep it elevated. As tight as you can." He let go of her hand after she wrapped her free hand around it. "Scout, you watch him. I have to get more light. I need to be able to see. If he moves, let me know."

"Are we the last three?" Lyn asked as Jake dashed into the cabin for a lantern, then back out and into the two tents for two more. "You, me, and my mother?

"Winter and Summer have hunted us near extinction."

Lyn noted his lack of answer and choked down follow-up questions.

"You know I'm not your daughter."

"Yes. I knew before you were born," Nix said. "A species can not be repopulated with limited participants, but that is another tale. Do you intend to rescue Anada without meeting her."

"Is that my mother's name?" Lyn sat back down in her chair. She kept her hand clutched to her chest while she watched Nix.

The dark skinned man nodded.

"Then yes." Lyn nodded once. "But so far, I don't see how. I have more going against me than for. I wouldn't be able to get close enough."

Nix's confidence puffed out his chest. "If Summer comes to you, so will Anada." A look of sadness passed across his face."If you fail to strike a deal with Summer, I'm certain Anada will be forced to take you out." There was little emotion in the last of his words. He stated fact, only his face betrayed his feelings on the subject. As if it was a foregone conclusion and he had no say in the matter.

"Will she?" Scout asked.

"Deals are binding." Nix nodded once.

"Do you know what Anada traded her loyalty for?" Lyn asked.

Jake pulled another chair close to Lyn and laid a sterile blue paper over her leg. He pulled Scout's chair over and set the lanterns in the seat so that he could see her hand more clearly.

Nix nodded again. "My safety."

"But you're hunted," Scout said.

"Only by Winter. I can pass through Summer safely, if I'm careful."

"Why haven't you tried to rescue Anada, yourself?" Jake asked without looking. He focused instead on Lyn's hand and the deep wound she had inflicted on herself.

"My safety only extends so far. If I were to go directly against Summer, she would find a way to end me. It need not be by her hand. How did you hide from the sisters for so long?"

Scout squeezed her shoulder in warning.

"I won't answer that for now," Lyn met Nix's eyes, "not with Winter so close and Summer on her way."

Nix nodded. "That is wise."

"Why are you here?" Scout asked.

"I am tried of running. I will help you with Summer, but you must deal with Winter. "

"Fair enough." Lyn accepted and looked down as Jake slid a thin curved needle between two layers deep within her palm. Tears formed at the corner of her eyes and flowed down her cheeks, but she didn't make a sound.

She looked away, hoping that she'd feel less if her eyes were not involved. "Scout, can breakfast come early? And coffee. I'd love 8 hours of sleep, but I don't think it would be a good use of my time." She winced and held her breath. "And I need you to change my music. Something slow and instrumental please." Her voice shook with pain and tears and exhaustion.

Jake looked up at her as he pulled the suture through. "I'm sorry."

She closed her eyes and tears fell. She shook her head. "I've felt worse. But I'm exhausted and can't ignore the pain this time. Just shut me out and do your job. The faster, the better."

"Speed will leave a scar. But I'll do my best." Jake waited while Scout lifted her phone out of her pocket and subbed out Eye of the Tiger for Pachelbel's Canon in D, the base of most modern music. She could sing almost any song with these few chords.

She let the music soothe her as she felt Jake puncture and pull the next suture through. She focused on not holding her breath and keeping her pulse steady. She did not need to have her wolf close to the surface while Jake poked a needle in her flesh.

"Which is your mate?" Nix pulled Lyn's focus.

Beside her, Scout choked and Lyn turned to see him wave her off and grab a half full water bottle from the ground beside the fire.

"Neither," Lyn answered.

"But they stand with you?" Nix asked.

She looked at Jake who met her eyes and nodded. "They do."

"Which would you trust at your back?"

She considered. She would trust both of them at her back and at her throat. "Both, but if I have to choose." She pointed to Scout. "No offense."

"None taken." Jake poked her again without looking up.

She stiffened and took a deep breath to keep from whimpering.

"Then I will ask this one." Nix turned toward Jake.

"Not right now you won't." Jake said. "I'm going to finish this without distraction or the damage to her hand will be on your head. Sit down and wait your turn." Jake's voice was firm.

"Can I still have coffee?" Lyn pouted.

"If you can drink it and stay still," Jake answered. "And quiet."

Scout stepped into the cabin and returned with the kettle.

CHAPTER THIRTY-NINE

Jake pulled the last suture through the top layer of Lyn's skin and tied it off. "It's good. It's not perfect but I doubt there will be a scar." He cleaned and bandaged the half inch gash then cleaned up the supplies he used before he turned to Nix. "Okay, what do you want to ask me?" Jake took the mug that Scout held out for him.

"For your wolf," Nix said.

"My what now?" Jake held the mug low.

"If Nix mimics your wolf, he can stand by Lyn unknown." Scout looked at Nix. "Right?"

Scout must have been using the quiet time to strategize, which was smarter than Lyn, who had wasted it. She wiped tears from her face with the sleeve of Scout's hoodie. Now that the deep wound was stitched, she could relax a bit and maybe get her emotions in check.

Nix nodded.

"What about me?" Jake asked.

"You can stand by her on two legs," Scout said.

"Alternatively, I can use your face. I would not mind looking like you from time to time. Winter has seen your wolf, she will not think too hard when she sees it again. A new human face however, will garner her attention."

"Hold up," Jake said. "I am not at all sure I want anyone besides me having this face." Jake looked from Lyn and Scout to Nix. "This mimic thing won't keep me from shifting if the need arises, right?"

Nix nodded.

"Sis?" Jake looked at Lyn.

"It's your choice, but I'd be more confident with another person on my side."

"You trust him?" Jake asked.

Lyn took a sip of her coffee. She wanted to trust Nix. He was the only person she knew that was like her. The only person who was able to teach her about being a mimic. But she couldn't be sure. He was fae, and in theory, that meant he didn't lie. However, lies were not always obvious constructs. Sometimes the avoidance of a truth was lie enough, and it's completely possible to let someone lie to themselves when you've said nothing at all.

Nix turned to Lyn. He kneeled and lowered his head. "Your companions are right to be wary. Tell me how I can prove myself."

Lyn's eyes went wide. Why was he kneeling at her feet? What in the world has her life come to? Less than a year ago she was a nobody. Why was she important now? Because she was a half-breed? A mutt? A mix of predators? *A weapon. That's why.* She sighed. *My life is never going to be simple, is it?*

Lyn considered Nix on his knees in the dirt. Her mind flitted through scenarios as fast as butterfly wings. "Did you send the butterflies to the cemetery? Was it you who called me from the woods beyond the fence?"

"What butterflies?" Nix looked up.

"The ones that led me to my mother's grave. Then found me again on the stream when I followed you."

"I know nothing of your cemetery. But the day we met, pixies led me to you."

"Tiny things, white wings?" Lyn asked.

"Or invisible, depending on who you ask." Scout added.

"That sounds like pixies." Nix stood. "They sometimes show themselves as butterflies to humans, but prefer to remain hidden. They are a wild species thought inconsequential to the courts and are considered by most to be pests, a mere nuisance. However, they are extremely loyal to those that earn it. When our kind were more plentiful, we would protect the wild fae, pixies included. We have not been able to do that in many cycles. Pixies have short life spans for fairies but they have long memories and a penchant for curiosity. How does sharing this knowledge test my trust?"

"It doesn't." Lyn sighed. "I need four hours of sleep, or more coffee, whichever I can more easily afford. The butterflies that spoke to me were pixies. Okay. Is there a fairy creature that presents as a dog to humans? Maybe golden retriever shaped?" All eyes turned to look at Lyn. She folded back into her chair. "Never mind. It's silly. I'm tired. I've been known to imagine things." She closed her eyes and tried to ignore the gazes of her companions. Now was not the time to bring attention to her past hallucinations.

Scout moved to her side and lifted her from the chair. He whispered in her ear. "We're going to revisit that another day." He sat back down with her in his lap. She laid her head on his shoulder and closed her eyes as Jake moved to refill the kettle.

"I'm not crazy," she whispered back.

"Which is why I want to talk about that later. But we need to focus on the now."

Lyn nodded.

Several breaths later, Scout spoke up. "You could make a deal, skewed in Lyn's favor. If you work against her in any way, you will forfeit your life."

Lyn pulled her head away from Scout and stared at him. "That's a little drastic."

"Is it?" Scout asked. "Winter asked much the same of you and you accepted." Scout looked pained.

She noted that he could use a few hours of sleep too. "I didn't accept."

"Not yet, but you're going to and as much as I hate the fact that you would be putting your life in danger for a stranger, I can't fault you for it. I just hope she has as much family loyalty as you do."

"I stole it from Jake," she mumbled, a tear slipped from her eye. She didn't try to hide it.

"The deal is acceptable." Nix said. "I value my life, as much as Anada's. She did much the same for me, and I would rather Lyn hold my life in her hands, than have it in the queens' grasps." He knelt in front of Scout and Lyn's chair.

She faced Nix and lifted her not bandaged hand to the still kneeling Nix. He accepted with two hands to her one. "I will forfeit my life rather than put yours in danger."

Lyn looked at Scout.

He shrugged.

Lyn blinked away her tears and her near frayed emotions and ran though the semantics in her head. She didn't speak until she was satisfied at the wording. "Deal," she said and electricity sparked between their hands. The scent of electricity and white flowers wafted into the air.

"Fine. What do I have to do?" Jake asked, holding a warm kettle for Lyn's mug which she gladly let him refill.

Lyn took a long sip of the brew and a small portion of her tension melted.

Scout smiled and looked at his brother. "You look deep into the man's eyes while holding his hands." Scout couldn't contain his mirth.

Jake glared at him. "You know I'm doing this for your girl, right?"

Scout choked. "She's not my girl." He squirmed uncomfortably under Lyn's weight.

"Not with that attitude, she's not," Jake said and unzipped his pants.

Lyn turned toward Scout. "After this mess is cleared up, there will be a grocery store trip and a full night's sleep and time where we talk about complications. Yours and mine." She inhaled the steaming hot caffeine from her mug.

"My house or yours?" Scout agreed.

Lyn heard a whimpered growl and turned back to Nix and Jake.

Jake's wolf looked at Nix. A flutter of tension vibrated down his spine, the fur on his back moved with it. Nix put his hand on Jake's pelt, but Jake did not relax.

Nix's transformation was fast and clean. Like a state of the art copy machine instead of Lyn's own decades old copy process. She envied his speed and his lack of pain.

Scout snapped a picture of the two wolves touching each other.

The wolves separated and Jake shifted back to two legs, barely giving Lyn enough time to look away or risk turning a bright shade of fuchsia. "Is that what I look like?" He asked.

"Yeah. Pigment for pigment." Scout confirmed, unconcerned with his brother's nakedness.

"Cool." Jake smiled and eyed the copy. "I'm a good looking wolf," he said as he zipped up his pants.

"Can we talk about the deal with Winter now?" Lyn asked. "I'd like to avoid slitting my own throat if I can."

~

"*D*awn is close." Nix said.

The sky had lightened considerablt while they had discussed the meeting with Winter.

"I'm still not sure about this." Scout said looking down at Lyn.

She had managed to find a comfortable position in his lap. One that allowed her a few moments of peace and Scout had held her as she drifted off to the spot between waking and sleeping while the other three had continued the discussion.

Lyn blinked awake. "But you're sure about me, right?"

Scout nodded.

"Say it, please. I need to hear it." Lyn's voice had an edge of worry to it and her eyes pleaded with him to chase it away.

She had no idea how much he admired her strength. How brave she was. He stood up, letting her slip slowly out of his lap to stand on her own feet.

He took her arms in his hands and met her eyes. "Lyn, I have absolute faith in your abilities and I trust you with my life." He saw the doubt cross her face momentarily before she pushed it way.

"Thank you." She closed her eyes before the moisture in them could fall.

"I mean it. Every word." Scout pulled her close and kissed the top of her white haired head. He pulled away and shifted to his wolf as the moment collapsed and their ears popped.

Jake stood beside the fire with his wolf by his heel.

It was a little weird to see his brother standing beside his own wolf, but that was not the only weird thing over the past few days and today promised a few more.

Lyn joined him and placed her hands in the scruff of both wolves' necks. Her bandaged palm resting lightly between Scout's shoulder blades.

"Winter, take two." Lyn sighed and walked around the cabin as snow fell. The wolves walked at her calves while Jake walked slightly behind.

CHAPTER FORTY

Lyn walked toward the center of the open space. The snow melted in her wake.

Winter approached from the opposite side dressed in fur lined armor underneath a thick white cloak. She was flanked by four wolves of her own in varying shades of grays and whites.

Lyn noted that the armor was more visually appealing than practical. More of a costume for an audience. However, the wolves at her side were real and growled low and slow, a sound of caution that amplified their mistress's air of danger.

Lyn was glad to see Winter trying so hard. That meant that Winter viewed her more like a threat and less like a bug to squash.

"Do we have a deal?" Winter said curtly as she met Lyn in the center of the glade.

Lyn breathed in fresh snowy air and confidence. "I will remove the mimic from Summer's ranks and never fight on Summer's behalf in exchange for neutrality and safety for myself and all mimics."

Nix had made the addendum, insisting that she consider future generations. He wanted the deal to have lasting implications beyond her. That made Lyn wonder again if she were the only hidden mimic child in the world. But she didn't question him. She didn't want to put anyone else at risk and since she knew the courts were close, she let it go.

"That is not the deal we had." Winter crossed her arms and her wolves' growls turned up the menace factor. The closer two took a step forward.

"It's the deal I'm offering." Lyn's posture stayed open, but her wolves tensed at the threat and added their own growls to the thunderous mix.

"Who is this?" Winter pointed to Jake.

"My second."

"If you fail, he will take up your banner?"

"If she falls, her fight becomes my own." Jake answered.

"So be it."

Lyn felt electricity wash over her in a wave from the Winter Queen's position in the snowy glade. They were close enough to touch, but making deals with Fairy Queens was not bound by touching, apparently.

"It is done," Winter said. "You have until midnight tonight."

"Wait, that's not…" Lyn started.

"Fair?" Winter laughed.

The sound of glaciers breaking apart chilled Lyn to the bone. A shiver ran up her spine and Scout's wolf nuzzled her hand. Lyn stood speechless as the Queen of the Winter Court turned and disappeared, taking the snow, her wolves, and the darkness with her.

CHAPTER FORTY-ONE

*E*arly morning birds chirped as the sun crested the horizon.

"One down. One to go?" Lyn closed her eyes and Scout watched as her white hair became curly brown. When she opened her eyes they changed from amber and silver to the shade of spring grass Scout was familiar with.

Jake caught Lyn as her legs buckled and lifted her off the ground before Scout could shift from his wolf.

"I think I can buy myself a little time," Lyn murmured, "but I really need some sleep,"

Jakes handed her prone form to Scout.

"Then sleep you shall have." Scout walked her back behind the cabin toward their tent.

He tucked her into the tent and walked inside the cabin to grab a set of clothes, since Lyn was wearing his. "Her fight will become yours? Really? We don't have enough problems as it is?" He called to Jake.

"Yeah, if Lyn falls, I'm taking it out on both courts." Jake smiled. "That's what she's really fighting for, right? To control her own life."

"That and…" Scout stepped to the dying fire.

"LALALA." Jake cut him off with his fingers in his ears. "Look, little bro. Sometimes details complicate life, and it's the broad strokes that really matter."

"This is a broad stroke?" Scout asked.

Jake shrugged. "I'm playing fast and loose with the spirit of the rules. So what?"

Scout lifted one eyebrow.

Jake lowered his voice so only Scout could hear. "She faced Lady Snowflake when she had nothing on the line. She'll have to go all in to get something from the other one. It won't be near as easy."

"That was easy?" Scout said. "She nearly made a deal to slit her own throat."

"Yeah," Jake smiled, "but did you hear how she skirted the issue? Luck was on her side and Lady Snowflake forgot it in the final agreement. Do you think she was afraid of Lyn? Intimidated? She came back with wolves." Jake shook his head. "Anyway, your girl knows how to take control and throw in a little verbal sleight of hand. Now, it all hinges on how she does face to face with Lady Sunshine."

Scout turned to Nix, the wolf. "Summer will come to Lyn?"

Nix changed from wolf to fully clothed man without so much as a grunt. Scout envied that ability. One day he'd be used to the pain of his shift, he might not even feel it anymore, but it would never be that smooth and he would never come out of it fully clothed.

"News travels fast in Fairy. Winter will use her meeting with Lyn for other turns. Summer will have no choice but to seek Lyn out."

"How long do we have?" Scout wanted weeks or days. He'd settle for hours, but he knew they needed Summer to make a move soon if they planned to have Winter's deal sealed up before midnight.

"It depends on what the girl does to hide herself." Nix

considered. "If she can teach me, I will be forever in her debt."

"One thing at a time." Scout said and sat in a camp chair near Nix. "May I ask you some questions about your kind?"

"You can ask. I can answer or not, as I choose."

"Fair. Was Winter intimidated by Lyn?"

Nix nodded. "Not Lyn so much as what she is. When we were plentiful, our kind did more than most to maintain balance. In the past, our kind has had reason to depose a Queen and the means to do it. Winter holds her power because we helped her get it."

"And Summer?"

"She knows it happened and is afraid we'll do it again."

"Would you?"

"To maintain balance? Without question." Nix nodded.

"Wouldn't having Anada on the inside make it easier?"

"Deals were made, hands are tied. Summer has both Anada and I in check for the moment."

"But Lyn is a new piece on the board."

"More like a piece gone from the game for too long." Nix agreed.

It was Scout's turn to nod. "What did you mean when you said strong emotions could make her lose control?"

"Emotions are volatile. She will have to learn to temper them, but it's not always easy. If you love the girl, you will have to be comfortable with every face she takes."

Jake let out a long whistle. "You better believe my imagination is flying away on that one. Can you imagine you kissing her, but you open your eyes and you've been locking lips with yourself?"

Scout threw the first thing he could lay his hands on at his brother, but Jake dodged the empty water bottle projectile and laughed.

Scout looked at Lyn sleeping inside the tent. "Knock it off. Lyn needs to sleep."

Jake lowered the volume, but didn't stop laughing.

"Enjoy it, brother." Scout said and stood up. He walked to the open door of the tent.

"Oh, I will." Jake called quietly, but Scout heard the amusement in his voice.

Scout slid into the tent beside Lyn, leaving the door unzipped, and pulled her to his chest. Her brown curls tucked under his chin.

"Not yet, please," Lyn whined. "I just got here."

"No, not yet," he whispered over her head and closed his eyes. He was asleep in minutes.

CHAPTER FORTY-TWO

*L*yn woke to Scout's breath on her ear. She waited for him to stir, but his breath was rhythmic and his muscles relaxed.

She checked the time on her phone, 11:47 a.m., and turned off the alarm before it sounded. The air was warm inside the tent. Even nestled underneath the shade of a tree.

She ran her fingers through her hair and pulled it over her shoulder to confirm it was brown. She didn't know if Scout's idea held or if it was just a coincidence, but she wasn't willing to question it yet. If she could name the time and place, she would.

She stayed still, thinking, not about the impending conflict with Summer, but about things more personal. She told herself she had been fighting for a year to control her own life, but she knew that wasn't true. She had gotten lazy and slid back into old habits. Blending into the background. Letting other people lead while she followed.

The binding spell the witch placed on her was gone, but her learned behaviors were harder to break.

She made a deal with herself that she would fix that as soon as she survived Summer in Texas. She would regain the control she had allowed her friends to take from her and she would keep it this time.

Lyn listened for sounds outside of the tent, but heard only Jake snoring from a camping chair, even the nature sounds were subdued in this heat. She wondered what Nix was doing. He didn't seem the type to lounge around a campfire.

She looked at Scout while her head rested on her hand. She didn't want to wake him, but she couldn't afford to wait any longer.

He blinked awake. "Now?"

"It's almost noon. I only have twelve hours to pull this off."

"Let's do it then." He stretched, drew in a deep breath, and filled his lungs with fresh air. "It works, by the way. Jake said that the sight transfers from wolf to human, but we're still not sure if it washes off."

"I guess I'll have to kiss your brother again." Lyn sat up.

"At least he's not August."

Lyn shook her head and turned to face Scout. "That boy and his dog biscuits." Lyn sighed. "Did you know he'd push those tiny ones through the vents on my locker door?

Scout shrugged his shoulders. "He's mostly harmless and he likes you."

"Tell him to show it with steaks."

Scout let out a deep belly laugh. "Trust me, we tried."

"A steak would be awesome, right now." Lyn moaned, and fanned herself with her hand. The weather felt toasty warm after the snow from earlier this morning. "I'm so hungry."

"I think we have sausages."

Lyn pouted. "No, thank you." She stuck out her tongue. "We need to get this show rolling. I'm calling for sunshine." Lyn pulled the fabric of her dress away from her body to allow air to circulate near her skin and wished for cooler weather. "The air is stifling, do you think she's already here?" Lyn looked out of the tent.

Sunlight filtered through the leaves in the trees, creating a brightness that made her shade her eyes.

She stepped out of the tent and stretched. "Anyone not ready, needs to get ready fast. And if anyone can find the air conditioner controls, that'd be great. Thanks."

Scout laughed from the tent door and Jake doused his head with the emergency bucket of spring water to wake up.

"Where is Nix?" Lyn asked.

Jake looked around. "I don't know. He was here when I crashed." He shook water from his hair. "Do you think that is going to be a problem?"

"I'd rather have him here than not know where he is or what he's up to, but he knew the plan." She shrugged. "We'll find out if that's a bad thing or not, I guess."

"Do you want me on two legs or four, sis?" Jake asked.

"Two. Let's hold wolves in reserve in case we need a surprise attack. We'll also assume Nix has a good reason to be gone, but be suspect if he comes back. Jasmine and gardenias or it's not him."

"He said there were only three of your kind left." Jake's eyes were watching her.

"Actually he didn't." Lyn sighed, "and we haven't met the third."

"We can't be sure of her intentions." Jake concluded and stood up. "Got it."

Lyn nodded and took his face in her hands. She quickly sniffed for his orange, clove and clean sheet smell before she kissed his eyelids and stepped back. "Just in case the water washed it off.

"Are you ready?" Scout asked as he slipped a white shirt over his head.

"If you mean would I rather run and hide, the answer is yes, I would, but I can't." She sighed. "Last night... this morning? Anyway, whatever it was, was the first time I have slept and not woken up feeling trapped. If I ran, I'd never be able to be free again. And I don't know how long I can hide from fairies. So, yes, I guess I'm ready and one way or another it ends today." She looked away from the brothers. She had sidestepped a deal with Winter to slit her own throat if she failed, but Summer or her mother might still end her if things didn't go her way. She promised herself that she would do her best to make sure Scout and Jake walked away unharmed even if she couldn't. "I'm also hungry."

Scout ran inside the cabin and when he returned, he tossed her and Jake a granola bar each.

Lyn opened the wrapper and took a bite. "Thank you."

"Let me see your hand." Jake stepped closer. She held out her hand and he unwrapped the bandage. "I know you had a reason to do this, but as the nearest thing you have to a doctor out here in the middle of nowhere, can you…" Jake began.

"I'll refrain from puncturing myself again, Dr. Jacobs." She cut him off. "Sorry, about the extra work."

"No." He forced her to look at him. "You do what you have to do, sis. I'll clean up the mess, but don't do it in the same spot. Stitches on top of stitches would be too much for me and the nearest hospital is not so near."

She nodded.

Jake picked up the discarded bandage and held his hand out for her empty granola bar wrapper. He took both inside the cabin. "No need to leave your blood lying around," he said as he stepped inside.

Lyn's breath hitched. She should have known better after Ms. Evans. A tremor ran through her legs but she maintained her upright stance. She took a steadying breath and calmed herself as much as possible, pushing the past away. It wasn't witches this time, it was fairies and fairies didn't need blood to control her. They were more subtle than that. Still, she made sure the cut was no longer bleeding and was happy she had enhanced healing from her shifter genes.

Lyn let her old self, brown hair and green eyes, melt into her true self. White hair fell down her back and her eyes went from green to amber and silver.

She peered around the edge of the cabin to the empty glade. Her phone now said 11:57.

"How long, do you think?" Scout asked.

She took his head in her hands and stood on her toes.

Scout leaned his head down and closed his eyes for her to kiss them.

"Three minutes, give or take," Lyn said. "Should we wait for her out there or wait for her to get here first?"

"You need to be in control from the beginning," Jake said. "I think you need to be waiting on her."

Lyn nodded and gathered her courage. She walked to the center of the open space.

Scout took her injured hand lightly as he came to walk by her left shoulder while Jake walked on her right. She felt like she was leading them into a trap and her nightmares flooded back. Lyn froze in her tracks. She tried to turn back toward the cabin, but Scout put his hand at her back.

"You can do this."

Lyn was about to object when flowers sprouted up in a wave toward her feet, bringing with it an even more oppressive heat.

Lyn stood in the middle of the flowers in Umiko's pale green dress and bare feet as a cloud of monarch butterflies resolved into a blonde wearing a sheer sky blue floor length asymmetrical dress.

Umiko would love that dress. Lyn felt a pang of guilt. As much as she enjoyed spending time with Scout and Jake, she just realized how much she missed her BFF, who was probably worried sick.

"I might need Lyn's music distraction today." Jake startled

Lyn out of her thoughts. He was staring at the stunning Queen of Summer.

"What about Veronica?" Scout asked.

"Yep, she'd need music too." Jake said, not taking his eyes off of Summer.

Lyn pinched him. "She'd burn you to a crisp."

"Veronica or Summer?"

Lyn watched as Jake struggled to look away from the very embodiment of Summer standing in front of them.

"Both." Scout said with a low growl.

"True enough." Jake took a deep breath. "I will not fly too close to the sun." He said under his breath and Lyn heard him repeat it twice more.

"Good afternoon." Lyn stepped forward. She needed to take charge and get her head on straight. Jake would have to be in charge of his own. "Summer, I presume. Well met." Lyn said. "I'd like to make you an offer."

Summer looked at her and Lyn was happy to see that the woman was caught off guard for a flicker of a moment.

Scout stepped closer to Lyn.

"May I offer you refreshments," Lyn asked Summer. "My offering pales in comparison to what you are accustomed to, I am sure, but what human refreshments I have are yours for the asking."

"Your manners are refreshing in one raised as you were, but I will decline, nonetheless." Summer made a motion and her people stepped out of the tree line and provided a table, chairs, and a large white lace umbrella to sit under.

Her people were just as varied as Winter's. However, Summer surrounded herself with more appealing faces, even the green skinned among them were oddly gorgeous, distractingly so.

Once the scene was set, Summer sat in a large ornate blonde wicker chair and invited Lyn to sit across from her.

Lyn was thankful for the shade provided. It was a flimsy

respite from the increased temperature brought on by the height of Summer and her court, but at least the sun would be kept at bay. Lyn hoped it would be enough protection to keep her skin from burning.

She expected to be turned down and was pleased because she wasn't sure what food was left beyond the sausages that Scout had threatened her with.

"What would you offer me beyond refreshments?" Summer asked.

"As you well know, Winter has paid a visit," Lyn began.

"Indeed. I also heard that you had accepted her generosity." Summer smiled and Lyn had to remember she was a predator in fancy clothes.

"But you did not kill me on site." Lyn kept her appreciation a silent one. *Rule number 4: Do not say thank you.*

"Hospitality dictates I not shed your blood while in your territory. We are in your territory, are we not?"

"We are." *Thank you, Jake!* His claiming her as a sister had far more benefits that she had originally thought. "And while your intel about my acceptance was true, the terms were misleading. I did not agree to what she wanted most."

"I see. So my sister is playing games with me as usual."

"I can not speak to that, but I can tell you I am prepared to offer you a similar arrangement to the one I made with Winter."

"Which is?" Summer leaned forward slightly.

"I will promise never to fight for Winter in exchange for a boon."

"You have a boon in mind, I imagine." Summer sat back making Lyn feel all but dismissed.

"I do." Lyn saw Nix, pale skinned and white haired, step out of the woods from the East. Jake turned his body to follow her gaze.

Scout did not move from Lyn's side. He kept his eyes on the gathered fairy court.

Lyn knew the brothers hunted better than any partnership she could imagine. The trust was absolute. She also knew, beyond a doubt, that Scout would not leave her side for any reason as long as her safety was in question, which it was as long as Summer was sitting across from her.

Summer snapped her fingers and two attendants flanked her chair. One looked almost exactly like Maria Davis, only younger. Lyn clutched at Scout's leg below the table's edge. She tried to keep the emotional response from her face. She couldn't afford to show weakness, but she was looking at the face of her dead mother reflected on her biological mother's. She hadn't thought her biological mom had met her adoptive mom, much less known her enough to take her looks. If Lyn was wrong about that, what else was she wrong about?

Lyn's pulse increased as the doubts started piling up.

Did her bio mom know about Ms. Evans? Did she know that the witch took her blood for sixteen years to give herself a power boost and ageless skin? Did she care? Did she just need to get Lyn out of her hair? Did she want Lyn at all or was she just an inconvenience? An inconvenience that she would be fine with killing if Summer asked her to.

Lyn's pulse increased again when she looked at Maria and Maria smiled back. *Is she looking forward to killing me?*

Scout leaned down and whispered in her ear.

Lyn nodded and he slipped two earbuds into her hands.

Lyn put them in one at a time while hiding what she was doing with her hands behind her long white hair.

Scout already had a playlist queued up and Lyn was grateful. She took a slow, deep breath in and out.

"Is he a danger to you?" Lyn asked the queen as she tilted her head toward the newest arrival.

Lyn tried hard to keep her doubts from overwhelming her. She did not have the time for a panic attack. Lyn focused on the long draw of bow strings over a violin while she waited for an answer.

"Not as such." Summer said, but her shadows were tensed, ready to intercept.

"Then allow my man to intercept him for us."

"By all means." Summer waved her hand in acquiescence.

Jake walked off to meet Nix away from the Summer party, and hopefully figure out what was going on. Where had he been? Why was he here now?

"No matter." Summer brushed off the incident. "What is your boon?"

Lyn spoke without thinking. "The release of my mother from her loyalty to Summer."

Summer laughed and it reminded Lyn of a bubbling brook. A refreshing feel on an overly warm day.

Lyn relished the thought of giving into the sound, of putting her bare feet into the calm water and letting all her worries float away. She didn't need to confront. Summer she could walk away and...Lyn came back to herself when a somber note from a violin vibrated in her ears.

Lyn pinched her thigh just beneath the hem of her dress. She had allowed herself to be distracted and she hoped it wouldn't cost her.

"You'd have me give up my best weapon against my sister in exchange for a promise of neutrality." Summer sat back in her chair and snapped her fingers.

Lyn's mother knelt down for Summer to place her feet on as she lounged back in her chair.

Lyn felt the familiar rumble of her wolf in her chest and the volume of the music in her ears increased.

"Why shouldn't I just kill you?" Summer asked.

Lyn tried to stamp down the challenge she wanted to offer the Summer Queen. She met the woman's eyes and unfolded her fingers that had formed fists without her permission. The tug on the stitches was the only thing that clued her in to the involuntary action.

She took a deep breath and watched as Jake returned, leaving Nix a good distance behind him.

He knelt down at her side and whispered a single word in her ear, "Troy."

Summer looked intrigued by the exchange. "What news does your man bring?"

"It's unimportant. He assured me he will deal with it if it becomes necessary, and since you have said the man is of no threat to you, we should return to our meeting." Lyn's voice mirrored the overly charming tones of her companion, since she had no intention of answering the Queen's question.

Jake returned to stand a bit farther away than necessary. Almost as if he were keeping Nix far enough from the table to not be a threat. Lyn wondered why and regretted that the distance also meant that without a breeze in the right direction, Lyn would not be able to scent either of them.

Lyn let it go. She had to trust him, as Scout did. Instead, she focused on the Queen and smiled. She needed to get back on track. She mentally ran through her play book. "You won't kill me now, because there are only three of my kind left. One you have claimed as your own, in exchange for the safety of the second." Lyn leaned back in her own chair, faking confidence.

"That sounds like another good reason to kill you."

"It does, but you'd open yourself up to repercussions from the neutral party you tolerate, not to mention the animosity of your loyal weapon. It's dangerous to hold your blade so close to your own chest. Did you know that most weapon related accidents happen in the home?" Lyn cobbled that fake statistic together but she hoped the queen wouldn't care about the details. The need to run was rapidly taking over the facade of calm in her body.

Her wolf wanted to end this with teeth and claws. She scented danger, and too many unknowns.

Lyn was on the verge of a panic attack and her wolf wasn't

helping. What if she snapped? Lyn did not like to see her mother on the ground under Summer's dainty feet and gorgeous legs. She knew that it wasn't really Maria, but the woman that loved her for sixteen years deserved more respect than this illusion offered.

A dull pain tugged as the stitches on her palm caught on the long sharp edges of her extending nails. Lyn couldn't watch any longer, not and keep her wolf controlled.

Lyn stood. "You have until sundown to decide." She walked away from the Summer Queen's table without another thought to the etiquette involved. Scout fell into place slightly behind, guarding her back.

Jake remained with Nix. Lyn glanced back when he didn't follow but tried to mask her confusion and the growl that grew in her belly.

Summer removed her feet from Maria's back and snapped her fingers. "Bring me tea and my musicians."

CHAPTER FORTY-THREE

*L*yn miscalculated how much the sisters would be alike. She had hoped for a break to gather her thoughts and get her emotions under control without Summer's presence. Seeing her mother's face disrespected kicked her in the gut.

She knew that wasn't Maria, but why that face? Why now? Was Summer toying with her? Was her bio mom trying to tell her something? Something Lyn didn't understand.

Lyn paced between the neglected fire and the open door of the tent she shared with Scout. She was too ramped up to sit and didn't have the luxury of a run.

The oppressive heat continued. Even in the shade, the temperature felt like the height of summer at the equator during the dry season and less like a normal June day.

Sweat dripped down Lyn's back. She felt horrible that Jake was out in the middle of the glade,= babysitting Nix, without shade or water or sunscreen. What was that about? Why did it look like Jake was keeping Nix at a distance. What kind of strategy was he playing? And what did he mean by 'Troy?'

Lyn growled and let some of her frustrations take wing on the sound as it escaped her throat.

Scout stepped to her side and handed her a bottle of water and an expandable paper fan he had made out of a snow damaged page from the notebook.

"Scout, is Jake okay out there? Should we take him water?" A drip of sweat rolled down her nose. "I don't like that he's out there, in this horrible sun, because of me."

Scout put a hand on her shoulder. "He'd be over here if he could. There's a reason he's staying and you need to trust him. You also need to remember who you are and what you can do. You don't have to suffer in this heat." He stepped closer. "Just remember what snow feels like.

"But…"

"No more names. Our brother would not want you to give yourself heat stroke or dehydrate." He motioned to the water bottle in her hand.

She lifted the bottle in the small space between their bodies and took a gulp. Heat radiated from his body and she doubted hers was much cooler. She closed her eyes and remembered the dusting of snow as it fell around her hours earlier.

"Good. Now, if you don't mind, I'd like to stand here a moment, just until my skin stops melting and my shirt stops sticking to me."

"You could take it off."

"You'd like that, wouldn't you." Scout winked. "I'd rather stand too close and watch your cheeks turn that light shade of pink they sometimes do."

"What do you think our brother meant by…"

He put his finger across her lips and shook his head. "Too many ears."

If Lyn could not talk to Scout or Jake, she couldn't confirm what Jake meant by 'Troy.' She was going on the assumption that it was Trojan horse related, but she could not be sure.

Scout turned his sweaty back to Lyn. She laid her forehead against it, unconcerned with the dampness of his shirt. The air around them cooled as she let her worry take a backseat and focused on colder temperatures.

Lyn's head lifted as music began in the clearing. A drum beat accompanied by a flute. Slow and rhythmic. She might not be able to run, but she had the space to dance.

She closed her eyes to listen to the beat and let the tension in her arms and legs float away on the melody. She let her hips drift left and right with the tempo of the music.

Scout turned back around to face her. "Lyn?"

A smile spread across her lips. She wanted to kiss him. To forget the world outside of her personal space and kiss the boy that believed in her, that trusted her with his life. She raised herself on her toes and leaned forward.

Scout pulled away, holding onto her arms with his hands. "Where are your earbuds?"

Lyn sighed and moved away from him. As much as she wanted to kiss him, her body ached to move. She closed her eyes again and let the music settle in her bones. She could dance forever.

Scout moved closer and swept the hair from her ears. He removed the in ear device and held it next to his ear.

There was no sound.

He put the earbud back in place and squeezed her hand. He took her phone out of his pocket, swore, and pulled out his.

Lyn tried to pull his hand closer to her body. "Can you hear the music? It's beautiful. Dance with me, Scout. "

"The battery on your phone is dead. Time to switch." He thumbed a few times at the screen with his free hand.

Lyn ripped her hands out of his and pulled the earbuds out of her ears. "Too loud."

"I'm sorry. I didn't realize how high the volume was. I'll turn the volume down, but please put them back in." He reached for one and slid his fingers down her head to brush her hair back away from her ear.

Lyn shuddered and closed her eyes as he replaced the tiny devices in her ears. "Lyn, are you still with me?"

She nodded but her eyes remained closed.

"Words, please, so I know for sure."

She opened her eyes. "I'm here. I'm okay, but you can't touch me like that..."

"I'm sorry." He cut her off and pulled his hands away. "But you have to be careful not to lose control this far into the game. You still have to out stubborn the Queen of Summer."

She nodded again. She had a strong stubborn streak, but was it stronger than the Summer Queen? "She's more obstinate than her sister."

He nodded and checked the battery level on his phone. "The battery is at fifty percent."

The stubborn slowness of time and the fickleness of battery power would force her hand and there was no way to know how long Summer would hold out.

She picked up the water damaged notebook and sat in her camp chair to begin brainstorming. She wrote "Plan B" across the top of the page. Nothing followed. She rubbed at her face to erase the tingle where Scout had touched her. The lingering feeling was as distracting as the fairy music. "Volume up, please." Lyn took a deep breath and focused on the words she wrote at the top of the blank page. She traced the letters again leaving the black ink thicker.

Scout sat next to her, his eyes focused on the corner of the cabin and his foot tapped on the packed dirt.

~

A while later her paper was still excruciatingly blank. She dug the tip of the pen into the page and pulled slowly down, leaving a gash in this page and several beyond it.

She looked down at Scout's phone. Twenty percent

battery. "I don't suppose we have any power bricks laying around?"

Scout shook his head. He didn't look at her. He sat in his chair with his arms crossed staring at the space between the cabin and the nearest tree. "I wish we'd left the generator running. We should have been charging something."

"We are going to need to make a move soon."

Scout stood up and extended his hand to help her out of her chair. Silence hung between them.

"You trust me that much, huh?" She wanted him to say something. Anything. She'd been sitting here for however long, failing to come up with a plan and she needed him to talk to her. "This isn't going to work out. I can't…"

Scout turned to her. His face looked crushed, like she had kicked a puppy and thrown it after him afterwards.

"I can't do this. I let you down and not even you think I can pull this off anymore." A tear slid from her eye. "You and Jake trusted me and Summer isn't folding. She's not intimidated by me. I'm just an inconvenience, she's probably figured out six ways to end me, while I have nothing."

Scout grabbed her by the shoulders. "Stop talking." He lifted her face gently with his hands so she would meet his eyes. "I have the utmost confidence in your ability to get yourself out of this crazy genetic nightmare. I believe in you more than you know. I wish Greg were here so I could force him to sit and watch as you best another fairy queen. I hate that witch for binding not only your genes but your confidence. I'd kill her myself if she hadn't age to dust the day you took her down. I hate Greg and Killian and even Umiko for not letting you see how powerful you can be when you make your own choices." It was his turn to hang his head. "I hate myself for not being able to show you and for not being as strong as you."

Tears fell down Lyn's cheek. "I'm not strong." She tried to pull her head away.

Scout held fast. "Bullshit," he said, more firm than he had ever talked to her. "I know you're struggling not to run right now. Run from me. Run from her. Run from everyone, but you haven't. You haven't run to hide since I stole you from your safe space with the noxious mushrooms. You didn't run when you were faced with your mother's grave or her face today. You are strong and you can do this. I am proud to be able to stand by your side and witness. I look forward to the moment I get to take you home and rub your accomplishments in their faces. I will gloat with the very best of the gloaters when I tell them that I was right and they were wrong." He wiped her tears away. "I'm sorry my brooding made you doubt yourself, but my attitude has nothing to do with my confidence in you and everything to do with that insidious music."

She nodded.

"Close your eyes." She did as he asked and her eyelashes forced the rest of the tears to vacate. Scout's lips brushed one eye then the other. "Maybe now, you'll see it too."

She kept her eyes closed and he pulled her close.

"So," he said over her head, "we have a battery problem, right?"

She nodded against his chest.

"What should we do about it?"

"We have to force the timeline. We can't keep waiting."

Scout nodded. "Lead the way." He let go of her. "Please don't take out the earbuds. The music is intoxicating and hard for me to resist and I'm not as sensitive as you are. If my phone battery gets too low we have to get to Jake's and pray there's a decent charge left on it."

Lyn straightened her spine and took a step back. She wiped her face on the hem of her skirt leaving a trail of damp and more than a little snot. Lyn ripped the current page out of her notebook and folded it into a neat square. She inhaled and exhaled as deep as she could and looked at Scout. He beamed at her.

Before she could second guess herself, Lyn turned and stepped around the cabin to see the gathered fairy guests dancing in opposition to the sound that was filtering through Lyn's head. The dancers were energetic but waning. The grass beneath them was trampled flat. The flowers Summer brought with her were smeared under their feet. One fell to a knee, but another helped her get to her feet again and continue dancing.

Jake and Nix were sitting on the ground where she had left them, unmoved by the music. Was Nix immune to the pull of the notes? But surely, Jake would be swept up, if Scout was having trouble.

"Does the music not affect our brother?"

"I've been fighting that infernal drum beat since it started. I've sung every song I can remember to myself twice, sometimes mangling the words because I can't concentrate. It might not affect me the same way it affects you, but it's taking a toll and I'm fighting back. Look at Bro's foot. He's tapping but the beat is off. He's doing something similar to counter whatever it is she's trying to accomplish. It's a gambit and it's failing and she knows it, but if you could make it stop, I'd be more than a little grateful. I've resorted to ear worms from children's TV shows that will probably keep me awake for weeks."

Lyn didn't have time to consider the implications of what she was seeing, because her battery would drain quickly from this point. Without looking at Summer, she walked toward Jake.

Jake said something to Nix that held him in place then met Lyn and Scout a decent distance away from Nix but not out of earshot of the Summer Queen.

Lyn leaned in to whisper and handed Jake the folded

square of paper. "Winter," was all Lyn got to say before the Summer Queen spoke up.

"What exactly was your deal with my sister?" Summer asked over the music.

Lyn turned to the Queen. "I'm not sure if that is your concern." Lyn started to turn back to Jake.

"Surely, if I am to agree to an equitable deal, I must first know the deal we are equalling."

Lyn sighed and considered. "Part of the negotiations was that if I failed, I would slit my own throat after that of my mother's."

"And you are prepared to do so."

Lyn didn't hesitate. She turned to Jake, and held out her uninjured hand, palm up. "Your knife?"

Jake blinked his eyes at her request. He leaned in to whisper. "I'm not comfortable with this. You've been crying."

"Loyalty, unconditionally and without bounds," she whispered back as low as she could.

Jake reached inside his pocket and retrieved his knife. He reluctantly handed it to her, gripping her hand longer than necessary.

Lyn pulled her hand away and flicked open the knife in an impressive display she didn't know she could pull off.

The queen snapped and the music halted. Her entourage fell to their knees, exhausted. She waved her people farther away and the few that could stand drug the ones that could not. "But you don't even know which of my people is your mother. Or if she is even here in my company." The Queen lowered her voice. "Surely you would not risk your life without first finding out."

"I would not, however, I know which of your people is my target." Lyn matched her volume and pointed to the woman standing over the queen's right shoulder. The one wearing Lyn's mother's face.

Lyn saw a flash of anger on Summer's face, followed

quickly by something akin to fear before it one again settled into a fake pleasant smile.

"You should also know that a second condition of the deal I struck with Winter was that if I fall, my second will continue in my place."

"With another knife?" Summer laughed. "Or is he fast enough to recover yours before my people end him?" The two figures flanking the Queen stepped forward with their hands on something at their hips.

Lyn pushed her advantage. "I have to admit, being raised by humans, I am ignorant of many things creature, but if I am not mistaken, you still bleed. My companions are deadly fast, even in this heat. They need only seconds to rip open your throat with their teeth. Surely, you have noticed that they are not as human as they seem." Lyn sat back down at her place by the table. "But I'm sure we can make a deal that won't lead to bloodshed between creatures."

Summer pulled her feet under her and snapped at her attendants to leave.

A thunderstorm rumbled in the distance, at odds with the sunny sky above them.

Lyn leaned forward and held the open knife in her hand on the table's top. "In exchange for the release of my mother from her bond with Summer, and the recognized neutrality and safety of every Mimic, I will never fight for Winter." Lyn leaned closer to whisper just to the Queen. "Or Summer."

"And if I don't?" The queen countered with her own whisper.

Lyn sat back and raised her voice to a conversational level. "Then I will be done negotiating and you will have forced my hand." Lyn pinched Scout's leg though his jeans and he let out a fierce animalistic growl which he held much longer than her fingers pinched. She knew his claws would be visible and his eyes more recognizable as wolf.

Nix shifted to a white wolf without a sound and Lyn heard Jake's growl added to Scout's.

Lyn smiled across the table. "Do we have a deal?"

Before the Queen answered, Anada's form shifted to Jake's wolf and bared his teeth. Lyn instantly knew what Jake had meant by 'Troy.' She now had a man on the inside.

"Well," the queen raised her voice for her people to hear. "I have tired of this handmaiden, her glamours are no longer pleasing to my eyes. I would kill her myself, but she is more useful to me as a trade. You can have her in exchange for your neutrality."

"And that of all Mimics."

"Yes, of course, if they will not fight for my sister. They can have their neutrality too." Summer snapped her fingers. "So be it."

Lyn felt the tinge of electricity in the air as the deal sealed.

The Queen stood and turned her back on Lyn. She walked out of the glade, leaving her loyal and exhausted subjects to gather the table, chairs, and other items.

Lyn stood and Scout placed his hand on her back to steady her weakened knees. She closed the knife and held it tight. They didn't move again until the last of the fairies vacated their land and the temperature dropped to a very cool and reasonable June temperature. Warm, but pleasant after the Summer Queen's influence.

Jake ran over and picked Lyn up. He swung her around in a circle fast enough that her legs spun out behind her like she was three years old. "Way to go, Sis." He let gravity pull her down again and hugged her.

She pulled away from him and he let go. He leaned close, keeping his face and voice from Scout. "Why were you crying before? Do I need to pummel Scout? I will. I'll take him out back and beat him blue if he made you cry."

"I'm hungry and my nerves are frayed beyond and I didn't run but I wanted to and I could really go for a burger and fries and maybe a strawberry milkshake." She felt her eyes filling with water again.

"I will get you whatever you want for dinner. You've earned it. But can't you just remember what it was like to be full?" Jake laughed.

"I'm not sure she's ever been full." Scout teased as he came up behind her and wrapped his arms around her shoulders.

Jake laughed "May I have my knife back, please?" When she handed it to him, he took off down the path to the cars as fast as Lyn had ever seen him run on two legs.

"Tell the gang, I'll be home tomorrow." Lyn shouted.

Jake flashed her a thumbs up before he disappeared into the brush at the far edge of the clearing.

Lyn turned to the figures embracing.

"I guess that's what Nix meant about all the forms." Lyn watched as the two figures kissed and melted between forms, not stopping on any one for longer than the moment it took to breathe.

She turned away and left them to their reunion.

CHAPTER FORTY-FOUR

*L*yn sat in the camp chair she had claimed as her own. Scout stood beside her, his hand feathered through his hair from front to back, leaving a trail of angry porcupine quills in its wake.

"That was amazing. I wasn't sure you were going to pull it off. I mean, Summer is stubborn. Worse than Killian and you combined."

His energy was bubbling out through his words and he wouldn't stop moving. She wondered if he was going to run off out of pure excitement.

"You didn't trust me?" She rounded on him. "I went out there thinking I could do the thing, because you told me I could do the thing, and you weren't sure I could pull it off?"

Scout lifted his hands and waved them in surrender. "Oh, no, I trusted you completely, but I still didn't know if you were going to pull it off." He crouched down in front of her. "When you asked Jake for his knife, I nearly had a heart attack." Scout placed his hands on her knees. "It took every ounce of will I had to stand down. My wolf was so close to taking over that I almost had a matching scar." He looked into her eyes. "You did it and now I get to gloat." His lips turned up in a huge grin. "I'm going to enjoy telling people that my girlf... what you accomplished today, without the details of course." He stood up and turned away.

"I still have to find the girl." Lyn sighed. She wasn't finished yet. She didn't know where the girl was or what she looked like or how to find her, but she made a promise to Jonathan, even if it didn't come with a joy buzzer shock ,and she would fulfill it even if he wasn't around to benefit. She owed it to the girl, if no one else.

Scout sat down at her feet and leaned back on her legs. "You'll do that, too."

"You mean you won't help?" She teased him.

He turned to face her. "Lyn Davis," he whispered, "I would do anything you asked me to, except walk away."

Lyn's chest tightened at the thought of him walking away from her. She didn't want him to ever walk away. She liked the person she was when he was around and he was pretty cool himself. "Then I won't ask." She smiled as she watched his expression puzzle over her words.

"Lyn?" Nix's voice called from beyond the cabin corner.

"Yes, Nix." Lyn called and Scout turned around. He leaned back on her legs.

"Anada would like to meet you." Nix said

A woman, paler than Lyn, but with the same long white hair stepped forward, slowly. Her cloud like eyes stared at Lyn like she was afraid Lyn might bolt if she got too close.

Lyn tensed her legs to stand, and Scout leaped to his feet. She reached for Scout's hand, he accepted it and stood at her side.

"Okay," Lyn said, "but I'm tired and hungry and my battery died and I don't think I can stay calm."

Scout squeezed her hand again.

Lyn's eyes filled with tears at each step her biological mother took toward her. Lyn wanted desperately for this woman, whom she had never met, to care and to understand,

and to want to be more than some vague memory and a source of unanswered questions.

Anada stopped when she was a foot away from Lyn. "I am so proud of you. Thank you." She folded and unfolded her hands in front of her stomach. Twisting them with the nerves Lyn felt strumming inside of herself.

Lyn nodded. "Now, you owe me." Lyn laughed, thinking about the rules of fairy. She wiped tears from her face with the back of the hand that wasn't clutching Scout's for support.

"I'm happy with that." Anada said, her own eyes more fluid than they should be. "Do you mind if I hug you?"

"I would like that very much." Lyn folded her arms around her mother and her mother folded back.

CHAPTER FORTY-FIVE

cool breeze blew in from the shallow creek and Lyn was mesmerized by the blinking of lightning bugs, like little moving stars.

Lyn shifted her eyes to fairy sight and smiled. They weren't all lightning bugs.

Jake returned with burgers, fries, and milkshakes from a little mom and pop burger joint nearby. Plus, several bottles of pre-chilled sparkling water. "To celebrate!" he said.

They ate in a comfortable silence as the sun continued to give way to darkness. Stars spread across the sky and Lyn breathed in the peace that had settled around the group. She took another sip of her milkshake. The burger and fries had filled the void in her stomach, but the milkshake soothed her. She looked around at the faces of the people around her. Her mom and her mom's husband. Her fake brother and Scout. It felt right, almost like a real family.

Anada and Nix sat near the fire, his arm draped over her shoulders. Her head leaned into the crook of his armpit. Jake sat in his chair, his phone in his hand, his thumb racing across the screen, probably texting Veronica. Scout sat next to Lyn with a grin a mile wide on his face. Every once in a while, he'd shake his head or laugh at something unknown to the rest of them.

Anada caught Lyn's eyes and smiled. "Tell me about your childhood?"

Lyn told her about everything except the witch, but assured her that the mother they placed her with loved her and took care of her as if she was her own.

Once one question was asked and answered, it opened a floodgate of others. Everyone had questions.

Lyn wanted to know about her dad. Anada said she didn't keep in contact, but that he was a shifter of notable rank and good breeding stock. She never told him about Lyn.

Anada explained how she had to give Lyn up when she found out that Lyn's life was in danger from the queens. "It was a risk I had to take, or you would have been raised to be a tool for one side or the other."

Lyn asked about the baby that Lyn was traded for. Nix said he had hidden her away the day of the birth and she was happy and content living among the wild fae. Her new family treated her as well as Lyn's had and she even picked up a knack for fairy magic in the process.

Hearing about the child pulled on Lyn's heart. She was going to find her, but tonight there were other things to talk about.

"You switched places with Anada in Summer when you disappeared this morning?" Lyn asked Nix. "How did you know what my human mom looked like?" She asked Anada, who looked to Nix. "I assumed you wouldn't have made contact if you hid me there. It's easier to keep a secret you don't know."

"You are right. I didn't know anything about the mother." Anada admitted. "As much as I wanted to keep tabs on my baby, on you, it was far safer for you that way."

Lyn shared a look with Scout, but stayed silent about her supposed safety.

"Nix found the witch and brokered the deal on my behalf." Anada said. "I knew she handled changeling swaps, but I was running out of time and couldn't stop running long enough to do it myself. He vet the mother, as well. We are very selective about where we place our children. I'm not sure how he convinced her to share her face, but he has convinced mothers to do far more and I am glad she agreed."

Children. Lyn latched onto the word and held onto it as the conversation flowed on. She wasn't the only one.

Nix spoke next. "I'm sorry to say that I tricked her out of it when the birth had her vulnerable, but you were the first Anada tried to spirit away. When we realized we would not be able to keep you safe ourselves, we wanted you safe for as long as possible. Even so, I knew that one day they would find you. How did you stay hidden?" Nix asked. Even Anada looked curious.

"You mean, you don't know?" Lyn asked, her face screwed up in doubt.

Nix and Anada shook their heads.

Lyn's pulse quickened. Lyn's chair shrank. Scout was too close. She couldn't move her legs or catch her breath. Her foot began to tap near Scout's hip. She hadn't wanted to talk about Ms. Evans and the binding and the blood and the nightmares.

"Breathe," Scout said to Lyn. To Nix and Anada, he spoke for Lyn. "The witch you chose bound Lyn's creature traits. Lyn's mimic skills, or the binding, or a combination of both, hid her as a human for sixteen years. When her human mother died, the binding started unraveling." His hand moved up and down Lyn's shin bringing warmth and a modicum of calm.

She closed her eyes and focused on his touch.

"She has been mimicking the binding off and on since it faded, but she didn't know what she was doing until recently." Scout finished.

"Do you know how?" Nix asked.

Lyn shook her head. Her nerves close to the surface. "I just...remember. Like you said."

"Can you show us?" Anada's eyes begged.

Lyn closed her eyes and shifted her features to the girl she had seen in the mirror when her mother was still alive. She opened her eyes and looked at the four people around her circle.

Jake sat quietly, watching the two new mimics, while Scout continued to rub her calf.

Anada and Nix looked from Lyn to each other and back again.

Lyn crossed her arms and ran her hands down her biceps as the two mimics examined her features. The pressure of their eyes on her was too much.

Anada and Nix shared a look and shook their heads.

"May we have that form?" Anada asked after a moment.

"If we can figure out what's different, we may be able to reproduce it." Nix added.

Everyone looked at Lyn. "You think you can reproduce a binding spell just from..."

Anada smiled. "You are just now coming into your skills, which I'm sorry about, but there are things which we can do that you can't even imagine right now. I'm not sure we can reproduce this binding, but that's not going to stop us from trying. The Queens might live up to their end of the deal for now, but we'd like every advantage we can get to protect our children in the future. Hopefully, without enlisting the help of a witch next time."

Lyn's foot still tapped by Scout's hip. She took a deep breath and looked at the faces around the fire. "I think being calm all day is ending. I'm not going to hold it in much longer. I need a run."

Scout stood up and reached for Lyn's hand. He pulled her to standing and took her seat. "Sit, please. I'm sure you have a little more calm in you."

She sat between his legs, her butt on the edge of the chair. Scout put his hands on her neck and found her pulse. He tapped it down, holding her together a little longer. He leaned forward to whisper in her ear. "We'll run before bed. There's a waterfall you should see before we leave and I think moonlight will be more than adequate." His breath on Lyn's ear made her pulse skip and his touch on her neck started a new, slower rhythm.

"Another time, perhaps." Anada's face showed no signs of disappointment.

Lyn nodded. "Where is the girl?" Lyn looked at Nix.

"I'll bring her to you tomorrow," he said.

"We will," Anada said with a look at Nix.

I'm going to see her. I'm going to get the meet the girl whose family I...stole. Lyn's face fell. "We won't be here," she said. "I have a mess at home I need to straighten out. We're leaving after breakfast. Can I give you an address? It's about an hour, maybe two, from here? Do you drive? Or would changing locations be an inconvenience?" Lyn felt her pulse speed up again.

"We can find our way to your address," Nix said.

"Your house or ours?" Jake asked. "If you go to yours, the whole gang will get involved. I can take mom and V out to lunch tomorrow and you can have our place to yourself."

Lyn shook off his offer. "My house." Lyn steadied her breathing, but a hitch caught in her chest. "It needs to be my house." Lyn felt the tingle at the end of her nose that meant tears were coming. "It's her house too."

CHAPTER FORTY-SIX

Jake put away his camping gear and headed back to town to meet up with Veronica for a late movie, leaving Scout and Lyn alone in the woods. Again.

"Race?" he asked, pulling the shirt off his back.

Lyn turned around to face him. "Yes, please!" She reached down and grabbed the hem of her dress in her fists.

Scout turned around and listened for her stifled shift-growl before unzipping his pants. His head shot up. "Hey! You don't have to shift that way, anymore." He turned around, but Lyn's snow white wolf was already running. He shifted with a pained grunt turned howl and dashed after her.

Lyn ran to the fence between Scout's family land and state park land, then doubled back. When she met up with Scout's wolf, she leaped at him, throwing him to the ground before she leaped away again.

Scout gathered his feet beneath him and raced to tag her back.

Three tags later, Lyn's snowy white wolf laid on the ground with her neck exposed and her tongue hanging out.

Scout's wolf crawled over to her, his belly low but his legs ready to push up in case of an ambush. When none came, he laid nose to nose and watched her breathe.

After catching his breath, Scout shifted and, when he was fully clothed, brought Lyn her dress and his hoodie for warmth.

He walked to the center of the open grove and laid on his back. Lyn joined him a shift later.

"What about the waterfall?" Scout asked. "It's a bit dark, but..."

She shushed him. "We should save something for next time."

Scout rolled over on his side and looked at Lyn. He was beyond excited that there would be a next time.

Lyn looked at the sky, undimmed by light pollution.

He took her hand in his. "I promise to never tell anyone your creature types."

Lyn tried to drop his hand as the static built, but Scout held on until the feeling faded.

"You didn't have to do that," she said. "I trust you." She turned on her side and put her head on her bent arm.

"I know. But I wanted to. I don't think anyone should know. If the wrong people found out, then..." He didn't want to think about it, much less say it out loud. She would always be in danger. The world might eventually accept some creatures, but Lyn was too dangerous to be accepted and allowed to live on her own terms.

"Then I would have to negotiate my freedom all over again." She sighed.

He nodded. "It was tricky enough the first time."

Scout was moments away from telling Lyn how he felt when she turned her head back to the sky.

"It will be hard to keep it a secret. I'll need to get Umiko to stop trying to figure me out. I'm not sure that's even possible."

"Greg too," Scout added. "Killian at least will be easy. He couldn't care less what you are, just who you're with."

Lyn nodded with a sigh and closed her eyes.

"Lyn," Scout said.

"Scout," Lyn said at the same time.

He nodded at her to go first.

"I want to tell you something," she looked away, "but I need to talk to Greg first. Can I get a rain check on our talk for twenty-four hours?" She turned her green eyes toward Scout. "No longer. I promise."

Scout searched her face. His chest ached with unspoken words. He already knew he would follow her anywhere, now he knew he'd wait for her too. "Okay," he laid on his back and looked at the stars. "How many constellations do you know?"

"Ummm, probably zero. Give or take another zero."

He smiled. "Want to?"

"Sure."

Scout wiggled and squirmed on the ground until his head was as close to Lyn's as he could make it. He lifted a hand to point to the sky. "Ursa Major and Ursa Minor are the easiest to find, although most people just stop with a small portion of their constellations. You might have heard of them. The big and little dippers."

Lyn punched him in the arm.

Scout laughed and took her hand. "Roman mythology holds that Jupiter's wife, Juno, discovered he was hung up on a girl named Callisto. Juno believed Callisto's son, Arcas, to be Jupiter's and turned her into a bear so he would no longer be attracted to her. Arcas, a hunter at the time, almost shot Callisto but Jupiter interfered by turning him into a bear as well and putting them both in the night sky."

"If you know a story about every constellation it's going to be a long night."

"I can keep the stories to myself if you like, and just point out the pretty pictures."

"No, I like hearing you talk, but you might have to carry me to the tent if you tell too many." Lyn yawned.

Scout was tired too. He knew that tomorrow was going to be the longest day in the history of long days, and if Greg fought for her it might never end.

They stared out at the galaxy in silence.

I'll fight for you.

CHAPTER FORTY-SEVEN

Scout and Lyn woke up with the sun early the next morning to clean up camp, but it took much longer than it should have.

Lyn scrubbed the dishes well past the point of clean and dried them until there wasn't a hint of moisture left, while Scout tackled the tent, and refolded the sleeping bags.

Once the tent was stored, he stuffed the rest into a laundry basket and set it outside the cabin's front door. They'd have to hike it out and take it home in order to wash and return the next visit.

Scout did other small jobs while Lyn swept the cabin floor. She suspected that the fire pit did not actually need to be mucked out, and that he was stalling, but she was fine with that. After all she had to go home and piss off three people. She'd rather clean the cabin until it sparkled.

Lyn tossed the contents of the dust pan into the trash bag and gathered the scant laundry that she had borrowed into the basket with the sleeping bags. She was relieved when the pants and shirt she had borrowed reverted back to their normal shape, but they needed a wash as badly as she did.

Scout gathered up the trash and checked the gas levels in the generator and the ATV.

Finally, there was nothing else to be done. The cabin was cleaner than when they arrived. Scout walked Lyn out of the front door and fumbled with his keys at the lock.

Lyn picked them up when they fell. "Are you okay?"

"I'm just not sure I'm ready to go back to the real world." He locked the door. They divided up the gear to take with them and walked away from the cabin.

"Where are the sim cards?" Lyn asked as they neared Scout's Land Rover.

He tossed the trash bag into the back of his car along with the laundry and dug in his pocket for his phone and both sims, as well as the safety pin he had neglected to return to Jake. He handed all of them to Lyn as he opened her door.

"Which is whose?" She held the identical tiny rectangle pieces of plastic in her palm.

"I have no idea." He chuckled and closed the door.

She picked a card at random and slid it into her phone, then did the same with his. "New sim cards tomorrow?"

He nodded and backed the Rover out of its hiding place and down the thin wooded driveway.

She plugged both devices into the car's outlet as Scout backed out onto asphalt. "Or we can figure out whose is whose and go back to the way things were," Scout said.

She hesitated for a moment before answering. "I'd rather not," Lyn said. She meant it about the sim cards and her life. She hoped he felt the same. "If you don't have plans tomorrow. Let's do phones and lunch."

Scout looked at Lyn, then at the lack of traffic as he drove back toward town. "I would love to have lunch with you."

"Good," Lyn said and looked out the window. "I'm throwing a party tonight at my house. Will you come?"

"Of course."

As soon as Scout turned onto the highway, the phones had

enough power for notifications to start blinking awake the screens.

Lyn ignored the phones until the flashes stopped.

"What are you going to tell them?" Scout asked.

She looked at the phones as if they were tiny bombs about to explode. She picked up hers and dialed Umiko.

Her best friend picked up on the first ring. "Scout, where's Lyn? Is she okay?"

"It's me. I'm fine." Lyn held the phone out from her ear as questions tumbled out of the speaker. Of course she had questions. Lyn had neglected to tell her anything for days. Lyn tried to ignore the stab of guilt.

When Umiko's questions were spent, Lyn put the phone back to her ear.

"Well?" Umiko asked.

"Want to plan a party?"

"Of course!" Umiko squealed, temporarily distracted.

Lyn needed to explain things to Umiko, but that conversation was best had in person.

Umiko had already begun running with the party idea. Her will to organize things far exceeded Lyn's. She would pull off the last minute party with minimal effort.

"Great. Q&A at five o'clock. My house. I have a meeting this morning that I need to have alone. If ANYONE shows up before five, I will be furious." Lyn said. "Got it?"

Umiko was silent for a moment.

"Umiko?"

Umiko sighed. "Sure, I got it. Five pm, your house, no earlier under threat of teeth and claws."

"Thank you. Can you tell the usual suspects? Killian too."

"Yeah. Are you sure about Killian? He and Greg aren't… "

"Five p.m. Both of them. Or no Q&A." Lyn only wanted to be grilled once, if that. She didn't see a way out of answering questions, but she'd have them on her terms or not at all. She knew Umiko's curiosity would see that Lyn's demands were met.

"Alright." Umiko agreed without further argument.

"Good. Then I will see you at the back gate at four." She would have invited her friend over earlier, but she had no idea when Nix and Anada would arrive. An hour would give them plenty of time to get party ready.

"Deal." Umiko agreed and Lyn knew she was excited to be getting special BFF privileges.

"Scout needs to use his phone, I'll see you later." Lyn hung up after waiting a suitable amount of time to listen to Umiko's closing.

"That's your phone." Scout said and turned on his blinker to change lanes.

"With your sim," Lyn said but didn't bother to change out the cards. She stared straight ahead and wished for road construction to delay her confrontation with her friends, then she thought better of it. She was going to meet her... Lyn struggled to find a word. *My sister? My sister!* She would not be adding complications to their relationship. This one would be simple.

"Are you going to change the sims?" Scout asked.

"Not unless you want me to." Lyn said. "I want Jake to come tonight. He can bring Veronica."

"You can call him while I drive. He'll like getting a call from his sister." Scout smirked.

She picked up his phone and looked down Scout's list of favorites for Jake's name, but didn't see it.

"He's listed under Jackass." Scout chuckled.

"You guys and your code names." Lyn pushed to call with a smile on her face. She wondered what she'd be listed under on both brothers' phones. She almost scrolled to find out, but the call to Jake connected before she could.

Scout spoke before Jake did. "You should see what he has me listed as on his phone. Or maybe not."

"Good morning, little sister," Jake said through a yawn. "How was your evening? And morning?"

"Sorry if I woke you up."

"Don't be. Just know, you are the only one that can get away with it other than V."

"Do you have plans tonight around five?" She paused while he spoke. "Do you think she'll be interested in a party at my house?" More pause. "That's fine. See you then."

"Is that everyone?" Scout asked.

"Yeah." Lyn said and put the phone to sleep. She didn't know what she was going to tell them. Certainly not everything. She'd have to be just as careful with her wording as she was with the fairy queens, and even then she'd need to fairy deal them to secrecy just in case. She picked up her phone and opened the notes app.

"Great, play me some tunes." Scout requested.

"What are you in the mood for?"

"Surprise me."

She picked up Scout's phone, made sure it connected to the Rover's speakers over bluetooth, and picked a playlist.

Straight No Chaser's version of "I won't give up" began playing.

CHAPTER FORTY-EIGHT

"I'll be back at five," Scout said as he pulled into Lyn's driveway.

"Unless you want to come earlier." Lyn hoped he'd come early. She got out of the car and Scout rolled down the window so she could close the door.

"As much as I want to spend the whole day with you, I think I will be back at five. I don't want to be third wheel to girl time with your..." He drew out the word as if searching for the next one.

"Sister."

"With your sister. I also have some things to do before tonight." Scout stayed in the driveway as she walked to her front door.

Two roses lay on her mat, one pink, one red, and an envelope with her name on it. She picked them up and opened the door. Once inside, she closed and locked the door and tossed the items from the mat onto the coffee table. She ran upstairs, discarding clothing as she went. She wanted a long bubble bath and a pair of jeans that were her own.

Lyn settled for a shower with two full rounds of soap, and

a second hair wash, since she didn't know when her guests would arrive.

~

*L*yn wore her favorite jeans and a pale pink scoop neck T-shirt. She decided on curly brown hair and green eyes, a little piece of her mom that could meet her real daughter. Lyn ugly cried at that thought, but she gave herself five minutes and when her time was up, she dried her face and went down stairs.

She was starting to worry they wouldn't come, that they wouldn't be able to find her house, or that her sister wouldn't want to meet her. Maybe she had taken too long in the shower and they had come and gone already? She was pacing the living room when she heard a knock at her door. She looked through the peephole.

A dark skinned man, with dark hair peeped back at her. A face she recognized. She flung open the door and it bounced off the wall nearly hitting her on the rebound.

"Nix! You're here! Welcome, please come in."

Nix stepped in and stood to the side of the door to give the two faces behind him a better view.

"Lyn, this is Nelu," he said as a girl Lyn's age, but shorter, lifted her hand in greeting. Her hair was the same curly brown as her mother's. Her skin had a warm honey glow, and her eyes were brown like Jonathan's.

Lyn was speechless. The girl was the perfect combination of Jonathan and Maria. "Nelu?"

"I'm named after a flower. Nelumbo nucifera, the sacred lotus. It was blooming the night I was born. Nice to meet you."

"It's a beautiful name. Please come in, Nelu. Anada."

"I've never been in a human house." Nelu said.

Lyn's heart broke and she took in a slow, deep breath to

266

keep from crying. She had stolen this girl's life, or rather it was stolen on her behalf. She'd have a long way to go to repay the debt. "Would you like me to show you around?" Lyn asked eagerly.

The girl nodded.

Lyn led her guests around the house that was too large for just herself and tried to figure out how to accommodate a sister. It would be easy enough to change rooms, unless Nelu wanted the bigger one. Lyn wouldn't fight her for it, if she wanted it.

"I could move into our mother's room and you can have mine." Lyn said as they made it to the second floor and she opened the door to her room. She was glad she took the time to straighten things a bit. "Or you can have the bigger one."

"Oh, no, I can't stay here. It's too… closed." Nelu gestured with her hands.

Lyn looked at Nix and Anada.

"When you get used to living under an open sky, people houses are…" Nix explained.

"Confining." Anada said, finishing her husband's sentence with a sad smile.

"But, it's …" Lyn started, but stopped. She understood the draw of an open sky now that she'd seen one herself. The pin prickling light of stars, the sound of crickets and other nocturnal animals.

"Nelu, tell Lyn about your home." Anada interrupted Lyn's thoughts.

"Can we go outside first?" Nelu asked. "The air is wrong and I don't like feeling trapped."

Lyn smiled at that commonality between them and led them to the backyard.

"You have no flowers." Nelu said as she dashed into the backyard and spun slowly around with her arms out. The sun shone down on her making her spiced honey hair glow. "Your trees are sad." Nelu looked at her feet. "Why is your grass crunchy?"

"I take it your trees and grass are much happier than mine?" Lyn smiled, a new idea forming.

"I live near a field of wildflowers that dance like grounded rainbows. In the warm months it is filled with the flower I'm named after. But the grass is always soft beneath my feet and I'm the only one of my siblings that can touch the tree branches without jumping."

Lyn listened as the girl told her about her home. She couldn't help but smile at the joy in the girl's face at the telling.

"She's happy and safe?" Lyn asked later of Nix and Anada when Nelu was occupied with a single wild onion growing near the fence line.

"Did you think otherwise?" Anada asked, puzzled.

Lyn shook her head. "I think humans get a lot of things wrong."

"Can I have your four leaf clovers?" Nelu called to Lyn.

Lyn didn't even know she had any, so she wouldn't miss them. "They are all yours, Nelu. Take as many as you can find."

"She'll take them all," Anada warned like they were precious and not just a weed.

Lyn smiled. "I want her to have them." Lyn turned to Nix. "Can you excuse me a minute? I want her to have something else, but I have to find it, first."

Lyn dashed through the house to the garage and turned on the light.

Mountains of cardboard boxes greeted her ominously.

She would need to take Scout up on his offer to clean out Jonathan's stuff. Most of it she was sure would end up being donated, but the few sentimental items kept her from wanting to start the process. She couldn't bring herself to open time bombs of a relationship she wasn't privileged enough to be a part of and had caused to self-destruct.

The box from the hospital with her mom's personal items was hard enough and this was a lot more boxes. It had been months since she had taken ownership and Lyn still did not know what was in any of them beyond her friend's handwritten sharpie labels.

"Thanks, Umiko," Lyn said aloud when she found the box she was looking for with her best friend's neat script on the side. "Photos," the box read.

She ripped the tape with a sharp creature nail and rummaged in the loose photos for one of Maria and Jonathan together. Both of them looked younger and Lyn didn't recognize the background. A college dorm, maybe?

She raced back to the yard with the photo clutched to her chest.

"Nelu?" Lyn said as she walked to the girl sitting in a small patch of green clover.

The girl looked up at her, several clovers in her hand.

"These are your parents, Maria and Jonathan. They very much wanted to meet you but..." Lyn choked on her words. It turned out it was harder than she thought to tell someone their parents were dead. She felt bad for the people she had snapped at now that she was in their place.

Nelu took the photo in exchange for a clover she was holding. She looked at it with her head tilted and rubbed the images of their faces with an index finger.

"What were they like?" Nelu asked.

Lyn sat in the crunchy grass and told Nelu all about Maria and what little she knew of Jonathan. She stopped several times to take a deep breath and wipe her tears away, but Nelu was patient.

Her sister leaned close to Lyn and whispered, "I'm not supposed to say it, but thank you."

"Thank you, Nelu." Lyn smiled. "Is it okay if I call you my sister?"

The girl nodded. "Sisters get to see a lot of each other. Will we?"

"I'd love that. You can visit anytime you like," Lyn said.

"My mom might want to meet you, my brothers and sisters for sure will," Nelu said and stood up. "We can go now. They'll be so excited."

Lyn stood up and walked with Nelu back to where Nix and Anada were standing on the porch. "Um…I can't today," Lyn said.

"Tomorrow, then?" Nelu said.

Lyn looked at her new sister with sadness. " I don't think tomorrow will work for a visit either."

"Nelu," Anada took the girl's hand. "We still need to be careful."

"We'll try when we can." Nix added.

Nelu nodded and turned to Lyn. "When you can."

Lyn nodded and hugged her sister. She would have to make that happen sooner rather than later.

"But I can come here. Anytime." The girl said into Lyn's hair and hugged her back.

"I'll show you where the key is," Lyn agreed, pulling her sister back to the porch.

Lyn wanted Nelu to stay for the party, but she also didn't want to bombard the girl with the drama that would surely unfold. They sat on the porch and had their own little question and answer session. Lyn was excited to learn that Nelu liked to dance as much as she did.

Lyn turned on a short playlist and the girls danced around the backyard until Lyn's alarm sounded and Nix and Anada stood up.

"We should go." Nix held out his hand for Nelu. "You're mom will be wondering why you aren't home yet."

Nelu took his hand, but pulled away just before they entered the house and rushed back to Lyn.

The two girls held each other and promised to see each other very soon.

Lyn walked the three of them to the front door and pushed back tears as she said good-bye to her sister, her mother, and an ally.

She closed the door and pressed her forehead to the cool surface.

"Lyn?" Umiko's voice called from the backyard.

Lyn brushed the damp from her eyes and prepared a smile for her best friend.

CHAPTER FORTY-NINE

*U*miko came through the back fence at exactly four p.m. She barely closed the gate behind her before she turned and ran through Lyn's yard. "Spill it! Are you okay? Where were you? What were you doing?" Umiko asked. "What about Scout? Why didn't you tell me you were going out of town?"

Lyn gave her friend a big bear hug. Umiko squeezed back and tried to pull away, but Lyn didn't let go.

Umiko hugged tighter and this time, she held on.

"Umiko, I need you to promise to stop trying to figure out my creature type." Lyn said into her best friend's hair.

"Why?" Umiko tried to pull away again. "Don't you want to know what you are? Aren't you curious?"

"I need you to stop trying to figure me out because you care about me and want me to be happy."

"Of course, I want those things." Umiko said and squeezed her friend again.

Lyn pulled back and let her hand slip into her friend's. "Then you promise?"

"Lyn Davis," Umiko put a hand on her hip. "I will stop

trying to figure out your creature type, if you tell me what's been going on the past few days," Umiko said.

"Deal." Lyn said and the familiar static sealed Umiko's deal. "But it will have to be over party prep because we have less than an hour." Lyn took off into the kitchen with Umiko on her heels.

～

"Okay, hair is done. What are you wearing?" Umiko unplugged the curling iron and snapped Lyn out of her reverie.

"This." Lyn indicated the clothes she was already wearing. "Jeans and a T-shirt." Lyn pinched the shoulder and pulled out until it snapped back in place. She wore an old rock band T-shirt. The screen print was aged and faded and she could no longer make out which band it was, but it reminded her of her mom and it was super soft after years of wear.

Umiko's shoulders sagged. "Really? With that hair? That is fancy party dress hair." Umiko pouted.

"Yes. Really. But, if you feel that strongly about it, you can pick a different T-shirt." Lyn was proud of herself or not giving in. A compromise was acceptable, since Umiko would need to be weened from making Lyn's every decision.

Umiko smiled and looked in Lyn's closet, then around on the floor. "Your mom's closet, too?"

"Sure. The best, cutest T-shirt you can find in the whole house."

Umiko raced out of the room.

Lyn looked at herself in the mirror. Her jeans hugged her curves like they were tailored for her, because they were, courtesy of a creature trait that she was going to use more often.

"Found it." Umiko came back with a white shirt with a screen printed unicorn in the center that read, 'One of a kind.'

Lyn took off the faded black shirt she was wearing and slipped into the cute white one Umiko had found.

"So, you met your sister. What was she like?" Umiko asked.

Lyn had spilled everything after she made Umiko the same secret keeping deal Jake was held to. She felt bad about doing that to her bestie, but she clamped down on those feelings and did what she had to do, for now.

She felt a bit better when Umiko had agreed with Scout's assessment that the fewer people that knew the better.

Lyn smiled. "I know it sounds weird, but I think she's part fairy. The grass in the backyard was crunchy before she visited and she said my trees were sad."

"I thought the grass felt healthier than usual. Maria or Jonathan?"

Lyn shook her head. "I thought they were both human."

"Interesting." Umiko smiled.

Lyn raised her hand to cut into Umiko's thoughts.

Umiko spoke up. "Just interesting. Not a challenge."

Lyn hugged her best friend and heard a car door close.

Moments later the door bell rang.

Lyn looked over at the clock on her bedside table. 4:52. "Someone is early."

"I told them not to be. I threatened them just like you said."

"Well, I guess it's party time." Lyn said and looked at Umiko's reflection in the floor length mirror. "Are we good?"

"The blue dress would be better, but..." Umiko started.

Lyn picked up the band T-shirt and started to put it on over the unicorn T-shirt.

"Just kidding, you look great!" Umiko finished and Lyn tossed the shirt onto her desk chair.

"Thanks." Lyn said. "You too."

Umiko was wearing a red princess cut dress that enhanced the tones of her hair. She checked herself out in the mirror once more before both girls rushed down the stairs. Umiko stopped on the bottom step and Lyn opened the door.

"Yo, sis. You look hot." Jake said, holding two cases of soda. "Love the shirt."

"Thanks, Jake." Lyn took a case from him and welcomed him into the house.

He pointed to his closed eyes and Lyn kissed one before stepping away. He stepped back and smiled. "Veronica, this is my sister, Lyn. Lyn, this is my girlfriend, Veronica," Jake said. "I'm going to get some more groceries from the car. I'll be right back." He set the other case on the ground and walked off, leaving Veronica with Lyn.

Veronica was wearing a black, slim-lined dress with a light weight burgundy sweater and pearls. Her shoes were taller than Lyn could imagine walking on, but made her legs look fabulous.

"Please come in." Lyn stepped back so she could enter. "It's nice to meet you Veronica, can I ask you for a favor?" She held out her hand in greeting.

Veronica put a hand in Lyn's. "Sure." In her other she held a bouquet of dying flowers.

"Would you keep my secrets? And not share anything you learn here tonight. I know it sounds weird, but I need to deal with a few complications, and we just met."

"Deal." Veronica said.

Lyn smiled as the static sparked between their hands.

"Ouch." Veronica pulled her hand back.

"Sorry about that, you'd be amazed how often that happens," Lyn said with a sideways smile.

"It's just a little static." Veronica said. "Jake's mom said these were yours." She handed the flowers and an envelope to Lyn. "You have a beautiful home and those are the most perfect curls I have ever seen, how did you get them to stay in ringlets?"

"Thanks. I had help on the curls, actually," Lyn said. "My best friend, Umiko…"

"Sister?" Umiko asked from the stairs when Jake returned with bags of snacks.

"Hey, Sunshine. I didn't see you there." Jake closed the door with his foot and took the box in his arms to the kitchen.

Umiko side eyed him and turned to Lyn. Lyn tossed the flowers and envelope on the coffee table without looking at them.

Lyn had forgotten that little detail. "Jake doesn't like names. He asked if he could claim me as his sister and I said yes. Nothing more, so stop whatever it is you're thinking and take a breath."

Jake winked at Lyn and she smiled back with a slight sigh.

"Sorry," Jake whispered as he and Veronica walked past.

"The party will be in the backyard." She said to Jake's back.

"Anything else you forgot to share?" Umiko crossed her arms in front of her chest.

"Not that I can remember." Lyn smirked. "But if I did, it was not on purpose. I would tell you everything."

Umiko nodded and walked through to the kitchen as the doorbell rang.

Lyn opened the door and welcomed in two large vases of flowers.

"Sidewalk sale?" Lyn asked the arrangements that hid Clark's face.

"Yeah, but these are for you." Clark handed her one of the vases, "As long as you don't mind dead people flowers."

"They are beautiful. Thank you." Lyn smiled. "Umiko just stepped into the kitchen, hopefully you can find your way there through the jungle you're carrying."

"I'll manage." Clark said and Lyn heard the smile on his lips even though she couldn't see it because of the flowers.

Lyn put the vase she held on the ground for lack of a

better place and turned back to the door. She looked up and down the street and saw Greg and Killian coming from different ends. She gave into the growl in her belly and felt the rumble pass her closed lips. Maybe it had been a bad idea to invite them both. They already looked ready to trade punches.

She wanted to get things done and over with so she could move on to something way less complicated, like a movie marathon and a pint of ice cream. The tempting image of rocky road ice cream made her mouth water.

"Are you guys gonna throw a few punches or come inside?" Lyn called. "Because I'd rather you do the first one out here than in my house." She crossed her arms over her chest.

The pair glared at each other but both turned to walk up the sidewalk to her front steps.

"No fighting tonight. Not once you cross this doorway." Lyn told them as she blocked their entry.

They mumbled their assent and she moved aside to let them into her house.

Greg leaned down to kiss her cheek and she turned away.

"Little bro says he's running a bit late, sis." Jake called from the back porch, waving his phone.

Greg pulled back from Lyn's face and he and Killian stared at Lyn.

Lyn rolled her eyes. "You all know Jake, right? He's horrible with names so he calls people whatever he wants without thinking," she yelled the last bit over her shoulder.

Jake laughed.

"It's a nickname, get over it." Lyn looked as far down the street in both directions as she could before she closed the door. She left it unlocked for Scout. "The party is out back."

Lyn herded her new guests to the backyard. She froze in the doorway as she stepped out into the smell of her own patch of wildflowers. She smiled at her gift from Nelu, only slightly puzzled how a human child could pull off fairy magic. With luck, she'd get to know more about her claimed sister in the near future.

Lyn flipped on the twinkle lights strung around the patio ceiling and stepped outside into the fresh air.

Where is Scout? She patted her pocket where she usually kept her phone, but it wasn't there. It was still upstairs in her bathroom. *He said he'd be here and he will.*

Jake and Veronica busied themselves opening chips and soda boxes.

Lyn took a breath and ran through the deal she had prepared for her friends. She didn't need Scout here to get started. Jake would have her back if it came to it. She took a breath to address her friends, but was interrupted.

"Scout said you left because we were too controlling." Greg said from beside her elbow.

"He was right," Lyn confirmed and took a step to get her personal space back.

"I'm sorry," Greg hung his head. He was tall enough that it didn't hide his face from her.

"Thank you." Lyn said and turned to him. She put her hands on her hips. "Do your people keep tabs on me?"

The color drained from Greg's face. He stood frozen.

Lyn watched as an excuse bubbled to the surface and fizzled out.

Lyn nodded. "I'll be getting a new phone number."

"Done." Scout said as he came out of the house with two wrapped boxes in his hands. One roughly phone sized, the other much bigger.

Lyn smiled at Scout and turned her attention back to Greg. "Will you excuse me for a moment?" She walked over to Scout without waiting for an answer. She wasn't asking for permission. "Jake said you'd be late. What are these?"

Scout looked at his watch. "I am late, it's 5:11, and these are the things I had to do before tonight. I'm sorry I wasn't here earlier, I had trouble choosing. I texted Jake, because you didn't answer your phone. Um. My phone. We really need to fix that." Scout looked toward his brother.

"I left my…the phone in my room when Jake knocked."

Scout put the wrapped boxes on the table inside the kitchen. "Want a drink?"

Lyn nodded. "A drink would be great."

He nodded and stepped away.

Lyn looked back over her guests. She found Greg standing with Clark in the yard a little ways away from the crowded patio. Clark thumped Greg on the shoulder and excused himself as Lyn stepped near.

She lifted her hand, palm up, to Greg "If you want my new cell number, we need to make a deal."

Greg put his hand, palm down on top of hers without argument.

"You and yours will not track me, rescue me, manage me, or control me without my permission. And you will call off any people you have searching for my creature type, including yourself."

Greg looked at her, mouth slightly open.

Lyn saw the hurt in his eyes. She leaned close and lowered her voice. "I am not the damsel you want me to be. I can take care of myself and I've proven that twice now. I need you to accept it."

Greg looked at her as the silence grew arms and threatened to choke her.

"Is this the end of us?" he whispered back.

"We're friends, like we have been. Nothing more." She stepped back, still gripping his hand.

"I want to amend the deal," he said. "Me and mine will not track you, manage you, or control you without your permission. I retain my prerogative to rescue you, in certain circumstances. I will stop trying to figure out what you are, but not who you are. In exchange, we will remain friends and I will work to earn back your trust."

Lyn stared into his eyes until she felt a slight tingle and realized hers must be changing from the green she last saw in the mirror to the blue looking at her. "Deal." She blinked to end the mimic before it got too far. The deal's charge sparked and spread up their arms. Lyn held Greg's hand until the spark died away. Then she loosened her grip and Greg let her hand slide out of his.

"Has everyone here made a deal with the fairy girl but me?" Killian said as he walked over to their quiet spot. Lyn was sure he was here just to jab at Greg.

"Back off, Killian." Greg said.

"I'm coming to you." Lyn turned her new ice blue eyes on Killian. She held out her hand in his direction and felt her pulse increase, as anger bubbled up.

"Nope. I'm good." He shook his head.

"Are you afraid of me?" Lyn asked louder than necessary and stepped closer to the pack leader.

The chitter chatter of conversation on the patio died away.

"No," he said as everyone watched what was unfolding.

"Then give me your hand," she said.

"Tell me what you want first."

"First? Alright. You're fired." Lyn dropped her hand. "You will no longer be in charge of training me."

"What?" Killian snorted. "You think you know everything you need to know about being a shifter?"

"No, but I think I've learned everything I can from you." Lyn stared him down while the rest of the party waited.

She was glad she had respected Greg enough not to put him on the spot, but she wasn't going to be as nice to Killian. He'd be better cowed with an audience watching. She hoped Scout would keep his musical intervention to himself this time because she was no longer playing with Killian.

"Here's the current deal, adjusted a bit to be just for you."

Lyn held out her hand, her crystal blue eyes still staring into his, unblinking. "You and yours will not track, manage, or control me in any way. You will not try to figure out what creature type I am and you will stop trying to claim me like a prize in a competition."

"In exchange?" Killian held her stare.

"We can remain friends for as long as you earn it."

"Is that it?" Killian laughed. "That's your offer. There's nothing in there for me."

Lyn felt her wolf stir. "Agree to my terms or I will challenge you for alpha," she said without flinching.

Killian's laugh died and a growl grew in its place.

Lyn returned it with her own.

Killian's nails extended and hers followed quickly after. Lyn set her feet in a stronger base and prepared herself for a fight.

"Dude, I would not piss that girl off," Jake said. "You have no idea what …"

Scout elbowed his brother.

"…she is capable of." Jake finished and glared at Scout.

"Take the deal, Killian," Lyn's eyes shifted to those of her wolf. "What does it cost you? You were never going to win me in the first place."

The backyard was silent except for the sound of leaves dropping from the trees and the death of a fly that flew into the bug zapper on the corner of the porch.

Killian met Lyn's stare and the test of wills began.

Lyn let everything but Killian become background noise.

"What kind of soda do you want, Umiko?" Clark asked.

"Cherry Coke?" Umiko answered.

Lyn heard the pop and fizz of a can opening, but she kept her eyes matched to Killian's. She would not be blinking first. If she could out stubborn a fairy queen, she could out stubborn the shifter standing in front of her.

Jake came to stand behind her shoulder, and added a warning growl to the mix.

Killian abruptly put his hand in hers.

"Say it," Lyn demanded.

"I will not track, manage, or control you in any way. I will not care what creature type you are and I will never claim you. In exchange, you will not challenge me for alpha."

"And we'll remain friends?"

"I made my terms." Killian snarled at her.

Scout stepped behind Lyn's other shoulder.

He and Jake growled softly. A promise of more if her stipulation was not met.

"Fine. We can be friends," Killian said as he assessed the added threat.

"Deal." Lyn squeezed his hand as the static bloomed across her palm and his.

"Great. That's done." Scout and Jake walked over for munchies as if Killian had not just almost lost his alpha status to a girl who had known she was a shifter for less than a year.

Lyn turned away from Killian, who straightened his collar and grabbed the open can of soda that Scout offered on his return.

"So what happened this week?" Clark asked.

"I went for a run. Did some dancing. Camped for the first time ever, saw more stars than I thought possible, found my mom, and met my sister."

The collected mouths hung open, except for Scout's, Jake's and Umiko's.

"Oh, I also got a brother, and a new friend, I hope." Lyn turned to Veronica.

"You're my kind of fierce." Veronica said with a lift of her soda can. "Let's do mani/pedis. Tomorrow?"

Lyn smiled, taken aback at the the ease of making a new friend. "It's a date."

"Actually, V, she's busy tomorrow. Rain check?" Scout and Veronica discussed a compromise.

"What?" Clark said.

"Yeah, the brother thing was Jake's counter to a different deal. It's no biggie. It's not like I married into the family or anything." Lyn rolled her eyes.

"A bro can hope." Jake said lifting his own can.

"That's weird, but not where I was going." Clark's eyes were glued to Lyn's. "Did you say you met your real mom?"

"Oh, yeah. My mom is pretty cool, actually. I learned some things. Then she introduced me to the girl whose life I stole." She looked at the newest person in their circle. "Sorry, Veronica. You're probably not aware. I was switched at birth and bound to the people I thought of as my parents by a witch, who I had to take out in order to rescue my friends. That was in September. Both those parents are dead now and I might never meet my real father, but I found my real mom, a girl I owe everything to, and my inner strength. Anyone who threatens to take that away from me again is going to wish they hadn't."

"Is that all?" Veronica smiled.

Jake wrapped his arm around her shoulder and beamed at Lyn.

Lyn nodded and chuckled. "Yeah, I guess my life is boring like that."

CHAPTER FIFTY

Scout connected his phone to a set of speakers and picked a party music playlist. The first song was Wolves by Selena Gomez.

Lyn laughed as soon as she recognized the chords.

Jake and Veronica joined them at the patio table.

"Well chosen, bro." Jake slapped his brother on the back.

"I thought you'd enjoy that," Scout said.

"Does this list have a theme?" Veronica asked.

"Of course it does, V. You know me better than to ask a silly question like that."

Veronica put her hand on her hip. "I know, but I keep thinking I might catch you ill prepared one day. How did the one I helped with go?" Veronica looked from Scout to Lyn and back again.

He lifted his watch to his face. "If you could save your question for about three more hours, I'll let you know."

"Sorry." Veronica sealed her lips with an imaginary key and handed it to Scout. Who took it and slid it into his pocket.

Lyn's puzzled over the exchange for a moment and then went in search of snacks.

"Wait just a minute." Scout reached for Lyn's arm and gently pulled her back into the conversation. "In the meantime. I'd like to declare, yesterday, June third, 'Lyn is a Badass Day.'" Scout said.

Veronica's eyes lit up like the fairy lights. "Is this a gift giving holiday?" Veronica winked at Lyn.

"How well do you know us?" Scout asked her, indicating himself and Jake.

"Yippee." Veronica clapped her hands with quick small movements close to her chest.

Lyn couldn't help but snicker at her childlike excitement.

"It's a Jake and Scout thing," Veronica told her. "You'll get spoiled by it." She looked at Scout. "What was my day called? I forget."

"I think it was 'Veronica does not know what she's signing up for Day.' Or something similar."

"Right." She smiled. "I totally did, by the way." Veronica turned and kissed Jake on the lips.

Jake took her face in his hands and lengthened the small peck.

"Anyway," Scout ignored the show of affection. "Gift number one." He reached into his pocket and held up a brown key. "A key to the secret lair."

Jake let out a deep bellowing laugh and reached into his own pocket. "At least mine has a key chain." Jake dangled a silver disk in Lyn's face that read 'World's Best Sister.'

"Yeah, well, you can win that round, I brought two more gifts." Scout stuck his tongue out at his brother.

"Veronica should get the extra key." Lyn said, accepting the key ring from Jake as Scout slid the single brown key back into his pocket.

"Oh, no you don't," Veronica said. "You can be the girlfriend who takes them camping and does outdoorsy things. I'm an electricity and running water type of girl."

"She's not my girlfriend," Scout said.

The words caused Lyn's stomach to clench. Those few nonchalant words hurt more than her wolf clawing its way to the surface.

Jake got in his brother's face. "Do not mess this up, baby bro. I like this one."

"I don't intend to," Scout said, pushing his brother back. "But the stars aren't out yet." Scout pointed at the sky and winked at Lyn.

Lyn took a deep breath and ignored the butterflies in her stomach. She turned to Veronica, "I'm sorry that I hogged Jake for the past few days."

"Don't be," Veronica said.

"You're not jealous?" Lyn asked.

"Why should I be? He was with you and Scout. Wait, that did not sound right." She backtracked. "Look, I know there is a part of his life I will never be in, it's fine for us to have our own things."

"You're not a shifter?" Lyn asked but then worried that she might have shared a secret that wasn't hers to share.

"I am 100% human." Veronica said with a flourish, then looked at her phone. She whispered something in Jake's ear.

"True enough. We're heading out, fam. We have dinner and movie plans. Thank you for letting me watch you bring Killian down a peg."

"But I really want to plan that mani/pedi." Veronica leaned in to hug Lyn. "Scout can give you my number."

Jake leaned in and kissed Lyn on the cheek. "Family dinner is once a month. You're obligated to make an appearance, sis," he said as he pulled away.

"She is not." Scout popped his brother on the back of the head. "Get out of here."

Scout kissed Veronica's cheek and Veronica waved to Lyn as Scout walked them to the door, talking to his brother as they left.

"Seriously. If you mess this up…"

Veronica interrupted the threat. "Please, Scout. Please say I can keep her."

"She's not a puppy." Scout laughed.

Lyn blushed, but she wanted to keep Veronica too.

CHAPTER FIFTY-ONE

Greg stood in the yard watching Jake, Scout, Veronica, and Lyn laugh together. His chest ached that he wasn't standing by her and that her laughter wasn't because of something he said. Had he ever made her laugh?

As he was thinking back over his relationship with Lyn, Clark walked up to stand at his side.

"I really messed that up," Greg said not moving his eyes from the group at the table. He watched as Jake and Scout both dangled something in her face.

"Yeah, you really did," Clark agreed.

Greg rolled his eyes. "Thanks, man. I can always count on you to cheer me up." Greg shook his head and took a sip of his coke.

"Well, it's the truth. But the funny thing is, now you can learn from your mistake. She's not off the board yet. There's still a game to play."

Clark left his friend standing alone in the dark of the yard with only his thoughts and walked over to stand with Lyn as Jake, Veronica, and Scout walked away.

~

"*D*o we need to make a deal too?" Clark asked as he stepped up.

Lyn turned to address Clark's question. He was the only person she didn't deal into keeping her secrets. Did she trust him? Did she tell them something that could get her into trouble? She hadn't told them what type of fairy she was or what her final deal with the Queen of Summer had been. Those secrets were still locked up safe. Clark had never cared to know more about Lyn. He didn't need to be told to stop searching for her creature traits, did he?

"You haven't given me a reason not to trust you," Lyn answered. "But if you think we need a deal, I'm open to one."

Clark smiled. "I'm happy that you got to meet your mom."

"Thank you. One day I will be happy that you get to see your dad."

They stood sipping sodas in the light of the patio, shoulder to shoulder. Scout and Umiko chatted over the chip bowl and Greg examined wildflowers in the yard.

Lyn heard the the song change and the haunting tones of 'Come Little Children' started playing. A nod to Lyn's fae side. She smiled and let the music fill her. She started singing under her breath.

'Come little children, I'll take thee away, into a land of enchantment.'

"You know he loves you, right?" Clark's low voice cut through the music.

"I know he loves the idea of me, but I also know he doesn't know me well enough to love the real me." Lyn said watching Greg run his fingers through his hair.

Clark turned to meet her eyes. "Did you give him a chance?" He held her gaze for a moment longer before he walked over to Umiko and the snack table.

Killian walked over as Lyn stood processing Clark's

parting words. "I'm out. I have better things to do with my evening. Training tomorrow six a.m.," Killian said.

"I'm sleeping in," Lyn said, "and you're still fired."

"You still have things to learn," Killian countered with a finger toward her chest.

"I will agree with you there, but they will be learned on my terms."

"Who is going to teach you?" Killian asked, crossing his arms over his chest.

"Jake said he's up for it," Scout moved to stand next to Lyn and faced Killian, "and my mom has been wanting a new project." He turned to Lyn. "If you are interested."

Lyn faced Killian. "It looks like I have options to consider. Maybe you can join us sometime." Lyn smiled. "I like sparring with you."

Killian turned to Scout. "Six a.m., Jacobs."

"I'll be there, Jacobs." Scout ushered Killian to the door.

~

"Y ou didn't have to buy me a new phone." Lyn said pointing to the boxes Scout had placed on the kitchen table.

"That's good because I didn't," Scout smiled, "and you have to wait to open those."

"But you said, 'done' when you got here?" Lyn's eyebrows rose in confusion.

"I did say that, but we already planned to go shopping tomorrow morning. He didn't need to know the details." He took a sip of his soda and lowered his can. "I noticed you tried to override our plans with Veronica and her mani/pedi date. Are you having second thoughts?"

She shook her head. "I'm sorry. I had a long day and I forgot. I'm looking forward to phone shopping with you." Lyn's lips fell into a pout. "Actually…it sounds boring."

Scout laughed. "It does, doesn't it?" He put his curved finger to his chin. "We will have to come up with a way to make it not boring." He titled his head to the dark sky above. "The stars are coming out."

"What are you going to do about Killian?"

"Go to practice, take a shower, grab coffee for two, and be here before you wake up to take you shopping for a new sim card. After that, I thought you could decide what we do the rest of the day, unless you're tired of me by then."

"So, nothing."

Scout laughed. "He's too bristly after your show of dominance. He needs time to cool down and I need a little semantics training before I rock that boat. Plus, he'll hold on more tightly now that you've shown interest."

"Sorry about that."

"Don't be."

"Do you think you'll go for it?"

"I'm not sure. It's what Jake wants, but I need to make sure alpha is what I want. It's a big commitment."

Lyn nodded as footsteps came up behind her.

"Lyn, thank you for inviting us. I think we'll head out. Do you want help cleaning up?" Greg asked.

Clark walked up with him but stepped away to talk to Umiko.

"No, it's just a few bowls and cans. I've got it."

"Scout," Greg lifted his hand to shake. "Thanks for taking care of her."

Scout took the offered hand. "I didn't take care of her. She took care of Jake and I."

Greg turned back to Lyn.

Clark joined them with a hand on her arm. "Good night, Lyn."

"Good night, Clark."

Greg leaned in to kiss Lyn's cheek and followed Clark through the house.

CHAPTER FIFTY-TWO

"I finished cleaning up the food," Scout said as Lyn walked back from walking Umiko to the back gate.

"Thank you," Lyn said.

"I also checked your grill. It just needs a little cleaning and it'll be ready for steaks."

"Are you volunteering?"

"I am. I can take care of it next weekend and we can have a cook-out to test it out. What do you say?"

"Let's do it."

Lyn turned off the patio lights and walked to the middle of the yard to look at the sky. "They look so weak from here," Lyn said, indicating the dim stars above them, "even with the lights off."

Scout walked over carrying two wrapped boxes. "I'll take you back anytime you need a fresh dose of stars." He handed her the first box. "Gift number two."

She ripped the paper off the smaller of the two boxes and let it fall to the ground. She opened the lid and lifted out a pocket knife.

"I can easily say that this is a surprise." Lyn opened the

blade and it glinted in the half light from the kitchen before she closed it back again.

Scout laughed. "You never know when a pretty girl might need a weapon on her person to make good on a threat."

Lyn dropped her hand with the knife and looked into this eyes. "I'm sorry I scared you. I had to improvise. The battery was dying and it was too hot and I was so tired."

Scout shushed her. "Don't apologize for being fierce." His eyebrows rose when he used the word Veronica had used to describe Lyn earlier. "Finally, for tonight at least, gift number three." Scout handed her the last, larger box.

"What do you mean for tonight?" Lyn asked as she took the heavy box.

"I have big plans, Lyn Davis." Scout said tilting her chin with his bent index finger. He looked into her eyes and smiled.

Lyn's breath caught when she realized he was going to kiss her but he pulled away.

"They start with you opening that box." He pointed.

Lyn punched him playfully in the shoulder, but then set the box on the ground to open it.

Scout squatted next to her.

She ripped the paper and pulled off the lid. "Chocolate, my favorite." Lyn smelled the wrapped bar she found inside the box since she couldn't read the label this far from the light. "Raspberry?"

"Yep. Is it alright?"

Lyn nodded. "Thank you."

"Keep going."

Lyn eyed him suspiciously.

"Bubble bath." Lyn pulled out the bottle and sniffed the cap.

"It's the closest I could get to your signature scent. It baffles me that no-one sells bottled lightning." He laughed.

She held the bottle in her lap. "Thank you, Scout."

Scout leaned close to look into her eyes. When she leaned forward to meet him, his eyes shifted to the box. "One more." He pointed inside.

Lyn reached back into the box and pulled out a wooden tray. "I don't even know what this is."

"It unfolds..." Scout indicated, "and goes over the rim of the bathtub and will hold everything you need to relax. Chocolate, your phone for tunes or a book, a stem glass. Oh crap, I could have put a bottle of something fizzy in the box."

"Scout Jacobs! Stop apologizing for not spoiling me rotten on our first night without complications," she snapped at him, but it had a playful edge. "Spread it out a little." She paused. "I'm not going anywhere."

He stopped talking and found her eyes. He stood up and lifted her off the ground with a hand in hers. "Does that mean I'm allowed?"

"Allowed to what?" she asked looking up into his face.

"To spoil you for the foreseeable future." He looked down into her hers.

"What are you thinking?" Lyn asked with a shrug. "A week? Two tops?"

"I cannot get enough of that snark." Scout smiled and picked her up. He spun her around in a circle before he set her back on the ground and took her face in his hands. He brushed a stray hair from her face and looked deep into her eyes. "Lyn, I'm going to kiss you now."

"Finally," Lyn said and closed her eyes.

Scout leaned down and gently pressed his lips to each eye before finding her lips with his.

Lyn relished his touch and his scent. She focused on remembering every tingle and irrelevant detail. She wanted to remember this moment forever.

ACKNOWLEDGMENTS

As with any book, this would not have been accomplished without my readers. Thanks for coming back and checking to see what Lyn and her friends were up to this time.

Also, thank you to my team: Chuck C. for once again finding the plot holes and making suggestions on how to make the story better, Betsie E. for reminding me that no matter how well spelling and grammar check works, it will never catch everything, and my husband who actually read this one before it went to print.

Once again, Callie R. at Literary Designs created the cover and I am beyond happy at how it turned out.

www.literarydesigns.com

And lastly, thank you to every single one of you for believing in me.

ABOUT THE AUTHOR

Jennifer L. Moore grew up in central Mississippi and moved to central Texas. She dreams of one day living in a place that has four seasons and magic, whether or not it's central to anything

For more books and updates check out:
www.jenniferlmoorewriter.com